For John Tomlinson, who first commissioned Dante.

A Black Flame Publication
www.blackflame.com

First published in 2006 by BL Publishing, Games Workshop Ltd., Willow Road, Nottingham NG7 2WS, UK.

Distributed in the US by Simon & Schuster, 1230 Avenue of the mericas, New York, NY 10020, USA.

9 8 7 6 5 4 3 2 1

r illustration by Simon Fraser.

84416 324 3
6 324 5

his book is available from the British Library.

y Bookmarque, Surrey, UK.

2673 AD: Russian outlaw and all-round daring rake Nikolai Dante is summoned to Britannia by crazy King Henry who believes assassins lurk round every corner. For once the king is proved right as one of the Royal Family's most beloved members is brutally slaughtered. But it is Dante and his sidekicks who get blamed for the bloody murder.

The Russian rogue escapes but his friends are taken to the Tower of London, awaiting execution for a crime that – for once – they didn't commit. Britannia's borders are sealed and Dante becomes public enemy number one, a stranger in a strange land with only five days to find the real killers. To make matters worse he is stalked by DNA-sniffing sadists, every bounty hunter in the country, and Britannia intelligence's deadliest operative, the secret agent codenamed Goodnight. Britannia may rule the waves, but Dante waives the rules in this riotous romp!

By the same author from Black Flame

Nikolai Dante

THE STRANGELOVE GAMBIT

IMPERIAL BLACK

Fiends of the Eastern Front

OPERATION VAMPYR

Judge Dredd

BAD MOON RISING

KINGDOM OF THE BLIND

A Nighmare on Elm Street

SUFFER THE CHILDREN

Nikolai Dante created by **Robbie Morrison** and **Simon Fraser**.

NIKOLAI DANTE

HONOUR BE DAMNED!

David Bishop

Black Flam
Workshop L
around the w
ISBN 13: 978
ISBN 10: 1 844
A CIP record for
Printed in the UK

ONE

"Laws are not written for the lawless."
– Russian proverb

"2673 AD: King Henry Windsor McKray continues to enjoy his status as ruler of Britannia, despite openly supporting the Romanovs during their doomed revolt against Tsar Vladimir Makarov. It is the first time in Imperial history a monarch has retained powered by pleading insanity. King Henry remains popular among the majority of his people, but the ruling upper class consider his eccentric behaviour a grave embarrassment. They would much rather his daughter Princess Marie-Anne Britannia took charge, but she is still a prisoner in the Tower of London after being found guilty of conspiring against her father.

The princess has sworn to avenge herself against Russian rogue Nikolai Dante, who supplied the evidence leading to her incarceration. Meanwhile Britannia remains a nation divided, its parliament stuck in a mire of political manoeuvring, scandal, sleaze and corruption. Some would say it was ever thus. The most popular member of the royal family was the Queen Mother, Barbara 'Babs' Windsor McKay. Her title stemmed from the fact she had been queen before Henry was born, but also acknowledged that she was mother of the current monarch. To confuse matters further, she looked younger than her son, thanks to the remarkable effects of ingesting royal jelly..."

– Editorial commentary from *The Imperial Times*

It was one of those days when it seemed to Nikolai Dante that all life, as someone put it, was nothing but a heap of six to four against.

Dante prided himself on being a gambling man. He was prone to taking on impossible odds and winning through, escaping almost certain death to emerge smiling from the other side of any adventure fate might throw in his path. But diving from a stained glass window on the Palace of London's tenth floor without bothering to look first was pushing even his legendary good luck to its limits and beyond. If he had any doubts about this, the disapprovingly patrician voice inside his mind had little hesitation in confirming it.

Dante, when I said evasive action, I did not think even you would be so foolish as to jump to your own death to avoid an assassin's bullet!

"I was improvising," Dante replied as he plummeted toward the stone courtyard below.

That much was obvious. The voice belonged to the Weapons Crest, a sentient battle-computer bonded to Dante's DNA. This remarkable piece of alien technology was created to train its genetic host as a potential ruler of the Empire. *My presence may significantly enhance your body's natural healing abilities,* the Crest observed, *but even I cannot resurrect the dead. Seven seconds to impact, by the way.*

"At least I'm still alive!"

Only for another five seconds.

"Shut up, I'm trying to concentrate." Dante could see a row of flagpoles that protruded from the building below. The palace whistled past his face as he twisted in the air, trying to get close enough to grab one of the poles. Miss these and he would be a red smear in–

Three seconds.

"I said shut up!" His flailing hands missed the nearest pole, but got hold of the rectangular flag hanging beneath it. Dante's body jerked to a halt, the sudden deceleration nearly wrenching his arms from their sockets. "Gahhhh!" He hung grimly to the royal standard, his breath coming in short, ragged gasps as the bitter taste of adrenaline filled his mouth.

Gahhh? Not quite what I'd call famous last words, the Crest commented dryly.

"Why... W-Why should they be... famous last words?"

The flag to which you're so gratefully clinging was not designed for such violent use. I estimate the fabric will tear itself free at any moment...

Dante looked up in time to see the material ripping apart. He tried to grab hold of the flagpole, but that only accelerated the disintegration.

...now, the Crest concluded as Dante resumed his rapid descent.

"Bojemoi!"

Mildred Barnstaple despised tourists. For thirty-seven years she had been a guide at the Palace of London, welcoming visitors to its grand halls and galleries, politely answering questions, aiding the helpless, the hopeless and the hapless. But never once in all that time had one of these ungrateful wretches thought to say thank you. An only child, both of Mildred's parents had died in a freak zeppelin accident over Walthamstow when she was twenty. The resulting inheritance had ensured she never need work, but left the young woman with a lifetime to occupy. A quiet passion for the beauties of the past led Mildred to the Britannia Heritage Society, a voluntary organisation striving to preserve the country's finest historic buildings. Since then she had more than done her bit – baking cakes, organising whist drives and running raffles. To her eternal shame, Mildred had even agreed to pose for a nude calendar. The results had proved an underwhelming failure and so Mildred had returned to her post by the green velvet canopy outside the Palace of London's entrance, wishing something exciting would happen.

"Look out below!" a voice screamed from the heavens. A man was plummeting towards the canopy, his arms and legs flailing violently as if he were trying to fly. Mildred took an involuntary step back and tumbled over, her eyes still fixed on the bizarre descent. The man fell on the taut green canopy, which bounced him towards Mildred. The man landed with a heavy thump, his face burying itself into Mildred's crotch.

"Oh my word!" she shrieked, suddenly aware of hot, masculine breath warming her in a way she hadn't experienced for at least a decade. At first she was shocked, then affronted and soon rather excited.

Mildred craned her neck forward to study the manly windfall positioned between her legs. He was around thirty in age, with a taut, athletic figure and shapely buttocks. Skin-tight grey trousers clung to his thighs before disappearing inside a pair of supple brown leather riding boots, while a crimson jacket with golden braid hugged his back. He had a thick mane of black hair, but his face remained hidden. Mildred felt her inner thighs being tickled by his beard. "I say," she sighed happily and clenched her legs together.

It took Dante more than a minute to prise apart the thighs holding his head captive. When he succeeded, a soft moan of disappointment issued from the middle-aged woman who had cushioned his impact. Dante scrambled to his feet, grinning sheepishly at her. "Normally I don't like to leave a lady unsatisfied, but my presence is required elsewhere – sorry!" He noticed a line of hover-taxis waiting on a nearby rank and waved at the first one.

"Take me with you!" the woman pleaded.

"Not today." Dante made a run for it, diving into the black cab. "But thanks for the soft landing!"

The taxi sped into the sky. "Can you take me to Nelson's Column?" he asked the driver.

"No problem, guv," a surly voice replied. "They've just finished rebuilding it after what happened during the war. Bloody disgrace it was."

"That's where the assassin fired from," Dante muttered darkly. "Take me there!"

Are you sure this is wise? the Crest enquired. *If the sniper was trying to kill you, getting closer only makes you a bigger target.*

"I don't think they were shooting at me."

"You talking to me?" the driver asked.

"King Henry suspected someone was planning to kill him," Dante continued, ignoring the cabbie. "Princess Marie-Anne can't wait to take his place on the throne. She must have hired an assassin to speed up the process."

"What you muttering about back there?" the driver demanded. "You got something to do with what happened at the palace? They was talking about it on the news – some kind of shooting."

"I was with the king when he was hurt," Dante admitted.

"Why'd you do it?"

"I didn't do anything!"

"What? You stood by and let somebody murder him? That's worse, you bloody coward!" The cabbie twisted round to glare at Dante, not bothering to watch where his hover-taxi was headed. Nelson's Column was looming ahead of them.

"There were two shots, moments apart," Dante protested. "By the time I reacted, the king was already down, blood everywhere. I saw what direction the shots came from, so I decided to go after the shooter. Now, will you watch where you're going, please?"

The cabbie lunged over the back of his seat to grab hold of Dante's jacket. "Don't you tell me how to do my job, you bloody foreigner! Look at you, in your fancy clothes! Come over here, telling us how to live our lives. There used to be a British Empire, you know, long before you bloody Russians started sticking your noses in–"

Dante, this cab is on a collision course with–

"I know, I know!" he said.

"I don't care what you know," the driver snarled. "I'm going to teach you a lesson!"

Dante–

The assassin was so intent on watching the palace he didn't notice the hover-taxi careering across the sky. The assassin clung to the statue on top of Nelson's Column, one eye closed while the other peered through a high-powered sniper's sight. It was only when a dark shape blurred across the his field of vision that he belatedly realised how imminent danger was. "Bloody hell!" The assassin reached back to pull the ignition toggle on his jet-pack but he was too late.

The hover-taxi smashed nose-first into the column, neatly severing the replica of Nelson from its base. The sundered statue fell on top of the taxi, impaling the vehicle on the specially reinforced column below. The assassin clung on to the statue, but his weapon tumbled to the ground far below. The shooter cursed in frustration; this had not been part of the plan. His client had been quite specific: a single shot, two at most – kill the king and get out of sight without attracting any attention. I doubt this qualifies, the assassin thought ruefully. But when he reached back to fire up his jetpack's twin engines, another hand was already resting on the ignition toggle. "Going somewhere?" a Russian-accented voice asked.

Not for the first time today, Dante was grateful for the augmentations he gained from being bonded with a Romanov Weapons Crest. Enhanced healing abilities had protected him from a brutal concussion when the hover-cab collided with Nelson's Column. The Crest also gave Dante the ability to extend razor-sharp swords of bio-organic circuitry from his fists. One swipe of these cut a path out of the crushed cab, enabling him to intercept the escaping assassin.

The two grappled on Nelson's toppled statue, the violence of their struggle threatening to send the golden effigy tumbling from its precarious perch. The assassin was wearing a slate-grey bodysuit and mask that hid everything but their eyes. "Who are you?" Dante demanded to know. "Why did you try to kill the king? Who sent you?"

The assassin tried to wriggle free, but Dante kept one hand clasped on the jetpack. "I won't let go until you tell me!" he warned. A lithe foot kicked Dante's groin with a sickening thud. He doubled over in pain, his grip loosening involuntarily. The assassin broke free and ran to the other end of the horizontal statue, one hand activating his jetpack. Still wincing, Dante flung himself at the killer as they lifted off. His clasping fingers caught hold of the assassin's flat-soled shoes and clung on. Then the two men were flying across London's twilight sky, the setting sun colouring the horizon in hues of orange and pink.

A magnificent vista, even if it is probably a localised side effect of air pollution levels.

"Crest, this is no time to be admiring the view!" Dante snapped. By now the assassin was kicking and thrashing his legs, trying to dislodge his unwanted passenger.

I fail to see what else I can do. You seem determined to kill yourself today, so I thought it best if I savoured my remaining moments. Sightseeing was the obvious option at this height.

"Diavolo!" Dante snarled as a knee connected sharply with the side of his head. "You could suggest some ways of bringing this bastard down to earth!"

I don't think that will be an issue for much longer, the Crest replied.

"Why not?"

In your earlier struggle you dislodged the jetpack's fuel line. It's been venting ever since. I doubt there's enough left in the tanks to keep both of you airborne for more than a minute.

Dante looked down and realised they were several hundred metres above the ground. If the jetpack cut out now, both of them would fall to an exceedingly unnatural death. He crawled up the assassin's still thrashing legs and yanked the jetpack sideways, sending them into a rapid, spiralling descent. Below, the Thames grew larger as it got nearer. Most of London's greatest attractions had been relocated to a cluster on the river's north bank, making it easier for visitors to savour the best of Britannia. As a result the Houses of Parliament, the Tower of London, Big Ben and New Covent Garden all stood cheek by jowl with each other, competing for tourist roubles.

The assassin flailed at Dante with both fists, pummelling him repeatedly until his tenacious grip began to loosen. When Dante thought he could hold on no longer, the jetpack's engines began to splutter and cough. Fortunately, they were now less than ten metres above the flower stalls of New Covent Garden. Beneath them a trader was trying to shift a cartload of yellow roses. "Five big bunches for a rouble, guaranteed thorn-free!" she cried out in a gravelly voice. "Get your roses. Show your good lady wife how much you love her!"

The jetpack died completely, sending Dante and the assassin tumbling toward the flower stall. They hit the rose pile with an almighty thump, Dante crying out as his trousers were sliced to ribbons by the foliage. By the time he had extricated himself the assassin was already fleeing on foot. The flower seller stared at her devastated stock. "Where the hell did you come from?"

"St Petersburg," Dante replied tersely, removing a sharp triangle of green from his posterior. "I thought you said these roses were thorn-free?"

"*Caveat emptor*," the stallholder said, folding her arms imperiously.

That means buyer beware.

"I know what it means, Crest!" Dante snapped, clambering from the cart to pursue the fleeing assassin.

"What about my bloody roses?" the flower seller protested as Dante ran off.

"Try making potpourri!"

The assassin could feel his energy draining away as the chase wore on. No matter how fast he ran, no matter what obstacles he left, the man chasing him kept coming – sprinting through the darkening streets as night closed in, implacable and utterly relentless. Doesn't this bastard ever get tired? Who the hell is he? There was no choice but to keep running. If I can reach the rendezvous in time, I'll be fine. Otherwise... No, there was no otherwise, the killer thought. I have to make it. He sprinted round the corner of an old sandstone building.

Dante ran round the same corner, straight into the waiting assassin. A fist punched Dante's throat, choking him. As he staggered back, a hand smashed into his nose, snapping his head backwards. A knee slammed into Dante's stomach and he crumpled to the ground, gasping for air. The assassin moved in for the kill but the sound of approaching sirens rent the twilight. The sniper ran off, leaving Dante spitting blood.

Britannia's law enforcers are closing in on this location.

"About time. Where were they when the shooting started?"

I also sense a skimmer circling nearby – it could be the assassin's getaway vehicle.

"Where?"

A few hundred metres ahead, at a river crossing known as Westminster Bridge.

■ ■ ■

The assassin ran onto the bridge, searching the sky intently. Fog was rising from the sluggish river below, casting a shroud across the city centre. Night had claimed the sky but a few foreign visitors still strolled over the bridge. Those close enough to see the assassin's curious garb and wounded leg hurried on, not wanting to get involved. Despite the rising mist, the illuminated dial of Big Ben was still clearly visible, its larger hand creeping towards apogee. Within a minute the mighty bell would chime seven times.

"You left in such a hurry we never got introduced," a voice slurred from behind the assassin. He twisted round to see one of Dante's bloody, bruised fists hurtling towards him. It smacked into the killer's facemask, sending him sprawling to the footpath. "My name's Dante, Nikolai Dante. What's yours?" Dante kicked the assassin hard in the groin, then flung himself on top of him, pinning his arms to the ground with his knees. "What's the matter? Cat got your tongue?" Dante punched the crumpled sniper once, twice, then a third time. He grunted in pain but still said nothing, gave no reply.

Dante–

"Not now, Crest!"

But you need to–

"I said not now!" Dante snarled. Then there was a sharp pain at the back of his head, followed by darkness and nothing more...

Dante was shocked back to consciousness when his body tumbled into the Thames. "Bojemoi!" he gasped, swallowing a mouthful of river water. He spluttered and sank beneath the surface, arms flailing uselessly. Someone had hit him from behind. Icy water was numbing Dante's arms and legs, cramping his already exhausted muscles. A glimmer of light danced overhead, pale and inviting. Dante willed his limbs into action, but the Thames seemed determined to hold him with its chilling embrace, extracting the maximum of effort for every stroke.

Dante could hear the blood pumping through his ears, while his lungs were screaming for air. He gave another kick and broke the surface, gratefully breathing in something other than water. To his surprise Westminster Bridge was some distance away. The Thames obviously had a powerful undertow beneath its slow moving surface. Rising mist made it hard to see the faces of anyone on the bridge, but Dante could make out a male silhouette watching him. He was talking with another, unseen figure, occasional words and phrases audible across the water. "I'll see you soon... Yes, the old man... Hoy..."

A low-flying skimmer dropped to the bridge, catching the man in its headlights. He was quite bald, with a solemn face and curling goatee beard. Then the vehicle's lights swung left and he was gone, lost in the thickening mist. Dante realised the current was dragging him further away. Treading water, he looked for the nearest riverbank but could not see either edge.

"Which side is closer, Crest? I can't tell in this accursed fog." Dante waited but got no reply. "Crest, this is no time to be sulking!" Still nothing. He sighed with exasperation. The Crest was the product of a superior alien intelligence, but it was not above extracting petty revenge for having its feelings hurt. "All right, look – I'm sorry I snapped at you before, okay? I realise you were simply alerting me to danger. I promise to pay more attention to your warnings in future."

The Crest laughed hollowly in Dante's head.

"How about if I promise to try?"

That would be more realistic.

"So – which side is closer?"

Swim to your left, the Crest advised. *Your other left*, it added a few moments later.

▪ ▪ ▪

By the time Dante reached the nearest bank the river had swept down to the next bridge. He tried climbing out but his cold, stiffening fingers could not get a purchase on the slippery surface. "Fuoco, is nothing ever easy in this country?" Dante cursed. As if in reply, a red and white life preserver splashed into the water beside him. It was tied to a rope which disappeared up into the fog-shrouded bridge. Dante grabbed the preserver and was dragged from the water. As he rose, Dante could see flashing red and blue lights tinting the air. Britannia's law enforcement agencies had arrived at last – but were they in time to catch the assassin?

Once the life preserver was level with the bridge's parapet he scrambled over the edge, shivering in the cold early evening air. "Thanks for getting me out of there," he said. "If you're quick there's still a chance you can get the shooter. They were on Westminster–"

The sound of a dozen weapons being cocked silenced Dante. He glanced at the surly faces of the policemen surrounding him and realised something was badly amiss. "What's wrong? You look like you're ready to kill someone!"

Dante, you might have been better off staying in the river...

"You don't think I had anything to do with shooting the king, do you?"

A trench-coated man emerged from the throng. "We don't think anything of the sort." The speaker struck a match, its flame briefly illuminating his middle-aged face and receding ginger hair. He was lighting a pipe, its rich, pungent tobacco smoke adding to the mist in the air. "We *know* you tried to murder him."

"That's ridiculous," Dante protested. "I've chased the sniper halfway across London!"

"An interesting interpretation of reality," the pipe-smoker replied. "I was told you were fleeing the scene of the crime, trying to make good your escape. Happily, you failed. Another triumph for Rucka of the Yard." He gestured to the surrounding policemen. "Take him into custody. If he resists, subdue him. Use force if necessary, but he's to be brought in alive."

Dante fought like a wounded animal but even with his bio-blades fully extended he could not hold off all twelve of them. The last sounds he heard were his own screams of pain and the thud of boots into his already bruised and battered torso. Then merciful darkness took him. It was hard to believe it was less than twelve hours since his arrival in Britannia.

TWO

"Any scrap of paper will please a bureaucrat."
– Russian proverb

"For the world-weary tourist, travelling by airship may be the slowest method of reaching Britannia but it is also the most delightfully decadent. It is well worth the exorbitant price simply for the stately way you approach this green and pleasant land. As the ubiquitous fog parts you get your first view of Dover's legendary white cliffs. These iconic surfaces are repainted every summer to ensure they retain that peculiarly lustrous hue, but don't allow that to spoil your appreciation. When the cliffs hove into view, your journey is almost at an end. Only one chore remains: clearing customs. Other parts of the Empire may favour free movement from one state to the next, but Britannia retains many of its sovereign rights despite being a Tsarist territory. As a consequence, gaining entry can take longer than the three-day journey from Paris..."
– Extract from *Around the Empire in Eighty Ways*,
Mikhail Palinski

"The queue is a great British tradition," Lord Peter Flintlock said to his travelling companion with a wan smile. "Almost from birth we are trained to form into long lines and wait patiently for anything and everything. You become inured to the process, you almost welcome it after a while. Getting into a queue gives you a feeling of security, of comfort – you know you're home when you join the back of your first queue."

"Is that a fact?" Spatchcock scowled while scratching at his lice-infested pubic hair. The two men were startlingly different in appearance. Where Flintlock was thin and aristocratic, Spatchcock was short and dishevelled. The Britannia nobleman was blond and blue-eyed, but his associate was foul smelling and even fouler looking. Spatchcock removed the scratching hand from inside his stain-ridden underpants and examined his fingertips with professional disinterest. A tiny white insect jumped from one finger to the next. Spatchcock popped it into his mouth. He munched happily on the crunchy creature, before belching noisily. "Do you usually have to strip half naked first?"

The unlikely duo had kept company with Dante occasionally since serving under him in the war. More recently the three men had helped foil a dangerous genetic experiment to create a terrifying new weapon for the Tsar and saved an ancient monastery from an army of murderous Imperial soldiers. Now Spatchcock and Flintlock were together again, stripped of everything but their underclothes, waiting for Dante in a featureless holding cell. It was something of a comedown after their luxurious journey on the Paris-to-Britannia airship.

Normally the threesome were forced to travel incognito, thanks to the hundred million rouble bounty the Tsar had placed on Dante's head. But this trip had been different, thanks to a communiqué from King Henry to Dante, offering the Romanov rogue full diplomatic immunity and a first class passage for this trip to Britannia. "What's the catch?" Spatchcock had asked when the letter arrived. "Nobody gives you something for nothing in this life, I know that for a fact."

Dante re-read the communiqué but could find no obvious danger. "The king requests my presence and says I am welcome to bring an entourage as large as I see fit."

"Perhaps he's set a date for the royal wedding?" Spatchcock suggested. Britannia's monarch rejoiced in numerous eccentricities – wearing a fruit bowl as his crown, trying to outlaw baldness and urging the creation of a welfare state for the underprivileged. Among his stranger quirks was a long-standing proposal of marriage to Dante, whom he insisted upon calling Nicola instead of Nikolai. Spatchcock smiled, his crooked teeth a greasy mix of black, yellow and green hues. "I can just see your face next to his on a commemorative tea towel."

Flintlock remained stubbornly opposed to the invitation. He had been born and raised in Britannia, but left the country under a cloud. The exact reason for his abrupt departure remained unclear, but rumours spoke of a crime so vile all detail of it had been suppressed to save the nation's embarrassment. Whatever the cause of his leaving, the exiled aristocrat had been back to Britannia only once in the past twenty years. That was a flying visit during the war, when the country was in chaos and his presence could pass unnoticed. It had taken all of Dante's powers of persuasion to talk Flintlock round. Now the wisdom of that was looking more dubious by the minute.

A door opened and Dante was propelled into the holding cell, like the others clad only in his underwear. In Dante's case, it was less than dignified: a black silk g-string he had acquired from a duplicitous prostitute at the Geisha House of the Rising Sun, the legend "GET IT HERE" embroidered in sequins within a Valentine's heart logo. Spatchcock raised an eyebrow at the unconventional apparel. "My mother always told me to wear clean pants when travelling," Dante said, by way of explanation, "in case you have an accident."

I doubt she had that sort of undergarment in mind, the Crest said despairingly.

"We should never have come back here," Flintlock fretted, an embarrassed hand hovering in front of his plaid boxer shorts. "I told you this was a mistake."

"There's been some kind of mix-up with our travel documents," Dante sighed. "The head of customs should be here any minute to sort it out, okay? Don't get your knickers in a twist!"

"That's good advice from a man wearing a whore's drawers," Spatchcock commented.

Fortunately, the doorway reopened and a sour-faced woman in uniform strode into the holding cell. The navy blue jacket and skirt did little to forgive her rotund figure, while the greying hair pulled back into a taut bun gave her face a stretched, arched quality. An identity tag pinned over her left breast identified the new arrival as STAINES, MURIEL. She waited until the door closed, then sternly addressed the trio. "I am Officer Staines, of His Majesty's Royal Customs Department. Which of you is Nicola Dante?"

"Nikolai," Dante said, correcting her. "My first name is Nikolai."

Officer Staines glared at him. "You were travelling under the name Nicola."

Spatchcock shrugged, grinning ruefully. "That'll be the king's fault. He insists on calling Dante here Nicola – even wants to marry him."

"Indeed?" Officer Staines's gaze shifted to the small, squat man. "And what is your name?"

"Spatchcock. Like the chicken."

"Like the chicken."

"That's right."

"A curious name..." the customs official said, noting it down.

"Not as bad as yours, though," Spatchcock replied cheerfully, failing to notice the frenzied gesticulations to be silent from his travelling companions. "I mean, I wouldn't want to be called Staines all my life! I can only imagine how the other kids teased you at school–"

"Yes, thank you for that," she snapped back.

"Dirty Staines, they probably called you," Spatchcock continued. "Grubby Staines. Maybe even Semen–"

"That's enough!" the woman shrieked at the top of her voice, the words echoing round the bleak cell. She paused to regain her composure, then moved on to the last member of the trio. "And your name is?"

"Flintlock," he mumbled in reply.

"A little louder please!"

"Flintlock. Lord Peter Flintlock."

"Lord... Peter..." she repeated, scribbling down his reply. Her writing tool snapped in two as Staines reached the last word. "Flintlock?"

"Yes."

"*The* Lord Peter Flintlock?"

"Yes," he agreed, nodding his head sadly.

"The one who... Who did *that* with... and then..."

"Yes!" Flintlock shouted. "It was me, okay? I did it, I bloody did it!"

All hint of colour drained from the customs official's pallid features. She gazed at Flintlock with undisguised disgust while slowly shaking her head, as if he was the vilest piece of excrement ever to sully the underside of her shoes.

Spatchcock took a step nearer to Staines.

"What did he do, exactly? I kept trying to find out but the old bugger won't say."

"Get away from me," she snarled, sending the little man scurrying away. Once he was standing alongside Dante and Flintlock again, Officer Staines glared at them in turn. "Never in all my years as a customs official have I had the misfortune to encounter such a vile, repulsive, ungodly trio of unwanted arrivals here at Dover – a cross-dresser, a vile and vulgar ferret of a man and..." Words escaped her when she looked at Flintlock. "It pains me more than I can express to say what I now must..."

"Here it comes," Spatchcock whispered out the side of his mouth.

Officer Staines swallowed hard before concluding her speech: "Welcome to Britannia." She snapped her fingers and three more officials entered, each carrying a pile of clothing. "We found nothing untoward in any of your clothing, although health and safety regulations forced us to have Mr Spatchcock's garments destroyed for fear of allowing an unknown number of bacteria into the country – replacements have been provided for him. The Palace of London confirmed your right to enter Britannia and a royal skimmer has been despatched to ferry you direct to his majesty's presence. It should be here within the hour. In the meantime, I am obliged to ask if there is anything else I can do to make your stay more pleasant?"

Spatchcock was about to speak, a lascivious grin spreading across his grimy features, but a sharp elbow into the ribs from Dante stopped him.

Flintlock replied instead. "Any chance of a nice cup of tea?"

It was nine in the morning when the royal skimmer carrying Dante, Flintlock and Spatchcock arrived at the Palace of London. The ornate gold and green vehicle had flown low over the city, giving the new arrivals a glorious tour of the sights, before approaching the royal residence. The palace was a perfect cube of stone and glass, a formidable gothic tower at each corner. In the middle of the structure was the former dome of St Paul's Cathedral, now used as the palace's centrepiece. Above that was a golden statue of Britannia herself, a flagpole bearing the Union Jack clutched in one hand whilst her other held a mighty shield bearing the royal crest. Beside her stood a golden lion, proud and regal. As the skimmer got closer the statue sunk into the vast dome, its place taken by a circular landing pad.

Inside the palace, Dante and his travelling companions were greeted by two soldiers in full ceremonial dress, complete with black bearskin hats and sabres. "If you'll follow us, we have orders to escort you to his majesty," they said in unison.

"Lead on!" Dante said grandly, waving for Spatchcock and Flintlock to follow. Within minutes they were outside the royal bedchamber.

Dante told his associates to wait by the double doors. "Best you stay here while I assess the king's mood," he said. "Henry may be pants-on-his-head-mad, but he's no fool. I want to make sure this isn't some kind of trap after all."

The others were happy to stay put while Dante ventured inside. The first thing he saw was a vast four-poster bed standing in the centre of the room, surrounded by courtiers and attendants in various states of undress, all standing to attention. Rich tapestries lined the walls, while naked soldiers stood in front of the windows, facing the glass exterior. Of King Henry, there was no sign. His bed was unmade but empty. "Er, your majesty?" Dante said nervously.

"Hello! I know those dulcet tones anywhere," a voice called from beneath the bed. "It can only be the lovely Nicola, come to rescue me again!"

Dante raised an eyebrow at the nearest member of the household staff. The attendant sighed wearily and shrugged. Dante stepped closer to the four-poster. "Where are you, your majesty?"

"Under the bed, of course! Safest place to be – come and join me!"

"Well, I don't know if that's wise..."

"I said *join* me," the king insisted. "Otherwise I'll be forced to give you a smacked bottom, you saucy little minx!"

Perhaps you'd best do as he says, the Crest suggested. *I doubt even you would enjoy receiving a spanking from an elderly man.*

Dante dropped to his knees and crawled towards the bed. A single candle lit the scene beneath the mattress, where the king was cowering in a blue and white striped nightshirt, clutching a white porcelain chamber pot to his chest. Henry had aged since Dante saw him last. The king's hair was now snow white where once it had been greying, and heavy bags underlined his eyes. The ruler of all Britannia had lost weight too, his short but rotund figure a shadow of its former opulence. "There you are!" Henry said, a hint of desperation audible at the edge of his rich, rasping voice. "Hurry along, Nicola, we haven't got all night you know."

"Actually, it's morning outside," Dante replied, joining the king in his refuge.

"Already? My, how time crawls." Henry offered the contents of his chamber pot to the new arrival. "Care for a drink?"

"No thank you, your majesty."

"Oh well, all the more for us!" The king supped greedily from the yellow liquid in the bowl.

"Us, your majesty?"

"Yes, of course! Haven't you ever heard of the royal wee?"

Dante decided to ignore Henry's latest flight of fancy. "You sent for me, sire."

"That's right, I did, Nicola!"

"Nikolai, sir."

"That's what I said, Nicola – don't contradict me, damn you!"

Be careful what you say, the Crest warned. *It seems his majesty is more unstable and paranoid than the last time you met here. Remember, he could have you executed on a whim.*

"Of course, sire. You were going to explain why you sent for me?"

"I was?"

"Yes, your majesty."

"Isn't it obvious?" Henry asked, gesturing at the naked legs of his attendants and courtiers standing around the bed. "They're trying to kill me!"

"Who is trying to kill you, sire?"

"Everyone, obviously. That's why I don't let anyone remain fully dressed in my presence, as a way of ensuring they don't have any concealed weapons about them."

"I see..." Dante replied cautiously. "Have specific threats been made against you?"

"Not since my daughter tried to have me beheaded in Trafalgar Square, but you and valiant troopers saved me on that occasion. What I wouldn't give for a squad of such soldiers!"

"That was during the war, sire. The Rudinshtein Irregulars were disbanded after the Tsar won, but I have brought two of my men with me."

The king smiled gratefully. "Good, Nicola, good. Besides Babs, you're the only person I can trust anymore. I knew you wouldn't let me down."

"Never, sire."

"There'll be a knighthood in this for all of you, if you can ferret out the conspirators."

"Well, we'll do our best," Dante promised.

"That's the ticket!" Henry enthused, shaking his chamber pot enthusiastically and slopping the remaining contents all over the floor.

"Coo-eee!" a female voice called out. "Anybody in here?"

"We're under the bed, my dear," the king replied cheerfully.

"Who's we?" the woman asked.

"Henry and Nicola – Nicola's come all the way from the continent to see us!"

"I don't think I've met her. Send her out so we can be introduced."

"Yes, dear," Henry said. "It's high time you met Babs, Nicola. She's been a boon to me these past few months. Well, off you go!"

Dante twisted round to see the new arrival. Most of her was obscured by the vast bed overhead but he could make out a pair of dainty feet leading to two slim, shapely legs. "Who is it? You never told me you had a lover, your majesty."

"A lover? Don't be disgusting!" The king's face crumpled disdainfully. "As if I'd do anything so unsavoury with a member of my family!"

That confused Dante still further. Princess Marie-Anne was still being held captive in the Tower of London. "I thought you only had one daughter?"

"I do," Henry insisted, pushing his guest out from under the bed. "Now go and talk to Babs. Don't worry, she won't bite – the dear lady should have had her breakfast by now."

Dante reluctantly emerged from beneath the royal bed, not at all sure what he would find waiting for him. Amidst all the semi-naked staff stood a beautiful young blonde woman, wearing a translucent black baby doll nightie. She was petite in height, the top of her head level with Dante's shoulders, but possessed a gently heaving bosom of remarkable proportions. She smiled at Dante with gleaming white teeth, a twinkle of mischief at the corner of her warm, friendly eyes. "Hello? I thought Henry said your name was Nicola? You don't look like a Nicola to me, duckie!"

Dante shook his head politely and smiled. "My name's Dante, Nikolai Dante." He leaned forward and kissed the back of Babs's left hand. "Delighted to make your acquaintance."

She gave a raucous giggle in response, her considerable décolletage bouncing in time with her laughter. "Ooh, ain't you a charmer? I bet you're a real smoothie with the young ladies!"

"They don't come much younger than you, Miss…?"

"Miss! You hear that, Henry? He called me Miss!" Babs giggled again, flapping her hands in the air. "You'll make me blush, you will!"

Dante, I'm searching all Imperial records for any mention of a Babs Windsor McKray. There's only one such name listed in my database.

But Dante was not listening to the warning voice in his head. "Perhaps we could get better acquainted, once my assignment for the king is completed," he said smoothly.

"Ooh, that would be nice," Babs enthused. "Normally young men run a mile when I try to persuade them to be my special friend." She winked heavily at Dante, then broke into another raucous round of tittering and hand flapping.

Babs Windsor McKray is better known as Queen Barbara Windsor McKray, the Queen Mother. This woman is a hundred and three years old!

Dante froze, his gaze still fixed on Babs's bouncing bosoms. "I..."

The king emerged from beneath his bed, still clutching the chamber pot. "Well, how are you two getting along?"

"I think this young man is coming on to me," Babs confided.

"I... I..." Dante repeated helplessly.

"Nonsense, mother!" Henry said brusquely. "Eating all that royal jelly may make you look younger than my daughter, but we all know what happens when the effect wears off – don't we?"

Babs nodded unhappily.

"Besides," the king continued, "young Nicola is already betrothed to me!" He illustrated the point by slapping Dante's buttocks and waggling his eyebrows suggestively.

Spatchcock and Flintlock stood outside the royal bedchamber, their arms folded, backs leaning against the glint-edged doorframe. A slow smile of satisfaction crossed the smaller man's face, closely followed by a look of disgust on Flintlock's features. "I say, where is that vile smell coming from?" He caught the mischievous glint in his companion's eye. "Must you break wind in every building we ever enter?"

"I like to leave something behind everywhere I go," Spatchcock said, grinning broadly.

"You could at least give me fair warning!"

"The element of surprise is half the fun."

Before Flintlock could reply Dante hurriedly emerged from the bedchamber, leaving behind two giggling members of the royal family. "Well, what's the story?" Spatchcock asked.

"The king thinks he is going to be assassinated soon."

"Not an unlikely event, considering the bloodline," Flintlock observed. Britannia's royal household had survived its last crisis through intermarriage with London's most infamous crime family. The result had secured the future of the monarchy but doomed its descendents to a lifetime of bloodletting and backstabbing worthy of the Borgias. Princess Marie-Anne's many attempts to usurp her father were notable for their lack of subtlety. The McKray blood was obviously more dominant in her genetic make-up. "But why should it happen sooner rather than later? And what does he want with you?"

Dante shrugged. "Apparently Britannia Intelligence intercepted a coded transmission of an assassin being hired to kill the king. They didn't get all the message, so we don't know who is behind it, but the hit is due to take place any day now. The king believes I'm the only one he can trust and it's our job to keep him alive." Dante tugged thoughtfully on the bristles of his beard. "I want you two to stay here and keep watch over Henry. He's madder than a three-pound note, but I believe he's genuinely afraid for his life. Whatever insanity he drags you into, play along – just make sure he stays safe until I return, okay?"

"Where are you going?" Flintlock asked.

"To see the person with the most to gain from Henry dying." Dante sighed. "Get one of the courtiers to call ahead to the Tower of London. Tell them Nikolai Dante requests a private interview with Princess Marie-Anne."

THREE

"Better free than in a gilt cage."
– Russian proverb

"The Tower of London's history dates back almost 1600 years when William the Conqueror had a wooden fortress built beside the Thames to keep locals from rebelling against the Normans. A stone keep known as the White Tower was constructed on top of old Roman fortifications and soon grew into a full-scale castle. The Tower was best known as a prison for many centuries, holding such celebrity inmates as Queen Elizabeth I, the explorer Sir Walter Raleigh and Twentieth century German war criminal Rudolf Hess. The famous structure later became a tourist attraction and home to the fabled Crown Jewels. Fifty years ago the historic structure was disassembled, moved a mile west along the Thames and reconstructed as part of the new look London tourist zone. Lately the Tower has resumed its role as a place of incarceration for out of favour royalty."
– Extract from *The Smirnoff Almanac of Fascinating Facts*, 2673 edition

Dante emerged from the king's private skimmer to find twenty-five yeoman warders waiting for him. Each was clad in full ceremonial uniform, their red knee-length tunics resplendent with gold piping. The midday sun gleamed on each warders' black patent leather shoes and glinted from the blades of their ceremonial swords. A dozen guards stood on either side of the grey cobbled path that led into the Tower of London.

"Bojemoi," Dante muttered under his breath. "Does this entire country like nothing better than getting in a queue?"

The yeomen are forming an honour guard for your visit, the Crest sighed.

"Oh!" Dante smiled. "I usually see the inside of a prison when I'm under arrest or trying to break somebody else out."

One of the warders marched toward Dante and saluted briskly. "Yeoman First Class Marcus Reynolds at your service, sir! Please accept our apologies for the paucity of this reception party, but we were only informed of your imminent inspection ten minutes ago, sir!"

Dante did his best to return the salute. "No need to apologise, er, yeoman – this is not an official state visit. I've come to speak with her royal highness, Princess Marie-Anne."

"So I understand, sir. If you don't mind my asking, is that wise?"

"Wise?"

Reynolds looked abashed. "It's simply that... Well, her royal highness is not the easiest prisoner we have kept in our custody here. She is prone to unhappiness and... outbursts."

Dante's eyes strayed to the other warders. Almost all of them bore bruises, livid scars or broken noses. Reynolds himself had a badly blackened eye, the surrounding skin purple and blotchy, while a savage cut extended through both lips. "So I can see. I trust you have a safe enclosure in which to keep her during my visit?"

The warder nodded grimly. "We've recently transferred her to our maximum security wing in the basement, as much for our safety as anything else, sir.

Her royal highness may have all the airs and graces of a princess, but you should never forget what she is."

"What is that?"

"Oh, she's a monster," another voice interjected. "Pure sociopath. It's so rare to have one in captivity – normally they occupy positions of power within the political system."

The person speaking was a tall, elegant man who had appeared from within the tower. He advanced toward Dante, hand outstretched in welcome. "Forgive me, I'm Doctor Eric Malvern, the Tower of London's resident psychiatrist. I've been counselling the warders in how best to deal with her royal highness – or the people's princess, as she likes to be called."

Dante shook the offered hand, struggling to mask his distaste at Malvern's moist, clammy grip. "She's always been prone to delusions of grandeur, in my limited experience of her."

The doctor's eyebrows shot up. "You've met her before?"

"Twice. I proved she had used the drug Psykd: Range 27 to drive her father insane. That led to her being imprisoned. I also stopped her having the king executed during the war."

Malvern could not disguise his delight. "You're Nikolai Dante!"

"In the flesh."

"This will be fascinating! To see her royal highness brought face to face with the man responsible for her downfall – psychiatrists wait years to witness such confrontations! Of course, she hates all of us, thinks I'm her nemesis."

Dante, you will get nowhere with the princess if Doctor Malvern insists on observing your meeting with her. He shows a level of fascination far beyond professional interest, to the point where it verges on sexual arousal. You need to dissuade his attendance, the Crest suggested.

"Indeed," Dante replied, "I couldn't agree more. Perhaps you could show me the way to her royal highness's cell?"

Malvern beamed happily and led Dante into the tower through a foreboding wooden doorway. They strode along ancient corridors, then descended a narrow stone staircase to an underground chamber where more warders were waiting. As they walked, the psychiatrist did his best to warn Dante how dangerous the princess could be. "I fought in the bloodiest battles of the Tsar Wars. I doubt I have much to fear from a single woman."

The doctor's eyes narrowed against Dante's sarcasm. "Good, then you should be able to remember the rules. Do not touch the glass. Do not approach the glass. Give her nothing. If she attempts to pass you anything through the food carrier, do not accept it. Do you understand me?"

Dante nodded. "If you are her nemesis, perhaps it would be best if I went in on my own?"

"But I–"

"That would be the sensible approach from a psychological standpoint, wouldn't it?" Dante added, prompted by the Crest. "What do you think?"

Malvern's face fell as he acknowledged the truth of Dante's suggestion.

"Very well," the doctor said huffily. He nodded to Reynolds, who had followed them down from the entrance. "When our guest has finished, bring him out." Malvern stomped back up the stairs, his fussy, leather-soled shoes squeaking with each step.

The chief warder smiled sympathetically at Dante, then unlocked an old but sturdy metal gateway leading to a holding chamber. "She's past the others, the last cell. You keep to the left."

Once Dante was inside the holding chamber, he could see a long corridor beyond another metal gateway. The walls were made of the same cold bricks as the rest of the tower, crumbling mortar visible between the stones.

Intermittent sections of glass and iron bars marked the presence of cells on the right hand side of the corridor. Light spilled in from a metal walkway overhead, but it could not remove the dank, dismal feeling that hung in the air. Dante had been in more than his fair share of prison cells but the tower was as bad as any of them. This place was despair made real. A folding chair was already positioned outside the most distant cell, facing the glass-fronted enclosure. Dante nodded his readiness to Reynolds.

"I'll be watching you," the warder said kindly, gesturing at a selection of security screens set into the stone wall behind himself. Reynolds signalled another yeoman and the inner gateway between Dante and the underground cells swung open. "You'll do fine."

Dante stepped into the corridor, unable to stop himself being startled when the gate closed again, even though he knew it would happen. The sound of prison doors closing was never comfortable for someone so familiar with the wrong side of the law. Willing himself to be calm, he strolled along the corridor towards Princess Marie-Anne's cell. Dante could smell her before he could see her, the sickening aroma of expensive perfumes cloying his nostrils. When he did reach the cell she was waiting for him, clad in an elaborate gown of silk and brocade, her blonde hair delicately coiffured, her make-up immaculate. She saw him and grimaced.

"Nikolai Dante," she sighed. "Why hasn't someone had the good sense to end your worthless, pathetic life once and for all?"

"Do you think anybody would mind terribly if I murdered the king?" Flintlock asked loudly as he strode into the servants' dining hall at the Palace of London. "I mean, if I accidentally stabbed him to death with one of those blasted paint brushes, or arranged for him to be impaled on something large and fatal – do you think anyone would raise a finger to object? I doubt it, I bloody doubt it!"

Spatchcock was next into the room and dismayed to discover half the palace staff had heard his associate's petulant outburst. "He's joking, he's joking..."

"I bloody well am not," Flintlock replied. "Henry may be king, but he is madder than a badger in a hot air balloon. We could pay an assassin to finish the king off – call it a mercy killing. How much money have you got?" The former aristocrat plunged his hands inside Spatchcock's pockets to search for cash but quickly withdrew them again. "My word, what is in there? Are you keeping worms now?"

"Just the one," Spatchcock replied with a smirk. "He's my best friend."

Flintlock shuddered with revulsion. "Don't tell me anymore, I don't want to know." He spun round to find dozens of staff glaring at him with ill-disguised disgust. "I say, what's the matter?"

A pageboy folded his arms, a sour expression on his face. "You are! Since you two arrived with your lord and master, the whole palace has been in uproar – routines disrupted, the king doing whatever he pleases, the Queen Mother amok amongst the pages – it's a nightmare!"

"What's your name, boy?" Flintlock demanded.

"Fitzwilliam. Darcy Fitzwilliam."

"Well, Master Fitzwilliam, our arrival may have upset the rhythm of your working day but that's as nothing to the indignities I've been subjected to! Your royal highness has required me to pose nude as a subject for him to paint in watercolours."

"Is that what he was trying to paint?" Spatchcock asked. "I wasn't too sure."

Flintlock ignored this comment. "When I got a glimpse of the painting in question, it transpired King Henry had me posing like a fool for nothing – he choose to paint a banana!"

"Are you sure it was a banana?"

"Look, you vile little man, I think I know a banana when I see one!"

Spatchcock shrugged. "I thought it looked more like a painting of your pen–"

"Don't be ridiculous. The thing in the portrait was shaped like a banana!"

"So's your–"

"It was covered in little black spots!"

"Still sounds like–"

"And it was yellow from one end to the other!" Flintlock concluded, glaring at Spatchcock. "And before you said another word, no, my willy is not yellow and it does not look like a banana!"

Spatchcock nodded gravely, waiting for his friend to calm down. Only when Flintlock's nostrils finished flaring did Spatchcock speak again. "Not a full-sized banana, anyway."

The two men were still fighting on the dining hall floor when a footman came in, saying the Queen Mother requested their presence. "Any idea why she needs us?" Spatchcock asked.

"Something to do with a corset, a crowbar and a pot of lubricant," the footman replied, struggling to keep the grin from his features. "And a feather duster, too."

Flintlock wailed bleakly. "Why did I ever let Dante talk me into coming home again? And where is that Russian rapscallion in our hour of need?"

Dante smiled blandly as the princess cursed his name, questioned his parentage and mocked the size of his reproductive organs. "It's a pleasure to see you again, too, Your Highness," he replied once her rant had come to an end. "Yes, I am a bastard. No, I don't mind you taking my name in vain. And as for the contents of my pants…" Dante paused to look down appreciatively at his groin, then grinned broadly. "I haven't had many complaints in that department lately."

"Because no woman is fool enough to sleep with you, most likely!" the princess replied.

"You've been behind bars too long," Dante observed. "Prison has coarsened you."

Marie-Anne hurled another mouthful of abuse and obscenities at him. "See what I mean?"

"Why are you here?" she demanded.

"Your beloved father invited me to Britannia."

"My beloved father is a simpering dolt who doesn't know one day from the next. He isn't fit to lead a dog, let alone rule a country!"

"King Henry is a delightful eccentric," Dante countered.

"King Henry is a doddering lunatic. The sooner he's dead the better."

"When have you scheduled the assassination?"

"What?" The princess glared at her visitor as if he was the madman.

"Your father believes there is a plot to have him murdered, something that would conveniently clear the way for you as heir to the throne." Dante folded his arms. "The king summoned me to Britannia to prevent that from happening."

Marie-Anne stared at him in disbelief, then a grin slowly spread across her pert, pretty face before she dissolved into a fit of giggles. "Y-You?" she spluttered between gasps for air. "P-Protect my father?"

"I've done it before," Dante protested. "I can do it again!"

The princess sniggered with quiet satisfaction. "The sole reason you saved his life last time was thanks to the intervention of an entire platoon of airborne Romanov troops. But for them I would now be in my rightful place as ruler of Britannia."

This bickering is getting you nowhere, the Crest pointed out. *If there is a plot to kill the king, you need details.*

"When will the assassination take place?" Dante demanded.

"I don't know," Marie-Anne replied smugly. "Not precisely."

"But you admit there will be an attempt on the king's life?"

She shrugged. "I certainly hope so. He's an embarrassment to the entire country."

"Answer the question!" Dante bellowed.

"Why should I?" the princess spat back at him. "I've been in this place for six years now, Dante. I know they'll never ever let me out while my father is still alive. What possible reason would I have for preventing his murder, assuming I even knew anything about this alleged plot?"

Game, set and match to her royal highness. New balls, anyone?

"Shut up," Dante said.

"Make your mind up," Marie-Anne replied, not realising his comment had not been directed at her. "Either you want me to talk or you don't."

"What I want doesn't seem to matter, does it?"

"Perhaps not, but I'm going to give you a piece of advice anyway," she said. "I may be a captive but I still have friends in high places. A whisper of conspiracy has reached my ears, no doubt the same whisper that has penetrated the befuddled mind of my dear, soon to be departed, father. In the next twenty-four hours I expect to be released, due to the untimely death of a royal personage not too far from this godforsaken prison. Is that what you wanted to know? Has that made your task any easier, you repulsive piece of Russian excrement?"

"No, but it should make your trial much shorter if I fail to stop the assassination," Dante replied. "You've admitted to complicity in planning a murder."

No, she hasn't, the Crest interjected. *The princess is no fool. She gave you hints without foundation, a glimpse of the truth but nothing more.*

"We'll see," was all Marie-Anne said, but her smile spoke volumes.

"If an attempt is made on the king's life in the next twenty-four hours, I'll make sure your neck ends up on an executioner's block," Dante vowed.

"If the king dies in the next twenty-four hours," she replied, "my first royal proclamation will be to have you hunted down like the dog you are. All the armies in the Empire will not be able to protect you from my wrath!"

"I've been hunted by the best," he said. "The idle threats of a disgraced royal jailbird don't frighten me, princess. You want to see me dead? Get in line. I'm Nikolai Dante and I'm too cool to kill! Or hadn't I told you?" He strolled away from her cell, ignoring the torrent of abuse that followed him along the corridor. Within minutes he was back inside the royal skimmer as it returned to the Palace of London.

Well, that was pleasant, the Crest commented. *It's safe to say her royal highness could swear for Britannia if she took it up professionally.*

"How did she seem to you?" Dante asked.

You're asking my opinion?

"Yes, how did she seem?" Dante waited but the voice in his head did not reply. "Crest?"

Sorry, I was calculating how many days had elapsed since we were first bonded together.

"Why?"

To see how long it has taken you to ask for my view on something, anything.

Dante sighed. "Sarcasm is the lowest form of wit."

Better to have some wits than only possess half of one.

"Crest!"

Sorry. What was the original question?

"The princess – how did she seem to you?"

Dr Malvern's diagnosis was partially accurate. She may be a sociopath, but her narcissistic personality disorder is a greater problem. As for her hatred of you, well, obviously, that's quite understandable in the circumstances. The remarkable thing there is how quickly she reached such a fever pitch of antagonism – most women need to meet you four times before their dislike reaches murderous levels.

Dante gritted his teeth. "Putting to one side her feelings towards me, I wanted to know what you thought of her general demeanour."

I would have to say calm. Yes, cool, calm and collected.

"That's what I thought too. Her raging at me was a smokescreen, a sideshow to distract from her real feelings. She fully expects to be Queen of Britannia before noon tomorrow."

I'm glad to discover all the years I've spent grooming you are finally beginning to pay off. You are, at last, showing some hints of perceptiveness and intelligence.

"Of course," Dante added with a smile, "it might just have been her sexual frustration at never having slept with me that fuelled all that rage and anger."

I take it all back, the Crest muttered despairingly.

As the skimmer approached the royal residence, Dante noticed black smoke rising from one of the windows on the palace's northern face. "Pilot, do you know what's inside that room?"

"It's one of the royal apartments, sir, where King Henry and the Queen Mother live."

"Bojemoi," Dante gasped. "We're too late. The assassins have already attacked!"

Dante sprinted through the palace, shouting for the nearest pageboys and footmen to follow him. By the time he reached the royal apartments smoke was billowing from beneath the doors. Dante kicked them open and threw himself inside, bio-blades already extended in anticipation of a battle to the death. Instead he found King Henry dancing naked around a pyre of burning furniture and paintings in the middle of the carpet. An equally undressed and somewhat sheepish Spatchcock was flinging more fuel on to the flames.

"Nicola, there you are!" the king proclaimed happily. "Come and join us, we're performing a rain dance to summon Cumulonimbus, the god of torrential downpours!"

Dante retracted his bio-blades. "If you don't mind my asking, sire – why?"

"Why? Well, why not? The more the merrier, eh, Cocksplutch?"

"Yes, your majesty," Spatchcock replied, throwing another painting onto the roaring fire before joining in the king's gyrations with gleeful abandon.

Dante folded his arms. "No, sire, I was asking why you were doing a rain dance indoors. Isn't it more traditional to perform such rituals outside?"

"I can hardly venture out with assassins lurking behind every corner, can I?"

"I suppose not," Dante agreed. "Then perhaps you could have foregone the fire?"

"I've never heard such arrant nonsense," the king spluttered, coming to an abrupt halt. Spatchcock blundered into the back of the monarch, unable to stop his forward momentum in time. Henry gasped in surprise before looking over his shoulder unhappily. "I say, old chap, careful where you're sticking that thing – I don't mind a bit of sport but there's a time and place for buggering about, Cockscratch, and this isn't it!"

"Sorry, your majesty," Spatchcock said apologetically, retracting the rolled up canvas he had accidentally jabbed into Henry's back.

"I should think so too!" The king turned back to Dante. "I was hoping to watch the annual cheddar cheese chasing championships from Cheshire, but the Britannia Broadcasting Corporation will insist on covering the real tennis tournament at Wombledin."

"Wimbledon?"

"That's the chappy! So I decided to summon some rain clouds to wash out play for the day." Henry peered through the smoke to the view outside. "No sign of success yet, alas!"

"And the broken window?" Dante asked.

"That was me," Spatchcock admitted. "The room started filling up with smoke, so I decided to create some ventilation. Smashing the glass seemed the only sensible option."

"I'm surprised you didn't set off every smoke alarm in the palace."

"Disabled the ones in here before we started, old chap," the king replied, absentmindedly scratching his dangling scrotum. "We're not madmen, you know!"

"Of course not, your majesty," Dante sighed. "But there are smoke detectors in other rooms besides this one." Not sooner had the words left his mouth than an alarm started ringing nearby. A monsoon of cold water gushed from the apartment's overhead sprinklers.

"By Jove, it worked!" The king resumed his rain dance, waving his arms in triumph. "I told you, Cocksnitch! Dull old Nicola didn't believe us, but we proved her wrong, eh?"

"Yes, your majesty!" Spatchcock replied, shouting to be heard above the deluge. Pageboys and footmen were racing round the apartment, trying to rescue antique furniture and artworks from the indoor rainstorm. Dante remained by the doorway, slowly shaking his head.

"Twenty-four hours," he told himself. "Just keep this lunatic alive another twenty-four hours and then we can get out of this madhouse."

Congratulations Dante, the Crest said. *For once in your adult life you are the most sensible person in the room. I suggest you savour the sensation while it lasts.*

Dante waited until Spatchcock danced within reach and then pulled him to one side. "I doubt the answer to this question will make me happy, but I don't suppose you know where Flintlock is right now?"

The grubby-faced runt shrugged. "Last time I saw his lordship, he was trying to escape the amorous advances of the Queen Mother."

A terrified scream from out in the corridor got Dante's attention. He looked out in time to see a naked Flintlock race past with what looked like a feather duster protruding from between his buttocks. Moments later Babs appeared clad in black stockings and a crimson corset, her not inconsiderable bosom bouncing playfully as she scuttled by, a crowbar in one hand and a large pot of lubricant in the other. "Come here, you little tease!" she shouted after the fleeing Flintlock. "You know you love it!"

Four hours later Dante had finally got the rampant royals back under some sort of control. King Henry grudgingly agreed to resume wearing trousers and stop setting fire to priceless Britannia heirlooms, while the Queen Mother was given a fresh dose of royal jelly to calm her down. The Crest had analysed the viscous purple foodstuff and marvelled at its restorative qualities. *One spoonful of this is enough to halt the ageing process – temporarily, of course. Two spoonfuls actually reverses the process. How much is the Queen Mother consuming?*

Dante had already checked with the royal chef Ramsey. "Two litres a day, every day, for the past twenty years apparently."

No wonder her behaviour is somewhat erratic. This jelly contains trace elements of mind-altering chemicals. After eating so much for so long it's astounding she can still form sentences.

"Try telling that to Flintlock." The beleaguered Brit had spent three hours hiding in a broom cupboard and was only coaxed out with the promise that Babs would be suitably restrained. Now Flintlock, Spatchcock and Dante were all gathered in the palace's opulent drawing room on the tenth floor, watching the king and his mother bickering on a chaise longue.

"I keep telling you to cut down on that blasted jelly, Babs! It's sending you doolally."

"That's rich coming from a man who wears a gorilla suit to the opening of Parliament!"

"At least the only lovers I chase were born in the same century as me–"

"Enough!" Dante bellowed, his patience utterly exhausted. "I've listened to you two fight, squabble and rant long enough! Bojemoi, you're meant to be mother and son, not competitors in a constant contest to outdo each other in acts of lust-addled lunacy!"

The abashed pair stared at the rich oriental rug on the floor in the front of them.

"Well?" Dante demanded. "What have you got to say for yourselves?"

Henry and his mother mumbled something inaudible under their breath.

"I can't hear you!"

"We're sorry," the royals admitted.

"That's better," Dante agreed. "Now, if the urge should take either of you to start a fire in the middle of a room, what should you do?"

"Ask for help from one of the servants?" Henry asked sweetly.

"No! You never start fires in the middle of a room!" Dante thundered, his fists shaking.

"Oh," the king replied sulkily.

"And what about sexually molesting the royal staff? And before anyone mentions penises, by staff I mean the household retainers – chambermaids, pageboys and footmen."

Babs stuck out her bottom lip. "We shouldn't exploit our status for our own gratification."

"Exactly."

The Queen Mother folded her arms. "But what's the point in having all this power and status if we can't exploit it?"

"Dash it, you're right, Babs!" Henry agreed. He jumped to his feet and began pacing back and forth in front of a large picture window that offered a glorious view of central London. In the late afternoon sun the city gleamed like a trophy, light glinting off the towers and spires. "I won't be told what to do in my own kingdom, not even by you, Nicola. We may be betrothed but King Henry Windsor McKray takes orders from no woman!"

"Oh, do sit down and shut up," his mother sighed.

"Yes, dear," the king said meekly, returning to the chaise longue. Dante's attention was caught by a flash of light outside the window.

"What was that? It almost looked like a–"

Suddenly the pane of glass exploded inwards, showering the drawing room with razor-sharp shards. Dante screamed a warning as he dived towards the king. "Everybody, get down!"

Spatchcock and Flintlock had not needed telling, having already taken cover at the first sign of trouble. Their time with the Rudinshtein Irregulars had drummed into them the need for speed when in danger, but both also possessed an unusually strong sense of self-preservation. The king and his mother lacked such killer instincts, which was why they both suffered mortal wounds in the next few seconds. The first bullet was sent askew when it shattered the window, flying sideways into a wall to emerge in an adjoining room, where it startled several servants.

The second projectile had no such problems. But for Dante's diving tackle the round would have exploded the king's head like a hammer smashing a ripe watermelon. Instead it entered Henry's left shoulder blade, punctured a lung and departed through his chest, a few centimetres above his heart. The exit wound removed a clump of flesh the size of a child's fist, along with a shower of blood and bone fragments. The third bullet missed the king altogether as he tumbled to the floor beneath Dante, but the Queen Mother was not so fortunate. Babs was standing up to see what all the fuss was about when the window exploded. She had time to gasp in shock before the third bullet shot inside her open mouth and removed the back half of her skull, taking much of her brain stem with it. The elderly nymphomaniac was dead before her body had slumped back on to the chaise longue.

Dante rolled off the king, glancing at Babs long enough to know she was beyond help. His right hand reached instinctively for his Huntsman 5000 rifle, but palace protocol had required he surrender it before entering the building. Dante cursed himself for giving in to such stupidity and twisted round to see if any more attacks were imminent. When no more bullets were forthcoming, he ripped a strip of fabric from the Queen Mother's gown and used it as an impromptu bandage on her son. "Crest, can you analyse the trajectory of those bullets, calculate where the assassin is firing from?"

Completing my calculations now, the voice in his head responded tersely. *All three rounds began from a position of not more than sixty-two metres above the ground.*

"Search your database – what's that high on the city skyline, within range of here?"

Two structures, but only one has a clear line of sight – Nelson's Column.

"Then that's where I'll find the bastard who did this," Dante snarled. "Spatch! Flintlock! Are you okay?" The two men nodded from their hiding places. "Good, then get over here and look after the king before he bleeds to death."

Spatchcock was immediately crawling across the glass-strewn floor. "What about Babs?"

Dante shook his head grimly. The Queen Mother had been a sex-crazed centenarian, but she never meant anybody any harm. Her murder deserved to be avenged as much as the attack upon the king. "Crest, how long does the fastest route to the palace landing pad take from here?"

Three minutes and seventeen seconds.

"Too long. I'll have to take a short-cut to our killer!" Dante pulled himself into a crouch, then ran to the shattered window and dived through the hole, falling towards almost certain death.

In the drawing room Spatchcock ignored Dante's daredevil departure and concentrated on tending to the king. Blood was coursing from Henry's wounds faster than it could be staunched. "Flintlock, get out from behind that chair and go for help!"

"Do I have to?" the inveterate coward asked feebly.

Spatchcock spat a curse at him and Flintlock scuttled to the drawing room door, calling for the royal staff. Within seconds a phalanx of footmen and pageboys was pouring into the room, Darcy Fitzwilliam among them, his young face shocked by the violence he found. "My God – they've butchered the royal family!"

"Don't be an ass," Spatchcock snarled. "We didn't do this – we're trying to save them!"

Fitzwilliam searched the faces of the others. "You heard them in the dining hall! They were shouting about killing the king! Now they've done it!"

Flintlock shook his head, pointing at the shattered picture window. "The shots came from outside. We were lucky not to get hit ourselves!"

The pageboy jabbed a finger into Flintlock's face. "Murderer!" he screamed.

Agent Penelope Goodnight was making love to a beautiful woman when the emergency signal came through. For six months Britannia Intelligence's finest female operative had been working on the French ambassador, breaking down her barriers. The ambassador was as careful as she was beautiful, a full bodied woman who kept herself in shape despite having been a widow for ten years. It had required all of Goodnight's cunning, feminine charm and guile to persuade the ambassador into having an affair that would make her susceptible to coercion and blackmail. Now, after all that delicate preparation, all those subtle romantic overtures, the Marquise de Rosemonde had finally given in to lust – Goodnight's mission objective was about to be consummated. But, just as the secret agent's fingers invaded the Marquise's lingerie, a voice of authority spoke in Goodnight's concealed earpiece.

"All agents, respond immediately!"

Startled by the harsh, patrician voice, Goodnight pulled away involuntarily pushing her long hair away from her face.

"No, *mon cherie*, don't stop now," the ambassador pleaded. "I resisted you for so long, don't torture me like this. I have surrendered myself to you. I can't live unless I make you happy. I promise – no more refusals, and no more regrets."

"All agents, respond immediately!" the earpiece said again.

Goodnight knew ignoring the message was impossible. It would keep repeating itself, louder and louder, until it got a response. Better to find out why the emergency channel had been activated, then return to the job in hand. "Forgive me, I am not sure I can go through with this."

"No, do not torment me," the French woman pleaded, her fingers grasping imploringly at thin air as Goodnight climbed off the silk sheets.

"Give me a moment to think – please?"

"Only if you promise to return and… fulfil me."

Goodnight smiled. "I promise." The secret agent retreated to the doorway, blew a lust-filled kiss to the Marquise, then slipped from the room. Once out of earshot, Goodnight activated the earpiece microphone. "What the hell is so important that you pull me from between the French ambassador's thighs?"

"The king is dying or possibly dead by now, the victim of an assassination plot. The Queen Mother's corpse is getting cold, and the government is in uproar. All operatives are being recalled to headquarters immediately for a full briefing."

"But my mission–"

"Can wait! F is allowing no exemptions from this, and you know what a bitch she can be if anybody challenges her orders."

"Don't remind me." Goodnight's department had undergone a brutal purge, courtesy of Britannia Intelligence's new commander. "So how do I placate the French ambassador?"

"You're creative – make something up. I'm sure her thighs will be just as warm and welcoming once this little emergency has past."

"I wouldn't count on that. It's taken me half a year to melt this ice queen."

"Nevertheless, F's command stands. Put your trousers on and get back here!"

FOUR

"Wrath is a poor adviser."
– Russian proverb

"Scotland Yard has served as London's police headquarters for close to a millennium. The original building was sited near a courtyard supposedly used by a Caledonian king, a myth that gave the area its name. In the many centuries since, the capital's police force has shifted headquarters more than a dozen times as a consequence of overcrowding, terrorist attacks or structural problems. Following the second relocation the building became known as New Scotland Yard. After that it was decided that adding further prefixes would verge on the ludicrous and all subsequent headquarters have been known simply as Scotland Yard. The current police HQ is a gross, intimidating cube of concrete and steel less than a kilometre from the Palace of London. What few windows it has are restricted to the top floor. Only the most dangerous suspects are ever taken to Scotland Yard for interrogation, usually for matters that threaten national security. Fewer still ever emerge alive."

– Extract from *Places to Avoid in Britannia*, first edition

Dante came round in a dark, dank cell. The air was thick with the stench of stale piss and fear, while a cluster of flies feasted on a clump of faeces in one corner. The walls were coarse, grey cement, as was the floor beneath Dante's battered and bruised body. The sole source of light was a small opening high above the blank metal door. Dante uncurled himself from a foetal position to find his hands were cuffed together behind his back. Manacles also bound his ankles, a few links of chain between them. His jacket and boots were gone, as was his leather belt. He shivered in his white linen shirt and thin trousers.

How long had he been held prisoner here? More to the point, where was this place? Dante rasped a hand across his neck below the line where his beard usually stopped. Not more than a night's growth, so that made it Wednesday morning. As for his location, he could hear murmuring voices outside the cell, gruff London accents clearly audible even if their words were not. So, he was almost certainly still in Britannia. The last thing he could recall was being pulled from the Thames and accused of trying to murder the king. Everything after that was a jumble of memories from the previous days.

The sound of approaching footsteps snapped Dante back to the present.

He heard a beeping noise was audible, then the door swung inwards, flooding the narrow chamber with light. Once his eyes had adjusted, Dante could see three men standing in the corridor, staring at him. The one in the centre he recognised from the previous night – an inspector of some sort. The man certainly displayed all the dull arrogance of a policeman, his stance redolent of self importance. The inspector nodded to the other two, a burly pair whose uniforms marked them out as guards. "He should be ready," the inspector said. "Take him to interrogation room two. Don't give him any water. If he soils himself, he can stay that way until we get some answers."

The two men produced truncheons and moved inside the cell, grinning from ear to ear. Before the still dazed

Dante had time to react blows rained down upon his head, beating all resistance from him. Blackness closed in, a blessed relief from the dull thuds of pain.

The second time he came round, Dante was strapped to a chair in a white room, his arms pinned behind him with both wrists clamped to the back of the seat. When he extended his bio-blades they were unable to find anything to cut. Someone had obviously done their research and found a way to negate the abilities given him by the Crest. "Crest, where am I?" But no reply came. "Crest?"

"Good, it can't hear you," a crisp, slightly nasal male voice replied. Dante twisted round to see the police inspector leaning against one of the clean, bare walls.

"Why not? Have you drugged me?"

The inspector smiled thinly. "The Tsar may possess the chemicals to overcome a Romanov Weapons Crest, but we are not so fortunate here in Britannia." He gestured at their surroundings: a perfectly square chamber, its walls, floor and ceiling all gleaming white. There were no light fixtures visible anywhere. Instead all the surfaces gave off a faint glow. "We call this the White Room. All the surfaces have a luminescent coating that also debilitates psychic abilities. This has the side effect of breaking the link between you and your Weapons Crest."

"Who are you?" Dante demanded.

"I told you my name last night, when I arrested you for the assassination of King Henry."

"He's dead?"

"Not yet, but it's a matter of time. His wounds are severe. The surgeons and doctors doubt he will survive another day." The inspector extracted a wooden pipe from his grey jacket and tapped the bowl against the side of Dante's chair. Next he produced a slim packet of tobacco from another pocket and began filling his pipe. Finally, he struck a match and used its flame to light up. "My name is Rucka – Inspector Rucka, of the Yard."

"Rucka?" Dante snorted derisively. "That rhymes so nicely with fu–"

The inspector lashed out with a fist, the vicious blow snapping Dante's head sideways. Rucka waited until his captive had recovered before replying. "Spare me any juvenile attempts at humour. Trust me, I have heard them all over the years and I do not intend to be insulted by a murdering misanthrope like you."

Dante spat a mouthful of blood on the floor. "Hope that doesn't ruin your interior design."

Rucka ignored the comment, preferring to suck on his pipe. "You may be interested to know both your accomplices were captured at the scene of the crime."

"Spatchcock and Flintlock? They aren't my accomplices – none of us had anything to do with the attempt on King Henry's life."

"You simply happened to be in the room when he was shot, is that it?"

"He invited us to Britannia," Dante insisted. "The king believed someone was planning to assassinate him..."

"So he wasn't quite the lunatic everyone thought, eh?" Rucka said thoughtfully. "But his judgement of character still leaves a lot to be desired."

"Henry wanted me to protect him!"

"Poacher turned gamekeeper, is that your story?"

"Sorry?"

"You claim to have been acting as his majesty's personal bodyguard, is that it?"

"Yes," Dante agreed vehemently.

"Then why did you flee the scene of the crime?"

"I didn't flee. I was doing your job for you – hunting down the assassin!"

"I see. Well, can you give a description of this person you claim to have been hunting?"

"The shooter was wearing a mask so I didn't see his face."

"But you're certain it was a man – why?"

"I..." Dante thought back to the previous night, trying to remember past the beatings. "I got a glimpse of him, after I was thrown into the river. He was bald, with a goatee beard and an unhappy face. His accent, it wasn't local. I heard him arranging a meeting with someone – I think he called them 'the old man'."

Rucka arched an eyebrow at his prisoner. "Bald, a goatee beard, an unhappy face – not exactly a description likely to make finding this alleged suspect any easier, is it?"

"It's not my job to make your job easy," Dante snarled.

"Quite the reverse, I would have thought." The inspector smiled thinly. "All of this is irrelevant. Every piece of evidence points to you as the assassin. Your partners in crime were heard by royal household staff loudly proclaiming how much they wanted to see the king dead. You fled the scene when your plan went awry and resisted arrest when my men intervened. You even told Princess Marie-Anne of your plans to murder her father! Hardly the actions of an innocent man, wouldn't you agree?"

"The princess hates me, she'd say anything to incriminate me. Diavolo, she probably hired the assassin. Can't you see I'm being framed? How stupid are you?"

"Stupid enough to have caught Nikolai Dante, supposedly the most dangerous man in the Empire. Stupid enough to have him bang to rights for murdering our beloved Queen Mother. Stupid enough to have found more than sufficient evidence to prove complicity in King Henry's slaying – assuming his royal highness does not survive."

"What about the shattered window? That broke when the first bullet hit it. You must have noticed the window was smashed in from outside – how did I manage that while I was still inside the room, inspector? Answer that!"

Rucka smiled. "Quite simple. You had an accomplice shoot the window from outside, in an effort to provide you with an alibi. For all I know your accomplice is this bald man with the goatee and unhappy face to whom you seem intent upon shifting all the blame."

"This is ludicrous!" Dante snapped. "I demand to see a lawyer. You do still have lawyers in Britannia, don't you?"

"There's no need to be insolent," the inspector warned. "Of course we still have lawyers. Some of the finest legal minds in the Empire reside in Britannia. Alas, they will be of little use in this case, since you have already been found guilty of murder."

"I haven't even been tried! What about due process, the letter of the law?"

"Overruled, in view of the national crisis precipitated by your heinous actions." Rucka smiled. "The people of Britannia are demanding justice and that is what we shall give them. Your accomplices are already en route to the Tower of London where they will await execution. Once we have concluded our little chat, you will be taken to join them."

"This isn't justice, it's a farce! No one has the authority to overrule an entire legal system!"

"I do," a woman's voice replied. A doorway appeared in the seamless white walls and Princess Marie-Anne entered, smiling broadly. She was wearing a pristine white gown, a diamond tiara perched atop her blonde tresses. Once she was inside the door vanished, leaving no chance for escape. "With my father so close to death, the government felt obliged to release me from the Tower – I am the heir apparent, after all."

"You're a figurehead," Dante insisted. "The monarchy has no real power in Britannia."

"Not as such, but I contacted the Tsar. Vladimir was most amused to hear of your travails and only too happy to vouchsafe me sufficient authority to overrule our tiresome legal process. He's hoping to clear a window in his schedule for an Imperial visit to Britannia, simply so he can attend your public execution – he must hate you almost as passionately as I. Isn't that sweet?" The princess nodded to Rucka, who produced a document and read aloud from it.

"Nikolai Dante, by the power vested in the nation of Britannia by Vladimir Makarov, Tsar of All the Russias, you are hereby found guilty of murder and sentenced to death. You are to be taken from this place to await execution, whereupon your lifeless body shall be transported to Saint Petersburg for verification and vivisection. Has the convicted felon anything to say?"

Dante spat a fresh mouthful of blood at the princess, spattering her gown with crimson phlegm. Her mouth remained fixed in a smile but her eyes glared at him with murderous intensity. "For that little indignity I shall ensure your execution is as slow and painful as humanly possible. I look forward to seeing you die, Dante – you have been a thorn in my side for far too long." She snapped her fingers and the doorway reappeared. "Get this filth out of my sight," she commanded. "Tell the warders at the Tower of London to put him in my former cell. He should find the accommodations less than satisfactory."

Agent Goodnight strode north across Westminster Bridge towards the most famous clock in the Empire, Big Ben. The covert operative moved unnoticed among the tourists crowding the bridge, each visitor battling for the best position to have themselves pictured in front of the legendary landmark. None had a clue the secret HQ of Britannia Intelligence was a few metres away, the agent thought, but then it would hardly have been a secret if they did. Goodnight nonchalantly descended a stone staircase on the bridge's eastern side, close to the Houses of Parliament.

The staircase passed an inconspicuous green metal door in one of the bridge's support columns. Goodnight rested a hand lightly against the door for five seconds, letting hidden circuitry identify and compare the palm-print, heat signature and DNA likeness with that held on file. Once the computer-controlled system was satisfied, the secret agent had permission to enter, the door slid open with a sigh and Goodnight slipped inside. Moments later the door was closed, nearby tourists still blissfully unaware of what they had missed.

There was a tiny elevator the other side of the doors, no bigger than a broom cupboard. It plunged thirty metres into the ground, far below the level of the Thames and the old Underground train tunnels. The elevator shuddered to a halt and a new door opened, allowing Goodnight access to Britannia Intelligence's headquarters. The secret agent strolled along the corridors, nodding to other staff members, saluting whenever a senior officer strode past. In less than a minute Goodnight slipped into the main briefing room, where the lights had been dimmed in anticipation of F's arrival. Dozens of other operatives and HQ staff were gathered in the musty chamber, most seated in rows of stiff-backed chairs. Those who had arrived late lined the walls, all facing the small podium at the front of the briefing room.

Agent Golightly noticed her colleague's arrival and sidled over. "Cutting it fine?"

"I made it, didn't I?" Goodnight said with a smile. "Where's the ice queen?"

"Due any second now. How's the ambassador?"

"I had to pull out at the last minute." Goodnight slid a hand across the other agent's buttocks, gently massaging them. "And we both know how frustrating that can be."

Golightly shook her pretty head, a rueful smile on her pursed lips. "Tease! Always leave them wanting more, that should be your motto."

"I'll try to remember that when I commission my epitaph," Goodnight replied. The low murmur of voices around them died away as their commander approached the podium.

▪ ▪ ▪

When Dante came round for the third time, he was lying on a cold metal floor, chains and manacles binding his wrists and ankles together once more. The first thing to enter his mind was an after-image of the last thing he could recall. Rucka had arranged for Dante to be beaten unconscious again once the princess had left the White Room. "It's the only way to make certain you can't escape before we get you to the Tower," the inspector explained as truncheons pummelled Dante. "After that, you cease to be my responsibility. You will be what one of our greatest authors called an SEP – Somebody Else's Problem."

Dante made a mental note to kick the crap out of Rucka if they should ever meet again. The inspector was the worst kind of bully, one who gets other people to do their dirty work, the sort who rarely sullies their own hands. But dealing with Rucka would have to wait. Dante had more pressing problems now, such as finding a way out of his situation.

Whatever you do, don't speak. Don't do anything to let the guards know you're conscious – they'll only beat you senseless again and your enhanced healing abilities are still struggling to mend a fractured skull and severe concussion. So, for once, keep silent and listen to me.

Dante nodded his head imperceptibly to let the Crest know its words were understood.

Good. You're in the cargo hold of a police hover-van called Black Maria. *By my estimation the vehicle should arrive at the Tower of London within minutes, so there isn't much time. There are three guards in here with you, and three more in the front. All except the driver are armed. Relax your mental defences and cede control of your bio-blades to me.*

Dante willed himself to relax but involuntarily tensed as the Crest flexed inside his mind.

I said relax! If you don't escape before this van reaches the Tower, you may not get another chance. Empty your mind of all intelligent thoughts – an easy task for you, of all people.

Dante ignored the jibe and concentrated on thinking about nothing. Gradually the Crest claimed control of his nervous system, an uneasy sensation akin to having a dozen spiders running back and forth across his brain.

That's better, the Crest said. *Extruding bio-circuitry... now.*

Dante watched as ripples of purple and silver danced below the skin of his hands. His fingernails slowly stretched themselves out into elongated talons, before curling round to infiltrate the locks on his manacles. Within moments each binding was undone. Dante tried to move but the Crest said for him to wait.

Your limbs are stiff and sore. Allow thirty seconds for your restored circulation to revive them, it urged. *All the guards are wearing body armour, but it only extends down to their thighs – they don't expect to be attacked at floor level. There are two men directly behind you within striking distance, and a third beyond them. He's the most dangerous target as you can't reach him straight away.* Dante gave another nod to show his understanding. *Good. Your arms and legs should have recovered. I'm releasing control of the bio-circuitry. Do your worst.*

Dante allowed himself a grim smile, extended his bio-blades to their full length, and then went on the attack. He swiped his swords across the floor, neatly severing the feet of the two guards within reach. They went down screaming, their blood spraying the air. The third man was still drawing his weapon when Dante dived full-length at him, bio-blades pinning the guard to the back door. When Dante ripped his blade free, the dead man slid mutely to the floor. "Three down, three to go," he muttered. "Crest, how far are we off the ground?"

About a hundred metres. Diving out the back door is not an option.

"Guess I'll have to land this thing instead." Dante strode to the front end of the cargo hold and flattened his hands against the wall. "How far am I from the other guards in the front seat?"

Half an arm's length. Why?

The woman known as F would never be described as beautiful. True, a mischievous sparkle sometimes appeared in the corner of her eyes and her bosom had a comely aspect to its sway, but her looks were no aphrodisiac. She knew her face was haughty and arrogant, with its high cheekbones and prominent, almost Grecian nose. Her mouth was unusually wide but it rarely had a chance to smile, such was her stern demeanour. She kept her body hidden behind an armoury of tweed skirts and polo neck jumpers, her hair clipped into a curt bob. Everything about her outward appearance indicated she meant business. Only the stiletto heels of her black, knee-length leather boots hinted at anything out of ordinary – sensible shoes were not F's style.

Power turned her on; the getting of power, the wielding of it, the delicious delight of having dominance over another human being. She savoured it as a gourmet enjoys fine cuisine. Her rise to prominence within Britannia's intelligence community had not simply been a matter of career fulfilment or proving she was the best of her generation. No, for F the acquisition of authority was a way of sating her most rapacious desires. Every order she gave, every memo she drafted, every underling she disciplined or humiliated – each of these acts was a dirty little thrill. Addressing a gathering of every available operative in Britannia, commanding their attention, holding them in her thrall... that was a multiple orgasm for F. But none of her staff would ever know that from her expression.

She glared at those assembled, hands clasped together behind her back. "By now you will have all heard about the tragic events at the Palace of London last night. The king remains in a critical condition, with surgeons offering little hope of recovery. The Queen Mother's body is being worked on by the finest undertakers. Once fit to be seen by the public, it will lie in state at Westminster Abbey before a full state funeral is held. With the king incapacitated, her royal highness Princess Marie-Anne has been released from the Tower of London and is already assuming responsibility for many of her father's day-to-day duties."

There was a murmur among the agents but it was silenced when F cleared her throat. "I do not recall asking for anyone's opinion," she snapped, a shiver of delight running down her spine. "Questions will be asked with regards to how the assassin got through our defences, why we did not anticipate this attack and what we could or should have done to prevent it. No doubt heads will roll, but not from within this department, you may be assured of that. However, we must remain vigilant, keeping one step ahead of the police investigation, to ensure the intelligence community does not take the blame for this lamentable incident. Your individual controllers have specific assignments for each of you. All other investigations and assignments are temporarily suspended until this matter is resolved. This is a black day in the history of Britannia – let our conduct show that we can respond to the situation with the verve and skill required! That is all."

F nodded curtly, then stepped down from the podium, moving among the operatives and headquarters staff as they filed out. Her eyes lit upon a particular agent who had been at the back of the room. "Goodnight!"

"Yes, ma'am?"

"Wait here, please – I have a special assignment for you."

"Yes, ma'am."

Once the room had emptied, F gestured for Goodnight to sit down. But the head of intelligence remained standing, to reinforce her position of dominance. "First of all, I must remind you of our policy regarding sexual harassment – groping fellow agents like young Golightly may help pass the time in staff meetings, but it is strictly prohibited under Britannia Intelligence's rules and regulations. Do I make myself clear?"

"Yes, ma'am," Goodnight said meekly, eyes not meeting F's gaze.

"You may be our finest seducer, but that does not give you leave to practice on my staff."

"No, ma'am."

"Very well," F said, moderating her tone slightly. "Now, this special assignment – you have been requested by Princess Marie-Anne for an unspecified task to be undertaken on her behalf. No matter what she asks of you or offers you as a reward, remember where your true loyalties lie. An unmarked hover-car will transport you to the palace. In the meantime, I suggest you have a shower and change into something suitable."

The agent frowned. "How can I know what's suitable if I don't know what this task is?"

F smiled. "Use your imagination. I'm told it's one of your strong suits."

Constable Jackson Shaw loved to fly. He loved to fly in planes, in hover-vehicles, even in airships. All his life he had been obsessed with flying, but his limited intellect had prevented him becoming a professional pilot. Shaw was big, he was burly and he was thicker than concrete, all of which left one career opportunity to him: Shaw became a policeman in the Britannia Royal Constabulary. His passion for flying soon shone through and he was given the job of ferrying prisoners in a Black Maria hover-van. It was poorly paid, often mind-numbingly dull work, but when Shaw took to the sky he felt a little closer to heaven.

Today's trip to the Tower of London was unusual, but not unheard of. The government was not afraid of locking away political prisoners in the ancient dungeons there. The poor sod in the back was supposedly the most dangerous man in the Empire, or so Shaw's boss had told him. That must be why the prisoner had been beaten unconscious for the journey, but it didn't sit well with Shaw. He didn't have the stomach for handing out punishment beatings. He preferred being behind the wheel of a hover-van, zooming across the sky.

The two men beside him in the front seat had resisted all attempts at conversation. The *Black Maria* started its final approach to the Tower, the driver gave up trying to talk with them. Surly buggers, he decided. Let 'em rot. Shaw didn't notice when a pair of purple and silver blades stabbed through the metal wall behind his passengers, neatly slicing their spinal chords. Both men slumped backwards in their seats, as if dozing off. They'll get a right rollicking if they're still asleep when we land, the driver thought.

Moments later the passenger side door was ripped open and one of the guards fell out. "What the hell–?" Before Shaw could finish his thought, a hand reached in and extracted the second passenger. The *Black Maria* swerved across the sky as Shaw struggled to control his amazement and terror. Then the prisoner climbed in from outside, slamming the door behind him.

"Who are–? How did you–? I mean, that's– T-That's impossible!" Shaw spluttered.

The prisoner smiled. "I always try to do six impossible things before breakfast."

"But it's nearly midday..."

"I haven't had breakfast yet." The prisoner pointed a hand at Shaw and the driver felt a razor-sharp blade press against his neck. "Now, either you land this thing or I throw you out and try to land it myself – you choose."

Shaw loved to fly, but he didn't fancy trying it unassisted.

• • •

Dante waited until the *Black Maria* had landed before disabling its systems with his bio-blades. The driver was quaking in his seat, a wet stain round his crotch ample evidence of the man's terror. "Look, I haven't done anything to you, okay?" the policeman pleaded. "I'm not even armed. You go and I promise not to raise the alarm for at least ten minutes. Better still, knock me out and then I can't raise the alarm, can I?"

Dante aimed a bio-blade at the driver's throat. "I could just kill you."

"All the others had guns, you had to kill them to escape. I'm letting you go. Kill me and it's murder. Do you want that on your conscience?"

He's right. Killing him will only confirm you're a murderer doing anything to flee Britannia.

"I don't need your advice," Dante said.

"I know," the driver said, closing his eyes. "But if you're going to kill me, at least make it quick – like you did with the others, okay?"

Dante drew back his bio-blade, then punched the driver in the head, smashing him sideways against the van door.

Dante slid out of the passenger door, looking round in search of a landmark. "Where am I, Crest?"

Two minutes from the Tower, but if you're planning a rescue mission for Spatchcock and Flintlock, you'll need help. The cells are in the most heavily guarded and fortified section.

"Which way is the Tower?"

To your left.

Dante retracted his bio-blades and strode briskly away to his right.

Your other left, the Crest sighed.

"I'm not going to the Tower," Dante replied curtly, "and I'm not planning a rescue mission."

Why not?

"Why should I?"

Spatchcock and Flintlock are your friends.

"Spatchcock and Flintlock are two good-for-nothing parasites who latched on to me after the war. The only thing they care about is themselves."

Mr Kettle, allow me to introduce you to this black pot.

"Spare me the riddles, Crest. Where's the nearest heliport or international train terminus?"

I was alluding to the fact you are frequently just as guilty as Spatchcock or Flintlock of the charges you accuse them of. Aren't you even going to try and save them? Flee the country and that will be taken as final, irrevocable proof of your guilt. Those two parasites, as you disingenuously describe them, will be executed in your stead for a crime they didn't commit.

"I never asked them to tag along after me."

No, but you never told them to go away, either. You were their commander during the war, you kept them alive when others could not care less. They respect you, consider themselves your friends and they would not abandon you like this.

Dante laughed bitterly as he quickened his pace. "Flintlock is a craven coward and Spatchcock thinks only of himself. There's been plenty of times when they've left me to die!"

True, but there have also been occasions when they risked their own lives to save yours. What about on Fabergé Island, when they helped you stop that madman's experiments? Or at the Forbidden Citadel – they could have fled when the Imperial Black troops attacked.

"Diavolo, I was there, I know what happened!"

Yet now you choose to ignore it. What kind of man are you?

"You said it yourself, I can't break them out of the Tower single-handed."

Then prove their innocence – and your own – before it is too late.

Dante rounded a corner and saw the London International Train Terminal ahead. "At last!"

Running away won't solve anything, the Crest insisted.

"Spare me the sermon," Dante replied as he approached the train station. "I gave up praying long before I reached puberty."

Perhaps. But I doubt getting out of Britannia will be as simple as you surmise.

Goodnight was escorted into Princess Marie-Anne's private office after passing numerous security checks. The princess gestured grandly to a chair, motioning for the secret agent to sit down. Marie-Anne remained behind an antique black desk lavishly decorated with gold leaf and elaborate carved motifs. Spread out across its surface were swatches of fabrics, dozens of vibrant colours fighting with each other for attention. To Goodnight's eyes it seemed the whole office had been decorated to match the desk, a sinister opulence about the black walls and golden ceiling. The high-ceilinged chamber was thick with the scent of expensive perfume. "Excuse the vile decor in here," the princess said, waving blithely at her surroundings. "My father had it done to irritate my late mother, who hated this desk. I intend this room to be my new seat of power so, of course, I've having it remodelled immediately."

Goodnight decided against pointing out the king was still alive.

The princess sighed, then swept everything from her desk on to the floor. "None of this will do, none of it. I want something that makes a bold statement about who I am – pinks and pastels are never going to achieve that!" Having finished her display of petulance, Marie-Anne sank into a high-backed leather chair and stared at the new arrival. "So, I'm given to understand you've never failed an assignment."

"Yes, your majesty."

"Give me examples of your latest endeavours – and don't worry, I have full security clearance for anything you might mention."

The secret agent outlined three recent missions: the ongoing seduction of the French ambassador, five months spent undercover as a croupier in the Casino Royale at Monte Carlo, and a torrid weekend spent in bed with the Tsar's senior financial minister that ensured a constant flow of information about the state of the Makarov fortunes.

"Very well. Your credentials are impeccable, so I am going to trust you with a difficult but not unimportant assignment. During his interrogation, the king's assassin alluded to having an accomplice, a bald man with a goatee beard and an unhappy face. He claimed to have last seen this person on Westminster Bridge, less than an hour after my father was shot. Assuming this individual exists, I want you to find them and bring them before me so I may determine their part in these tragic events. Is that clear?"

"Quite clear, Your Highness."

"I have one stipulation to add. You must not–" But the princess's words were cut off by an abrupt knock at the door. "Come!"

A footman entered and approached Marie-Anne. He whispered a message in her ear, then withdrew. Goodnight was startled by the effect this had on the princess. She became tense and agitated, her shoulders hunching around her neck. "Your majesty, is something wrong? Has the king passed away?"

"It's Dante. He's escaped." The princess rose from her chair and went to look out a window, her face hidden from Goodnight's view. "This changes everything."

"Perhaps you wish me to leave?"

"No, stay. I meant this changes the nature of your mission. No doubt the police will blunder about in search of this fugitive, along with fools from every other law enforcement agency in Britannia. I want you to find Dante first and bring him to me."

"Is that wise? If he shot your father–"

"I do not recall asking for your advice!"

Goodnight blushed, angry at having overstepped good sense. "My apologies, ma'am."

"You will find Dante and bring him to me. He is not to be captured by anyone else. If he is, I shall hold you personally responsible."

"Yes, your majesty."

"He must be brought to me alive. I want to look into his eyes as the death sentence is carried out." Marie-Anne looked over her shoulder. "Are you a creature of ambition?"

The secret agent frowned. "Yes. Yes, I suppose I am, ma'am."

"Good. Succeed and I shall make you commander of all Britannia Intelligence agencies. Fail and you shall know my wrath like no other person ever has. Do you understand?"

Goodnight nodded. F must have known the assignment would be something of this nature, it explained her reminder about loyalty.

The princess smiled. "I must ask you to reveal nothing of what we have said here today – not to your colleagues, your commander, your family or friends. Betray my trust and the consequences will be ruinous to you and all who know you. Good hunting!"

Goodnight realised the interview was at an end. But a thought occurred that had to be spoken aloud. "Excuse me, Your Highness, but I've seen official briefing papers on this Nikolai Dante before. His Weapons Crest makes him a dangerous, elusive quarry. I've little doubt I can find and catch him, but how do I hold him?"

Marie-Anne returned to the vast, imposing desk. "I was wondering if you would have the wit to ask that. F chose wisely when she sent you." The princess opened a drawer, removing a pair of black handcuffs and tossed them to Goodnight. "When the Tsar heard of Dante's presence here, he sent these bindings by overnight courier. The connecting chain is all but unbreakable, it requires a diamond cutter to sever any of the links. The cuffs themselves incorporate an experimental substance developed by the Tsar's scientists that should disable most Weapons Crest capabilities, such as Dante's bio-blades. While wearing those he will be no more dangerous than any other criminal. Find him, Agent Goodnight. Find him, catch him and deliver him to me – I will make certain justice follows swiftly afterwards."

FIVE

"A thief knows a thief even in the darkest night."
– Russian proverb

"Trains bearing the name *Flying Scotsman* have journeyed up and down Britannia for hundreds of years. The first such vehicle was a steam engine that travelled between London and Edinburgh in the Nineteenth century. The service was discontinued but the name remained alive and was applied to other trains. Most recently the soubriquet had taken on a literal meaning with the introduction of the *Flying Scotsman* hover-train. Predominantly a tourist service, this airborne locomotive and its passenger carriages offers a gentle return to the luxurious train travel of centuries past. It may be most popular with foreign visitors to Britannia, but the *Flying Scotsman* remains one of the most romantic ways of seeing the nation."
– Extract from *Around the Empire in Eighty Ways*,
Mikhail Palinski

The London International Train Terminal's concourse was awash with people, luggage and misery. Every face around Dante was tired or unhappy, the wan features of waiting passengers bleached yellow by harsh overhead lighting. The station was a vast space stretched out beneath a grime-coated glass roof. Three of the four walls were given over to overpriced traders with surly faces.

Never in all his days had Dante seen such a depressing, dispiriting place. It stank of body odour and hopelessness.

"Fuoco," he muttered. "I've been to funerals with better atmospheres. What happened?"

You did, the Crest replied. *Look at the departure boards.*

Above the gate of each platform floated a holographic display unit showing when the next train was due to leave, the stations it would visit and a final destination. All but one of the boards was bright red with the words "TRAIN CANCELLED DUE TO NATIONAL SECURITY ALERT" flashing on and off in large, unfriendly letters. "What's that got to do with me?" Dante asked.

News of your escape has obviously reached the authorities. They have cancelled all international train services out of Britannia. I will hack into the Imperial Net to see if there is another option still open to you.

Dante sighed. As usual, the Crest had been right. Getting out of the country would be all but impossible now. He needed to find a place to lie low, to plan his next move. So far he had been operating on pure instinct and it wasn't enough.

It's the same everywhere: no international flights, no ships are being allowed to leave port, nothing. For all intents and purposes the borders of Britannia have been sealed. It won't be long before they–

The Crest suddenly fell silent, leaving Dante waiting. "Crest? It won't be long before what happens?"

You need to get out of here, it replied. *While you still can.*

"Why?"

Because of what's about to be broadcast on every holographic display in the country.

Dante heard a crisp, slightly nasal voice speaking via the station's public address system. "Is this thing on? Good. People of Britannia, my name is Inspector Rucka of Scotland Yard. I have an important message for each and every one of you." Like everyone else in the station, Dante felt his gaze shift to the departure boards. Each display was filled by Rucka's unsympathetic face. "As you know, our king lies close to death following a cowardly attempt on his life. The same craven attack claimed our beloved Queen Mother Barbara. But you will be overjoyed to hear the Britannia Royal Constabulary has wasted little time in capturing the fiends responsible for this sickening act of terrorism. Two of the culprits await execution. Regretfully I must tell you their ringleader escaped during transportation to the Tower of London, killing five good men in the process. The driver responsible for allowing this fugitive to flee has been executed for his folly."

Dante began walking towards the nearest exit. So much for sparing the driver's life, he thought – my escape still got him killed. The station's outer doors opened to admit a phalanx of policeman, all carrying sidearms and murder in their eyes. Dante quickly retreated the way he had come. The only hiding place on the concourse was a row of antique red phone boxes in the central area, so Dante ducked inside the first empty booth. Even inside, there was no escape from Rucka's relentless broadcast. The Imperial Net screen inside the booth was also showing the inspector's stern speech.

"Every way out of the country has been sealed to prevent the fugitive escaping justice. I gave that order and I hereby apologise to all those innocent, trustworthy citizens whom it has inconvenienced. However, I feel certain you willingly make this sacrifice to help us capture the monster who murdered Queen Babs and mortally wounded our monarch!" Behind Dante all the passengers on the concourse simultaneously applauded, nodding their approval at Rucka's draconian actions.

Bojemoi, Dante fretted, they actually believe these lies.

Rucka's message continued over the clapping. "I show you now the face of the fiend we seek. As I speak policemen are entering all major train stations, airports and transportation centres in search of him. If you have seen this vile killer, approach a constable. With your help, this cowardly assassin cannot remain at large for long. The murderer's name is Nikolai Dante and this is what he looks like." Rucka's face was replaced with a particularly unflattering image of Dante, his face puffy and bruised from one of the many beatings he had taken recently.

"Is that the best photo they've got of me?" Dante protested. "I look terrible!"

It's not your most flattering likeness, the Crest conceded, *but you should be grateful.*

"Why? For making me look fat?"

The less accurate the image, the less likely you are to be identified.

Dante scratched his chin thoughtfully. "There is that, I suppose..."

He noticed the line of policemen was getting steadily closer, checking the identity of each and every person on the concourse – man, woman or child. Rucka was back on the holographic displays, a smug smile smeared across his face like excrement on poor quality toilet paper.

"To encourage everyone in Britannia to do the right thing, a reward of ten million roubles is being offered to whomever supplies information leading to Dante's capture. If you see him, contact the number listed below, and apply for your reward. Thank you for your time and patience. Rule Britannia!" The displays dissolved to static, then resumed showing their messages.

Once again Dante cursed himself for accepting King Henry's invitation. "For that reward every scumbag and bounty hunter in Britannia will make it their business to hunt me down."

Not to mention every law enforcement officer and intelligence agency operative, the Crest added. *In other parts of the Empire your notoriety keeps you safe, despite the Tsar's bounty on your head. Here you are fair game. Rucka has declared open season on Nikolai Dante.*

The fugitive was still cursing his bad luck when movement nearby caught his eye. Among the travellers being questioned by the police was a balding man clutching a heavy suitcase and a timetable. He was facing away from Dante, but once the police were done with him the man turned towards the phone booths. Dante was startled to recognise the traveller's goatee beard and sad face. "That's him! That's the man I saw on Westminster Bridge!" The traveller walked past the booth towards a nearby gate, not noticing Dante staring at him. He went on to the platform with a cluster of other passengers.

"Crest, what train leaves from that platform, number thirteen?"

The Flying Scotsman. *It's a leisurely tourist service, stopping at various scenic destinations en route to Orkney before returning to London in several days time.*

"When is the next one leaving?"

Any minute. But that train won't get you out of Britannia.

"I've decided to take your advice and clear my name. If I hunt down the real assassin and bring him in, Rucka will have to let Spatchcock and Flintlock go free."

Why the change of heart? Has your little used conscience got the better of you?

"I'm certain one of the assassins just got on the *Flying Scotsman*. I'd guess he's planning to blend in with the other tourists, then slip out of the country with them when the train trip ends."

Quite a coincidence, him catching a train from this station. Dante, it has all the makings of an ambush.

"Why would the authorities bother with an ambush?"

Not everybody will want you found alive, the Crest pointed out.

"It doesn't matter – I have to get on that train!"

Then get moving, the police are almost on top of you.

Dante turned his jacket collar up to conceal his face, then slipped out of the booth and walked slowly towards Platform thirteen. "Excuse me, sir, could you stay where you are," a constable called, but Dante kept walking. "Sir? I must ask you to stop immediately!"

Faster, the Crest urged as Dante quickened his pace.

"Stop now or else I will be forced to intercede," the constable shouted.

"Not the most threatening phrase I've ever heard," Dante commented, breaking into a jog. Around him others on the concourse were looking round to see what was happening. Several pointed at Dante, calling out his name. "Britannia's police must be the most polite in the Empire. All the others are usually shooting at me by now!"

Dante–

"Let me guess, evasive action?"

Evasive action, the Crest agreed. *Now!*

The first shot was a warning blast that skimmed over Dante's shoulder. The other officers felt no need to offer such a warning. Within seconds the concourse was a shooting gallery as dozens of constables opened fire.

"Diavolo!" Dante cried out, flinging himself towards the closing gateway. He slid beneath the metal gates just before they slammed down from above. Bullets thudded noisily against the reinforced steel barriers, but Dante was safely on the other side. Ahead of him the *Flying Scotsman* hissed clouds of steam as the final few passengers climbed on board the last carriage, among them a beautiful woman in a figure-hugging navy blue catsuit. She was struggling with several hat boxes and an antique trunk, shoulder-length strawberry blonde hair falling over her pretty, delicate face. "Crest, how long before the train leaves?"

Less than a minute, but the police will be through the barrier before then.

"I'll have to risk that." Dante sprinted to the last carriage. The young woman had got all her hat boxes inside, but was still trying to manhandle her trunk on board. Admiring the curve of her taut buttocks, Dante grabbed the other end of her awkward luggage. "May I help?" The woman nodded gratefully and climbed into the carriage.

Dante spared a glance back at the gates, where the police were shouting for the barrier to be re-opened. The woman followed his gaze, before raising an intrigued eyebrow at Dante. "Overdue parking tickets," he smiled. "You can never find a space when you need one."

"I know exactly what you mean," she said, her voice betraying a private education but with a hint of mischief behind the precise vowels and phrasings. "Thank you for helping me, Mr...?"

"Durward," Dante replied, reverting to his usual alter ego when in need of an impromptu alias. "Quentin Durward, at your service." He bowed his head to her, but let his eyes hungrily examine the contents of her catsuit. The woman could not yet be thirty, her breasts still proudly straining against their confinement, while narrow hips led to slender, athletic legs. As Dante straightened up again, he was struck by the sardonic arch of her eyebrows and pert, upturned nose. Everything about this woman said she knew how to enjoy herself and anyone invited to the party would have the time of their life.

Dante, try to concentrate on the matter in hand, not on the commands of your groin.

"You can call me Penelope," the woman said. "My car broke down on the way to the station and by the time I reached the platform all the porters had vanished."

"It's my pleasure to be of service," Dante smiled, all too aware of heavy footfalls rapidly approaching the train. His eyes lit upon a doorway behind Penelope. "If you'll forgive me, I have an urgent call of nature." He clambered over the trunk, then squeezed past Penelope to gain access to the toilets. As he passed her a waft of exquisite perfume filled his nostrils, causing a stirring in his loins. Dante slipped inside the bathroom and locked the door as pursuing policemen reached the carriage.

"Madam, an escaped murderer just got on this train – dark hair, beard, a scruffy looking creature by the name of Nikolai Dante – did you see which way he went?"

Dante held his breath, willing the woman not to give him away. But his heart sank at hearing her next words.

"Yes, I did see him actually!"

Dante extended his bio-blades and got ready to fight his way out of the cubicle.

"He ran to the far end of this carriage and jumped on to the tracks on the other side. I thought he must be crazed, he had a wild look in his eye. You say he's an escaped murderer; who on earth did he kill?"

"The Queen Mother. You're certain he got off the train?"

"Absolutely, and thank heavens he did! I mean, a murderer on board the *Flying Scotsman*, it doesn't bear thinking about!"

"No, madam, you're right. Thanks for your time."

Dante strained forward, trying to hear whether the policeman had disembarked yet. A whistle sounded shrilly in the background, along with a gruff voice from nearby on the platform. "Stand away, please, stand away – this train is leaving the station! Stand away!" A warning beep announced the doors were closing, then came the sound of someone jumping back down to the platform as the doors slid shut. The train slowly rolled forward, picking up speed. Dante retracted his bio-blades, listening carefully for any hint of a trap outside. Once he was certain the police had left the train, Dante emerged from his hiding place.

Penelope was waiting for him in the narrow space between her trunk and the door, lips playfully pursed. "Overdue parking tickets, eh?"

Dante offered his most winning smile. "I didn't kill the Queen Mother. Honestly."

"Would you tell me if you had?"

"That would depend."

"On what?"

"Whether you would pull the emergency cord and stop the train."

Penelope smiled. “I’m more likely to applaud you. To me the royal family is a wildly outdated anachronism that should have been abandoned centuries ago.”

“Really? I thought someone with your accent would be all for Henry and his kind.”

“Heavens, no! The Windsor McKrays are dreadful, they give old money a bad name.”

“Well, I didn’t try to kill the king.”

“What a shame,” Penelope teased. “Here was I hoping to dine out on stories of how I helped a cold-blooded killer escape justice.”

“However,” Dante added quickly, “I am considered quite the scoundrel in some parts of the Empire.” He gave a gasp of surprise as Penelope rested her left hand against his groin, gently sliding the palm up and down in time with the rhythm of the train.

“And which parts would they be?” she asked coyly.

Before Dante could devise a suitable response the train’s public address system crackled into life. “All passengers, please take your seats. The *Flying Scotsman* is about to leave the tracks and take to the skies.”

“Sounds like we should be getting to our respective berths,” Dante said, as the sound of the train’s wheels on the tracks faded. It was replaced by the wind whistling past as the train rose with stately grace into the early evening sky.

“Do you have a ticket?” Penelope enquired with a wicked smile.

“Not as such,” he admitted.

“Well, I have a luxury sleeper compartment to myself and nobody to share it with. It’s one of the perils of being a beautiful, rich heiress, I suppose – when you have everything money can buy, it’s so hard to find something you actually… desire.” She closed her hand firmly around his groin. “Perhaps you would like to join me? We could see the sights together.”

Dante felt his eyes bulging. They weren’t the only things. “I… I might well take you up on that offer,” he said, struggling to keep his voice from climbing an octave. "But first I have to locate another passenger on board. He has something of value to me. Once I've retrieved that, perhaps we could meet for dinner?"

Penelope stepped away from Dante, a shadow of disappointment evident in her eyes. "Fine. Well, don't let me delay you any longer."

"I'll be back before you know it," Dante promised, but the moment had passed.

"Don't hurry back on my behalf," Penelope snapped, sitting down on the edge of her trunk. "If you find a steward on your travels, could you send him back here? I still need to get my luggage stowed away."

Dante nodded, then started working his way forward through the train's many carriages and compartments, still bemused by how quickly Penelope's passions rose and fell. "Women," he muttered. "I'll never figure them out."

That much seems certain, the Crest agreed.

Sergeant Jones never enjoyed the company of bounty hunters. For the most part they were criminals, with a history of violence and few moral scruples. To them a target was merely a way of making money. Some enjoyed the chase, the thrill of hunting another human being while living on the edge of the law. Others needed the rewards to feed insidious vices, be they gambling, drugs or women. True, bounty hunters were sometimes able to find and catch fugitives the law could not touch, but that didn't make their existence any less repugnant to the veteran policeman. After twenty years with the Britannia Royal Constabulary, Jones still felt his skin crawl when a bounty hunter came into Scotland Yard. Now there were a dozen of these scum standing in front of his duty desk, waiting for Inspector Rucka to come down from the top floor.

The bounty hunters were a mixture of humans and aliens, most bearing scars from their bloody trade. Among them were two Enforcers from the colony world of Berezova, creatures with squat torsos and mottled brown hides, said to possess incredible strength and power. Cyborgs of varying shapes and sizes scowled at each other as best they were able, not easy for those who no longer possessed a face. The rest stayed near the fringes of the gathering, not getting in anyone else's way. They were the parasites, hoping to pick up a few crumbs when the action started. Jones was grateful for one thing about this gathering – at least Dobie and Boyle were not present. That pair was the last thing he needed today. But no sooner had this thought crossed the sergeant's mind than the screech of protesting rubber he heard from outside. "Cover me!" a burly, masculine voice shouted. The entrance doors burst open as a man dived into the foyer, his sidearm drawn and ready to fire. Moments later another figure flung itself inside, performing an entirely gratuitous forward roll in the process.

The pair went through a series of elaborate poses while still crouched on the floor, nominally checking the large, airless room was secure. Both men swept their weapons round the others present, before nodding to each other with a knowing smile. The pair stood and sauntered cockily towards the duty desk, sliding their pistols into shoulder holsters with practiced ease. Boyle was first to speak, a mass of brown curls framing his sensitive blue eyes and bruised cheekbones. He was wearing a loud plaid jacket of red, white and black over a taupe knit shirt and faded denim jeans at least one size too small. "Sergeant Jones! Still propping up the front desk at the Yard, I see. How's the BRC treating you these days?"

"Fine, Ray. Still hanging around with this mercenary?"

Boyle scratched the side of his head, not looking at his nearby partner. "Don't call him a mercenary, it only gives him delusions of grandeur."

"That's rich coming from you," Dobie interjected. He was dressed in tan slacks and a brown blazer over a cream shirt. His short brown locks were brushed forward over his scalp to mask a receding hairline. "An ex-copper who decided he was worth more than a badge!"

"At least I know which side of the law is the right one," Boyle remarked.

"I didn't know there was a right side," Dobie said with a smirk. He leaned nonchalantly against the front desk and surveyed the other bounty hunters already gathered. "Well, it seems the gang's all here. Bad news, boys – now Ray and I have arrived the hunt is already good as over. We need a new spoiler for the back of the hover-car, so this reward is ours, got it?" The others did not dignify his comment with a reply. Dobie smiled broadly at his partner. "I think they understand."

"Oh yeah, you definitely convinced them," Boyle agreed, rolling his eyes.

An inner door swung open, Rucka stepped into the room like a visiting dignitary, with a constable following him. The inspector moved along the bounty hunters, studying each one with disdain. The constable joined Jones behind the duty desk. The sergeant could not resist whispering a comment out of the side of his mouth to the younger policeman. "Bounty hunters. We don't need their scum."

"Yes, sir," the constable agreed quietly.

"The fugitive won't escape us," Jones added.

Rucka began addressing the gathering in his clipped, nasal voice. "There will be a substantial reward for the person who finds Nikolai Dante. You are free to use any methods necessary but I want him brought in alive." The inspector noticed two men slouching by the front desk and pointed a finger at them. "No executions!"

Dobie and Boyle gave Rucka a mock salute. "As you wish," they replied in unison.

The inspector waved for the bounty hunters to leave, then approached the duty sergeant. "Well Jones, what news from our bobbies on the beat?"

"A squad of constables saw Dante at London International Train Terminal a few minutes ago. He tried to throw them off his trail by boarding the *Flying Scotsman*, but a witness saw him run away across the tracks. The pursuit is continuing, sir."

"Very good," Rucka replied patronisingly. "I know the presence of bounty hunters is repugnant to most policemen, but such mercenaries have a proven track record in flushing out this type of fugitive. Think of them as a little insurance if your men don't catch Dante."

"Yes, inspector," Jones agreed, seething as the inspector went back upstairs. The sergeant muttered an Oedipal curse that neatly rhymed with Rucka's name, then got back to co-ordinating the search for Dante.

Outside Scotland Yard, Dobie and Boyle were slouching in the bucket seats of their tan Phord Capri hover-car, each man listening to the surveillance device they had hidden by the duty desk. The pair laughed out loud at Jones's turn of phrase. "Sounds like your old mate isn't too fond of the inspector," Dobie observed.

"Can't say I blame him. Rucka was always good at grabbing the headlines but he needed real coppers to catch the villains for him."

"Real coppers like you, you mean?"

Boyle made an obscene finger gesture to his partner, then started the Capri. "Let's go," he said, gunning the engine needlessly.

"Where?"

"King's Cross. It's a good place to pick up a few tips."

"It's a good place to pick up a few diseases," Dobie observed. "Still, it's not far from the train terminal. Our target might be trying to lie low near there until the heat cools off."

Boyle smiled wryly. "My thoughts exactly." He released the handbrake and the Capri roared along the road before leaping into the sky, tyres squealing in protest as usual.

■ ■ ■

Half an hour later Dante had reached the front carriage of the *Flying Scotsman* without finding his quarry. Ahead lay only cargo carriages and the locomotive. "I don't understand how I could have missed him," he fretted. "I searched all the seated passengers."

But not the sleeper compartments, the Crest pointed out. *Your target must be inside one of the first class berths. The only time he's obliged to come out is for during the sight-seeing stops, when the staff clean and re-supply all the individual compartments.*

Dante saw a steward approaching, clutching a handful of timetables. Like all male staff on the train, he was wearing full Highland costume including a kilt, sporran, white ruffled shirt and shiny black patent leather shoes. Dante gestured for attention. "I say, could you tell me, when is our first sight-seeing excursion off the train?" he asked, affecting a Britannia accent.

The steward smiled indulgently. "We pause above the Watford Gap so passengers can take pictures, but the first time we land will be tomorrow at Nottingham. There's a choice of day-trips on offer there: the castle, Sherwood Forest or the historic country estate of the Fforbes-Lamington family. You may have already selected one when you bought your ticket. Perhaps if I could see it?"

Dante made a great show of patting all his pockets. "Ahh, I think my wife has both our tickets. She's at the other end of the train. We were among the last to get on and our luggage is rather cluttering the gangway. Penny could do with some help getting things stowed away."

The steward nodded understandingly. "Of course, sir. Perhaps you'd like to take a drink in the lounge while I placate your wife?"

"Capital idea, capital! I shall do just that. Make sure you get a generous tip from her, by way of compensation for all your efforts on our behalf – they're most appreciated." Dante clapped the steward on the back and strode back to the first class lounge he had passed earlier.

Penelope was still sitting on top of her luggage when a rotund man in a kilt approached her with a menu for dinner. "Excuse me, madam, is your name Penny?"

"Penelope, if you don't mind. And you are?"

"Gordonstoun, head steward for this excursion," he replied, bowing slightly. "Your husband sent me along to get your luggage squared away, said you were having some trouble."

"My husband...?" Penelope said, her mind racing. "Oh, him!" She permitted herself the slightest of blushes. "Well, as you've probably surmised, we aren't actually married."

Gordonstoun clasped his chubby hands together and smiled benignly. "Here on the *Flying Scotsman* we pride themselves at being the souls of tact and discretion. Your secrets are safe with us, madam, even if your, er, travelling companion is rather less discreet."

Penelope sighed theatrically. "Yes, he can be rather a bore but he means a lot to me. Once this luggage is out of the way, perhaps you could show me to my sleeping quarters?"

"Of course, madam. It would be my pleasure." Gordonstoun bowed again, then activated a staff intercom and summoned other attendants to fetch the hatboxes and trunk.

Once they had arrived, the head steward escorted Penelope to her quarters. He opened the gold and green door, then politely stood aside to let her enter first. The compartment was surprisingly large and lavishly furnished, with a four-poster bed at one end and matching chaise longue at the other. A tall mirror was mounted directly behind the bed, making the sound-proofed chamber appear even bigger than it was. A thick sheepskin rug covered most of the floor, complementing the plush, decadent decor.

Once Penelope was inside, Gordonstoun pointed to the berth's many features – a separate dressing room with ample storage for clothes, shoes and other accoutrements, a bathroom equal in size to the bedroom with both a free-standing tub and walk-in shower, plus a heavily stocked private bar concealed in an oak cabinet. All the wood in the compartment was oak with gold leaf ornamentation, whilst small crystal chandeliers concealed the light fittings on the walls. Gordonstoun gestured at a control panel skilfully hidden behind a tapestry on one wall. "This provides you with an encrypted communications environment. Like all our first class compartments, this berth is sealed to prevent any noise from outside disturbing you or any sounds you make being audible when the door to the corridor is closed. Your discretion and privacy are paramount at all times while you are a passenger on board the *Flying Scotsman.*"

Penelope gave the steward an outrageously generous tip. His eyes flashed hungrily for a moment until his calm, collected demeanour reasserted itself. "If there is anything you require madam, do not hesitate to summon me – day or night. I am happy to be of service. Ask for me by name: Gordonstoun."

"I'll be certain to remember that," Penelope replied with a small smile. Her brow furrowed as a thought occurred. "There is one thing. Where did you see my... husband... last?"

"The far end of the train, madam. He was going to the first class lounge for a drink."

"Could you give him a message for me?"

Gordonstoun listened, then repeated the message to Penelope for her confirmation. "I shall ensure he does as you ask, madam."

Penelope waited until the steward had gone before throwing herself on the vast bed, letting herself sink into its down-filled quilts. This was the life, she decided. A discreet knock summoned her back to the main doorway.

Two more stewards staggered inside, bringing her trunk and hatboxes. "Put them into the dressing room, please," Penelope said. She made sure to tip them generously as they left.

An insistent beeping from one of her hatboxes soon demanded Penelope's attention. She retrieved a tiny, circular disc hidden within the brim of a hat and inserted it into her left ear. "Receiving loud and clear." Penelope returned to the main room, adjusting the position of the translucent device until it was firmly lodged inside her ear. "Yes, I have seen and locked on to my target." She went to the nearest mirror and twisted her head sideways, checking to make sure the disc was all but invisible. "No, the target does not suspect me, I'm certain of that. He thinks I want him sexually. You know what some men are like – all the world revolves around their groin."

Penelope paused, listening to the voice inside her ear. "No, I will not be able to get him off the train tonight. That will have to wait until we reach Nottingham in the morning." Another pause as a stream of words transmitted themselves to her. "I'm about to have a meal with him. After that I'll invite him back to my sleeping compartment – I'm sure you can imagine the rest." Penelope nodded, and then laughed. "No, Your Highness, I don't think you need fear for my virtue. If anyone should be afraid, it's Nikolai Dante. The fool doesn't seem to realise the danger he is in." She listened to one last comment from her caller. "Thank you, ma'am. I'll deliver him to you before dusk tomorrow. Agent Goodnight, signing off."

The first class lounge was packed with people, most of them talking in foreign accents . Despairing of his quest, Dante ordered the largest drink available and settled in for the evening. The barman set about mixing an elaborate cocktail involving almost every kind of alcohol known to man, while Dante passed the time examining the faces of his fellow passengers. Foreign tourists were obvious from their gaudy clothes and propensity for ugly facial hair, while those from Britannia tended to be ruddy-cheeked and uptight in appearance.

Do any of these people look familiar to you?

The Crest's question puzzled Dante. "No," he whispered back. "Why, should they?"

There's something nagging me about several of these passengers. I feel as if I have seen them before, but I cannot remember where or when.

"But they still look familiar?"

Yes. I cannot explain it.

Dante's eyes swept round the room, searching for anything that jogged his memory – a profile, a family resemblance, anything. It was only when his gaze reached the far end that he recognised anyone. "It's him, he's right here!"

Who?

"The assassin – he's here in the lounge!" Dante said, trying to push his way through the throng. Ahead, the sad faced man with the goatee was sat at the bar, finishing a drink. He drained the glass and left the lounge, a rectangle of paper falling from his pocket. By the time Dante had struggled past his sixth party of Scandinavian revellers the assassin was long gone. Dante cursed his own incompetence, until he noticed the discarded document. It was a timetable for the *Flying Scotsman*'s journey north, like those the steward had been carrying earlier.

Dante picked it up and studied the list of destinations. Three names were circled several times – Nottingham, Peebles and Orkney.

If this timetable was dropped by the assassin, it suggests he is staying on the train all the way to the north of Scotland. That gives you until Saturday to find and confront him.

"Three days," Dante calculated. "Plenty of time to get the truth from this bastard."

A chime sounded. The portly steward appeared beside Dante in the doorway. "Ladies and gentlemen, that is the first bell for dinner. Would those staying in the sleeping compartments at the far end of the train like to make their way back? You'll find the evening meal awaits you there."

Dante became aware of his empty stomach rumbling and realised a day had passed since his last meal. The rotund steward whispered politely in Dante's left ear. "Your wife is waiting for you in that dining car, sir. I suggest you do not delay joining her – she seemed less than pleased you left her to cope with all the luggage."

"Ahh! Yes, indeed, I have been rather remiss," Dante agreed. "I'd better pop along and soothe the old girl's furrowed brow, eh?" Dante set off, eager to re-establish his acquaintance with the delectable Penelope. I wonder what her last name is, he thought idly.

Are you forgetting something?

"Like what?" Dante replied under his breath.

Your manhunt for the assassin? The quest to clear your name of murder, saving Spatchcock and Flintlock from the executioner?

"You said it yourself, Crest – I've got three days to find this sniper and make him confess. One night of pleasure with Penelope won't prevent that."

Your friends could be executed at any time.

"They can look after themselves," Dante insisted. "Besides, I have my honour as a ladies' man to uphold, and you know how I feel about the importance of my honour."

This from the man whose personal motto is "Honour be damned!"

"No, Your Highness, I don't think you need fear for my virtue. If anyone should be afraid, it's Nikolai Dante. The fool doesn't seem to realise the danger he is in." F listened to the intercepted transmission, her stern face evidence of a growing anger. "Thank you, ma'am, I'll deliver him to you before dusk tomorrow. Agent Goodnight, signing off." The recording clicked to a halt. F sat back in the high-backed swivel chair behind her desk of pine and glass, glaring at the meek messenger standing opposite.

"Why am I only hearing this now?" F demanded.

"Ma'am, the transmission was intercepted a few minutes ago. It took our cryptographers time to decode the scrambler signal on the line," Agent Golightly replied quietly.

"Not good enough! From now on I expect all of Goodnight's communications with that bitch princess to be relayed to me in real time – is that understood?"

"I'm not sure that will be possible–"

"Is that understood?" F repeated.

"Yes, ma'am. I'll pass that on to the code breakers." Golightly turned to leave.

"Wait!" F rose from her chair, strolling round the desk toward the trembling, terrified agent. "Tell me, what do you think is the significance of this communication?"

"M-Me?" Golightly stammered. "You want my opinion?"

"Obviously, otherwise I would not have asked for it, would I?" F stopped behind the young woman. "Give me your assessment – dazzle me with your acumen."

"It seems clear that Agent Goodnight–"

"Traitorous bitch!" F snapped.

"She has been suborned into reporting directly to Princess Marie-Anne. Her royal highness has assigned Goodnight to find and bring back the fugitive Dante – alive, by the sound of it. This message was transmitted from aboard the *Flying Scotsman*, so it's clear Dante remained on board. Someone – possibly Goodnight herself – lied to the police about seeing him flee the train."

"Yes, yes, all that is obvious," F said. "What I wanted to know is your interpretation of this betrayal's significance. Does the heir to our monarch intend claiming control of my intelligence service for herself? Perhaps the royal bitch has plans to install Goodnight as her puppet in my place." F stepped nearer Golightly, close enough for the beautiful young agent to feel the commander's breath on the back of her neck. "Would that be your interpretation?"

"It would fit with the ambitious behaviour patterns the princess has previously shown."

"Quite," F agreed, allowing herself a cruel smile of anticipation before activating the intercom on her desk. "I want a squad of Rippers despatched immediately."

"Yes, ma'am," a voice responded. "Target?"

"The *Flying Scotsman*. It should be over the Watford Gap in the next hour or two. The Rippers should find Nikolai Dante – his DNA records are still on our system from his last visit to Britannia. He is to be executed on sight."

"Yes, ma'am."

"Agent Penelope Goodnight may well be with Dante when the Rippers kill him. I do not want her eliminated – yet. Is that clear?"

"Yes, ma'am."

"Very good. I am not to be disturbed for the next hour. After that I will leave for my house in the country. You may contact me en route or at my home when I get there." F switched off the intercom and glared at Golightly. "I'm sorry to say I'm disappointed in your performance in this matter. You will have to be disciplined." F undid the leather belt from the waist of her tweed skirt. "Bend over and touch your toes."

SIX

"Eat the honey but beware the sting."
– Russian proverb

"The Rippers are covert assassins attached to Britannia's secret service, often used in a death squad capacity. They are genetically engineered for maximum stealth and sadism, with olfactory nerves designed to literally smell the DNA of their intended victims. Rippers always maintain a particular look: black cloaks lined with red silk; black stovepipe hats; black suits and ties; white shirts and pallid faces. This sinister appearance is carefully choreographed to strike fear into the underclass of Britannia, tapping into hereditary memories of the original Ripper murders that terrorised London almost nine hundred years ago. For this same reason they are armed with viciously sharp blades as their weapons. Rippers usually fly into action on single-seat aerial mounts fashioned like black hornets with bulbous red eyes."
– Extract from *The Files of the Raven Corps*

"Well, this is cosy, isn't it?" Flintlock remarked, his voice dripping with irony. "Only yesterday I was thinking to myself I never get to spend enough quality time with my good friend Spatch – and now look at us. All the time in the world, just the two of us, as close as close can be."

"Shut your mouth," Spatchcock urged. The two men were manacled together in a dungeon at the Tower of London, their hands clamped to each other's ankles. The cell was cold, damp and dank, the stench of rat droppings and fear seemingly impregnated into its ancient walls. They had been shoved into this hovel within hours of the king being shot. The only facilities provided were a bowl of brackish water, a single straw-filled mattress and a metal bucket for urine and faeces. Forced to huddle together for warmth overnight, Flintlock had spent most of the following day complaining to the sentries about the lice Spatchcock had given him. After several hours of listening to this persistent whining, a guard came in and manacled the prisoners together. When Flintlock protested this would make the lice infestation worse, not better, the guard replied the shackles were a punishment, not a treatment.

"I will not shut my mouth, as you crudely put it!" Flintlock snapped indignantly. "I reserve the right to say what I please whenever I please and there's nothing you can do to stop me!" His words came to an abrupt halt as a sulphurous stench filled the air. "My word, what is that? It's as if the very bowels of Hell have opened to release their noxious gases."

"Close enough," Spatchcock smirked.

"That vile stench emitted from your posterior?"

"I told you to shut your mouth."

"Like most civilised people, I sense smells through my nostrils, not my mouth."

"Oh, stop whining for once in your bloody life. Nothing's ever good enough for high and mighty Lord Peter Flintlock, is it? You're no different from me or Dante – just another scoundrel, trying to stay one step ahead of trouble. You stink as bad as the rest of us at the end of the day."

"Only when I've been shackled to a foul-smelling wretch and denied decent facilities in which to carry out my daily ablutions. It must be twenty-four hours since I've had anything to eat. I feel weaker than a kitten," Flintlock said.

"You *are* weaker than a kitten."

"You know what I mean. We are being denied our basic human rights."

Spatchcock shrugged. "Since they've got us down for murdering the Queen Mother, I don't think the powers that be are much bothered about our rights – basic, human or otherwise."

"I fear your summation is accurate."

"Come again?"

"I think you're right," Flintlock replied. "Don't you understand the King's English?"

"Of course I do," Spatchcock smiled. "I wanted to hear you say I was right again, that's all."

"You are the most tiresome of creatures."

"Here he goes again," the ruddy-faced runt snarled, before twisting round to shout at the narrow metal grille in the cell door. "Guard! Guard!" A sour-faced sentry appeared on the other side of the bars. "When's our execution planned for?"

"The date hasn't been finalised yet."

"When are they thinking of having it, then?"

"A week from today, give more people the opportunity to watch."

Spatchcock grimaced. "Any chance they could bring it forward? I can't stand seven more days being manacled to this whining turd, listening to all his pissing and moaning."

"Shut your mouth!" the guard said before walking away.

Flintlock aimed a kick at his fellow prisoner, eliciting a yelp of pain. "You might be in a hurry to die, but I've no wish to meet my maker yet, so don't speak for me in such matters."

"I wasn't," Spatchcock explained. "I was trying to find out how long we've got to wait before Dante comes to rescue us."

The Britannia native laughed bitterly. "We're in a basement cell inside the Tower of London, one of the world's most infamous prisons. There hasn't been a successful escape from this place for centuries and it is guarded by a small army. Dante will not be coming to rescue us. If he does try, he'll be dead long before he reaches our cell door."

"He'll come for us," Spatchcock insisted.

"Your faith in our former commander is touching, old boy, but I fear it is also misplaced. If Dante has any sense he'll have managed to get out of the country before the borders were sealed."

"Shut your mouth!"

"I'm telling you the truth," Flintlock insisted. "We're doomed, quite doomed, both of us."

"I meant shut your nostrils," Spatchcock replied, as another waft of vile air escaped from his anus.

"What? Why– Oh no, not again!"

"Well, this is cosy, isn't it?" Dante said as he sat down opposite Penelope in the first class dining car. Around them a selection of wealthy, well-dressed passengers were studying the *Flying Scotsman*'s extensive menu and lengthy wine list. Like the rest of the hover-train, the dining car was sumptuously furnished and decorated. Gentle, sympathetic lighting cast a gold glow over everything, turning each table into a oasis of dining splendour. Penelope was already waiting for Dante when he came in, seated` an intimate table for two in a corner of the carriage, her back to the wall. She had smiled and waved, beckoning him towards the vacant chair across from her.

"You'll be happy to know I have taken possession of a rather grand compartment near this end of the train, where the steward has promised I will not be disturbed,"

Penelope said, smiling playfully at Dante. "There's a wonderful dressing room and I even had time to change before dinner." She held out her hands to display the plunging neckline of a black velvet gown that struggled to contain her jutting breasts. "Sadly, the magnificent bed looks far too large for me to fill on my own. I was wondering if you had any suggestions how I could resolve that problem?"

"Let me think... Were you expecting to be joined by another traveller later on the journey north? Your partner, or a lover?"

Penelope sighed theatrically. "I have no husband, nor a long-term companion to help fill the lonely evening hours. I am quite alone at present."

"Then I think you should take a lover," Dante said. "Being alone at night is most unhealthy. What if you should take ill and need someone to soothe your troubles away?"

"Are you suggesting I organise an infidelity?"

"Certainly."

"With someone on board the train, perhaps?"

"With me, for example."

Penelope appeared almost shocked at Dante's boldness. "Why, sir, I hardly know you."

"You seemed to have a firm grasp of my particulars earlier."

She smiled at the memory. "That's true. I have always favoured the hands-on approach."

"I'm much the same myself," Dante agreed.

"Yet before you left me to fend for myself with all that luggage."

"I apologise. Sometimes my manners leave a little to be desired, but what I lack in sophistication I more than make up for with... enthusiasm."

Penelope smirked. "I always applaud enthusiasm, as long as it is well directed."

"I aim to please." The cut and thrust of their flirtation was interrupted by the arrival of an obsequious waiter with the menu. Dante rashly chose a dozen Caledonian oysters, followed by a braised haunch of Aberdeen Angus beef, to be washed down by a rich red wine. Penelope was more circumspect, preferring the risotto with truffle shavings and a cheese soufflé. "Are you a vegetarian?" Dante asked once the waiter had left.

"In all places but the bedroom," Penelope replied.

"How interesting," Dante said, rearranging the linen napkin over his bulging crotch.

Try thinking with your brain instead of your genitals, the Crest interjected. *You don't even know this woman's last name, yet you are behaving like a lust-crazed animal. Find out something about her so I can check it against the Imperial Net.*

"Yes, indeed," Dante said. "After I got your invitation to dine from the steward, it struck me that I don't even know your last name. You know who I am, therefore you have me at a disadvantage. Perhaps you would care to even the balance?"

"Perhaps," Penelope teased. "To be honest, I find my family name something of an embarrassment. People always take it the wrong way."

"Well, I promise to keep an open mind."

"Very well. My name is Goodnight – Penelope Goodnight."

"Really?" Dante asked, trying to keep a straight face. He was aware of movement between his legs and glanced down to see his napkin being expertly moved aside by a probing female foot clad in a black silk stocking. The foot began massaging his groin, toes working their way into the folds of his ever tightening trousers. Dante realised the waiter was returning with their first course and hastily rearranged the napkin to conceal his embarrassment. "I can't imagine why your name would give anyone the wrong idea."

Penelope smiled at him, licking her lips hungrily as their food was placed in front of them. "You'd be surprised.

Some people are apt to misinterpret anything as a sexual overture."

A second foot joined the first between Dante's legs, coaxing and cajoling the contents of his trousers. He struggled to keep a straight face, both eyebrows popping upwards in surprise and delight at the movements beneath his napkin. "I pride myself at being able to... recognise and appreciate the difference between innocent flirting and the more intense cut and... thrust... of a genuine invitation to act."

"I do hope so," she replied, putting a spoonful of creamy risotto into her mouth and savouring every morsel. "Misinterpretations of one's motives can be so... disappointing."

"Absolutely. But I always try to... rise... to the occasion." By now beads of perspiration were forming on Dante's forehead, but he did not dare remove the napkin to mop his brow.

Penelope gestured to the neglected plate of oysters. "You've hardly touched your starter. Has your appetite deserted you?"

"Quite the opposite," he said. "I feel rather ravenous, but these aren't what I had in mind."

She nodded at his glass. "What about the wine? Does that not excite your palate?"

Dante's eye bulged slightly as a wave of pleasure surged through him. "I prefer something with a bit more... body."

"I know what you mean," Penelope agreed. "There's a fully stocked drinks cabinet in my compartment. We could retire there and see if there's anything that's more to your taste."

"That would be... delightful," Dante gasped. He stood up abruptly, using the napkin to hide his groin. "If you'll excuse me for a minute, I need a few moments to... compose myself."

"Of course. I'll be waiting right here."

"Good. Don't go away." Dante strode from the dining car, not meeting the eye of any other passengers. He brushed past their waiter, ignoring inquiries about the quality of the meal. Only when Dante was out in the corridor did he breathe again, panting excitedly as pleasure flushed his features. "Bojemoi, that woman has toes that could out-crush a boa constrictor!" he gasped.

She may be dangerous in other ways, the Crest observed dryly. *I can find no trace of a Penelope Goodnight on the Imperial Net. The name she gave you is an alias or else her identity has been deleted from all public records. Either way, this woman is not to be trusted.*

"I gave her a false name when I got on the train," Dante countered.

Yes, but you're accused of trying to assassinate the king. What is she hiding?

"A husband, or maybe an entire family. I don't know and, to be honest, I don't care," Dante insisted. "She is willing to give me a place to spend for the night–"

Between her thighs.

"–and I need a place to lie low."

I could not have put that better myself.

"Thank you."

That wasn't a compliment. Dante, how many times must I warn you against tumbling into bed with strange women?

"I'll take a wild guess and say two hundred." The Russian renegade grinned. "Am I close?"

As always, you are your own worst enemy.

"I know what I'm doing Crest, so leave me in peace, okay?"

Fine.

"Good."

But don't say I didn't warn you.

"Whatever."

Agent Goodnight smiled as she studied her reflection in the dining car window. With her strawberry blonde hair pulled back from her face in a delicate arrangement, she bore a striking resemblance to her mother. Mary Goodnight had been a top operative for Britannia Intelligence, also specialising in the age-old art of the honey trap. That was how Penelope's parents had met, when Mary lured an unsuspecting spy from the Imperial court into bed. Danilov defected to be with the woman he loved, but a Makarov assassin had killed him before Penelope was born. The daughter of two spies, Agent Goodnight often felt her career had been all but inevitable, a hereditary legacy. Unlike her mother, Penelope was determined to remain aloof, unaffected by any feelings for the men and women to whose seduction she was assigned.

Maintaining that professional detachment would not be a problem in this case, Agent Goodnight decided. Yes, Dante had a certain boyish charm and he was closer to her own age than most subjects she lured into bed and betrayed. But he had the subtlety of a sledgehammer and almost as little wit. He had been putty in her hands thus far, if somewhat harder when placed between her toes. Nevertheless, he clearly did not suspect her motives, believing himself to be worthy of her undivided attention and lust. The arrogance of the man! No, arrogance was the wrong word, she thought. Cockiness – yes, that best described Nikolai Dante: cocky.

A whisper of static through the train's public address system got her attention. "If those passengers on the eastern side of our carriages care to look out their windows, below us they will see the physical anomaly known as the Watford Gap. Decades ago a devastating and utterly unexpected earthquake tore a hole out of this area of Britannia. Within minutes a bustling metropolitan conurbation was gone, swallowed by the ground. All that remains is the hole where once the city of Watford stood – hence its name, the Watford Gap. According to legend, if you look closely enough you can see the ghosts of all those who perished in that tragedy."

Penelope had seen the gap before but never from this height nor at night. She peered through the window and was struck by how beautiful even a scene of such devastation could look at night. The jagged edge of the chasm was well lit but the yawning absence where a city had once stood was nothing but blackness, like a ragged mouth in the night. No, wait, there was something moving across the darkness – several somethings. Penelope looked closer and realised the shapes were between the train and the topographical anomaly below. They almost resembled insects, a swarm of them buzzing through the air, moving ever closer to the *Flying Scotsman*. But no insect should be large enough for her to notice at this distance, should it?

Within seconds Penelope was out of her seat and striding briskly from the dining car. She had to find Dante and find him fast. A death squad of Rippers was surrounding the train in mid-air and there could be little doubt who they were looking for. She had scant minutes to conceal their quarry before the Rippers boarded the *Flying Scotsman* and hunted Dante down.

Her mind raced with questions. How had they traced him here? Yes, their genetically engineered senses were remarkably effective tools, but even they could not detect a single person's DNA on a sealed train without having been directed to this location. Either someone had spotted Dante on board and called in the Rippers, or else her last communication to the princess had been intercepted. Either way, somebody wanted Dante dead by any means necessary. Unleashing the Rippers meant whomever gave the order did not care who got hurt in the process.

Penelope spotted Dante walking along the corridor towards her, still adjusting his bulging trousers. "I was coming to fetch you," he said warmly.

"No need. Come and see my cabin," she replied, grabbing his left hand and dragging him along after her. "I promise you an experience you'll never forget."

"Sounds intriguing," he said, jogging to keep up with her. "Why the rush?"

"I've had my fill of flirting for one night," Penelope said. "Appetisers are all very well, but eventually you want to savour a nice piece of flesh."

"I couldn't agree more."

"Good," she said hurriedly as they reached the door to her compartment. Penelope unlocked it and shoved Dante inside, then followed him in and relocked the door. "Strip!"

"Sorry?"

"Get your clothes off!"

Dante's face split into a broad grin, then he tore off his jacket. "I was wondering how long you'd be able to resist getting your hands on me. Not that I'm complaining about your use of the feet," he added, as he removed his leather boots, tossing one over each shoulder. "Your toes are remarkably skilful. But I find fingers have a lightness of touch that few other parts of anatomy can match, don't you?" In the time it had taken him to finish his speech, Dante had peeled his shirt off over his head and stepped out of his trousers. He was standing in the centre of the compartment, both hands doing their best to hide the borrowed g-string that singularly failed to conceal his rising excitement. "Now what?"

Penelope studied the words "GET IT HERE" emblazoned across Dante's underwear. "You seem like a broad-minded individual. How do you feel about trying a little bondage?"

For the last time, listen to me, the Crest insisted. *This woman–*

"I like to think of myself as tri-sexual," Dante replied. "I'll try anything once."

"Good," Penelope said, gathering the rest of his clothes. "Give me your underwear and then lie face-up on the mattress." She watched him comply, resisting the urge to laugh as he clambered willingly onto the luxurious, four-poster bed. Penelope made a neat pile of Dante's clothes by the compartment door, then reached for a small case resting on a nearby side-table. She extracted a pair of black handcuffs and held them aloft. "I'm going to give you a night you'll never forget."

As head steward on board the *Flying Scotsman*, it was Gordonstoun's job to ensure nothing disturbed or upset his passengers. A panicked call from the front of the train had brought him running, forcing the portly attendant to abandon his usual station during the dinner service. When he saw the sinister squad of hollow-cheeked hunters sniffing their way along a corridor, his heart fluttered with terror. A dozen knife-wielding maniacs in black cloaks, suits and stovepipe hates certainly qualified as disturbing in Gordonstoun's estimation. Despite his inner fears, the steward stood his ground outside the dining car, refusing to let the Rippers pass.

"I don't care whose authority you claim to have for your dreadful intrusion, I am responsible for the care and welfare of all those on board this train. I will not have you frightening the passengers or staff with your bully-boy tactics," Gordonstoun maintained.

The Rippers' leader sneered at the steward, a grey moustache quivering with repressed rage. "You shouldn't be takin' liberties with us, guv'nor – we slice and dice the likes of you for breakfast without thinkin' twice." He held the point of his left dagger close to Gordonstoun's throat while the right dagger reached underneath the steward's kilt. The blade scratched its way up one of Gordonstoun's legs, edging ever closer to his unprotected groin. "One slip of my knife and you'll be singing with the boy sopranos for a long, long time, if you catch my drift. Now, get out of my way, you officious nonce!"

The head steward stepped aside, his bottom lip wobbling as tears filled his eyes. Gordonstoun stared at the floor as the Rippers shoved past, too ashamed to meet their gaze. Dear god, he prayed, let them find whichever poor soul they're searching for quickly. Maybe they'll leave us in peace after that.

Penelope secured one end of the black handcuffs around Dante's left wrist, pulling his arm up over his head to the hefty wooden post at one corner of the bed. She stretched forward over Dante to feed the other end of the cuffs behind the post, her velvet-covered breasts brushing across his eager face. "Now give me your other arm," she commanded.

"Do I have to?" Dante asked. He was busy using his free hand to caress Penelope's firm but well rounded buttocks. "It's having quite a good time where it is." His fingers slipped sideways to explore between the top of her supple thighs.

Penelope sighed, reaching back to extract Dante's groping hand and yanking it up to meet the other end of the cuffs. "That's better," she said, clamping his wrists together.

"Ouch!" he protested. "Do those have to be so tight? I'm not big on pain."

"A typical male," she sneered, climbing off the bed. "Happy to savour the pleasures of sex, but you never stick around to face the consequences." Penelope stood back to admire her handiwork. Dante was lying naked on the mattress, his wrists clamped together above his head while each ankle was secured to the resolute wooden posts at the other end of the bed by carefully knotted silk scarves.

"So, what do we do now?" he grinned, waggling his eyebrows suggestively.

"I noticed earlier you were wearing a pair of women's underwear."

"Like I said, I'll try anything once."

"Good." Penelope disappeared into her dressing room for a few moments, then returned with several pairs of delicate lace panties. She held them up for Dante to see. "Which of these do you prefer? The black or the red?"

"They'd both look good on you," he replied. "Come to think of it, aren't you a little overdressed? Feel free to strip off and join the party."

"Oh, these aren't for me," Penelope laughed. "They're for you."

"You'll need to untie my legs first to get them on me."

"True," she agreed, approaching the bed. "But I had something else in mind." Penelope pulled down the front of her gown and let her breasts spill out in front of Dante's mouth. He stretched forwards and opened his lips wide, eager to put them around her aroused nipples. Instead he found both pairs of panties shoved into his mouth. Confusion crowded his face and he started to gag against the fabric. "Breathe through your nose," Penelope urged, "otherwise you're likely to drown in your own vomit."

Dante struggled to follow her instructions, puzzlement evident in his eyes as Penelope hoisted her gown back into place. "I haven't got time to explain," she said, "but this is for your own good." After that she ignored her captive, instead searching through a small case containing bottles of scent and eau de toilettes. "Yes, this should do the trick," Penelope decided, choosing one particular bottle of perfume from among the many. She removed the lid and tipped most of the contents over Dante's writhing, thrashing body. An overpowering odour of sandalwood and musk filled the compartment, eradicating every other smell. "This is called Bitch, it's the new fragrance from the House of Klein. In small doses it stinks like a tart's boudoir at low tide, so it should mask your natural body odour quite effectively."

Dante yelled and howled in protest but his cries were muffled most effectively by the mouthful of lingerie. Penelope looked at his crotch and smirked. "Not quite so cocky now, are you?" She strode to the outer door and pulled it open, then tossed Dante's clothes and boots out into the corridor. She emptied the last of the perfume over the spot where his garments had been lying. "There, that should do it. Now to lay a scent." Penelope went out into the corridor and closed the door, gently waving to her prisoner as she departed. Dante heard the door being locked, then the sound of something being dragged along the corridor towards the rear of the hover-train.

I tried to warn you, the Crest sighed.

Dante attempted to reply but his words were all but unintelligible thanks to the improvised gag in his mouth.

What was that?

Dante tried again.

The handcuffs? They must be made of a special compound that suppresses your cyborganics. Dante spoke again, another garbled collection of grunts and noises.

If I had to guess, I'd say Ms Goodnight is an operative for one of the local intelligence agencies. She seems remarkably resourceful and well equipped.

Another outburst came from Dante.

I was referring to the handcuffs, not her décolletage, the Crest replied. *Even tied up your libido is more active than your brain, isn't it?*

Dante simply shrugged.

Penelope hurried towards the back of the *Flying Scotsman*, dragging Dante's clothes behind her. As she approached the final carriage the translucent disc in her ear began to vibrate. She pressed a finger against the device, activating its two-way communications link. "Agent Goodnight responding."

"This is her royal highness, Princess Marie-Anne. Have you located the fugitive Dante?"

"You know bloody well I've located him! Why have you sent in the Rippers? I had the situation under control, now you've forced me to compromise my cover!"

"What are you talking about? I didn't send the–" A scream of static cut through the transmission, forcing

Penelope to pluck the tiny device out of her ear. It bounced against a window, then fell to the carpet. Seconds later the static was gone, no sound issuing from the comms disc. Penelope retrieved the small circle but could get no response from it. Someone was jamming the signal, cutting off the outside world. The Rippers must be closing in.

After checking the final carriage was unoccupied, Penelope threw Dante's clothes and boots inside it and locked the connecting door... Next she smeared her make-up and rubbed her eyes, forcing them to look red and weepy. Lastly she tore the top of her dress, letting it hang limply from one shoulder, and removed one of her shoes. The sound of heavy footfalls running towards her became audible. Penelope burst into tears and staggered slowly away from the final carriage. The Rippers appeared, knives drawn, the lust for blood all too obvious.

"Please, you've got to help me!" Penelope whimpered. "This man, I think his name was Dante – he attacked me! He dragged me into the final carriage and tried to have his way with me. I managed to fight him off and lock him inside. He was bleeding, I don't know if he's dead or alive!" She broke down in tears, her ordeal apparently too much to bear.

"Don't you worry, miss," the Rippers' leader vowed in a broad Cockney accent. "If that scum ain't dead already, he will be by the time we've finished with 'im!" The other Rippers leered their approval, light glinting off their blades.

Penelope pointed with a shaking hand. "H-He's through there..."

The twelve Rippers moved as one, storming along the corridor to the final carriage. The locked door was quickly dealt with and the death squad rushed inside. Their leader picked up the discarded clothes and boots, sniffing them suspiciously. "I smell his stench on these rags, boys! The Russian bastard must be in one of these compartments! Spread out and start searching."

Penelope waited until all twelve were busy with their manhunt before returning to the connecting doorway. She closed and locked it again, then smashed the glass on a small box marked with the words "EMERGENCY CARRIAGE RELEASE – WARNING! DO NOT ACTIVATE WHEN TRAIN IS IN FLIGHT". Penelope shoved her fist into the large red button. A warning klaxon sounded and a stern male voice announced carriage separation would commence within ten seconds. The leader of the Rippers reappeared in the corridor opposite Penelope, uncertain what was happening. His confusion turned to anger as the automated countdown began. He ran to the adjoining door but could not undo the lock in time. Penelope waved as the countdown reached zero, ignoring the Rippers' threats.

With a hiss of hydraulics, the *Flying Scotsman*'s final carriage uncoupled itself and tumbled away, turning end over end as it fell from the sky, plummeting into the black emptiness of the Watford Gap. Penelope watched as the Rippers' flying mounts raced after the descending carriage, but they could not catch up with it in time. In less than a minute the detached section of train had disappeared from view, along with its unscheduled cargo of DNA-sniffing psychopathic killers. "Secret agents one, Rippers nil," Penelope said with quiet satisfaction.

SEVEN

"However the devil is clad, he's still the devil."
– Russian proverb

"Traditional Highland dress for men has changed little over the centuries. Scotland may have been renamed Caledonia and transformed into a tartan tourist trap, but the kilt, sporran and Sgian Dhub remain much as they always have. A true kilt is made of eleven ounce quality pure worsted tartan, with a three buckle fastening and double fringed apron edge. Over the crotch any decent wearer will rest their sporran, a large pouch made of leather and fur that hangs from the belt. Below the knee is the kilt hose, usually an off-white sock or stocking often worn with flashes on adjustable garters.

Slotted into this on one leg is the Sgian Dhub, a small dagger held in an ornamental sheath. For the feet it is still traditional to wear ghillie brogues, the black leather shoes that have served Scotsmen for over a millennium. Above the waist a white shirt is most common, sometimes laced together across the chest. Last but not least is the Prince Charlie, a cut-off black wool jacket with gleaming silver buttons. Only the most crass of kilt wearers also sports a tam-o'-shanter, the brimless wool cap with a bobble in the centre. If you must indulge in this act of millinery madness, at least match the tartan of your hat with the tartan of your kilt. But whatever else you do, a true Highlander never wears underpants beneath his kilt. Your sporran will protect your modesty, so let everything else hang free as nature intended."

– Extract from *What's Scot to Wear*, 2670 edition

A polite knock at the compartment door woke Penelope shortly before dawn. With Dante handcuffed to the bed and snoring loudly, she had spent a fitful night on the chaise longue. The stench of *Bitch* still lingered in the room, like flatulence under a duvet, but with more acrid intensity. The knocking persisted so Penelope pulled a robe over her crimson silk pyjamas and approached the door. "Who is it?" she asked meekly.

"Gordonstoun, your steward," a familiar voice replied worriedly.

Penelope opened the door a fraction and peered out. The portly attendant was wringing his hands in the corridor, nervously shifting his weight from foot to foot. "Yes?" she asked, her voice becoming more forceful. "Surely breakfast is not for at least another hour?"

"You are correct, madam. This regards another matter entirely," Gordonstoun said apologetically. "It seems there was an incident late last night. We were boarded by Britannia Intelligence agents. They refused to explain their presence and began searching each carriage. Shortly afterwards the last section of the train fell into the Watford Gap, apparently with all the intelligence operatives on board. Our head office has asked me to take a full inventory of passengers, to ensure none were lost in this unfortunate incident."

Penelope smiled. "As you can see, I'm fit and well."

"What about your… husband?"

"Him? Well, his snoring remains as intolerable as ever, but he is otherwise well."

Gordonstoun nodded, his face still full of apologies. "I am glad to hear that, madam. Alas, I must ask to see him in person. My superiors have made it clear I must personally lay eyes upon all our passengers, to ascertain for myself nothing untoward has befallen any of them."

"Well, if you insist..." Penelope replied and opened the door wider, allowing the steward an eyeful of Dante's naked and bound body. A gust of *Bitch* escaped into the corridor. "Satisfied?"

"Yes, madam," Gordonstoun said with a blush, choking as the florid, cloying perfume flooded the air around him. "I see you have been busy."

"We've been tied up all night, you might say."

"Indeed. There has been quite a lot of that on board," he replied, shaking his head gently. "Well, I will delay you no longer. Breakfast will be served from seven onwards and we are due to stop at Nottingham a little after nine. Good day to you both." Penelope closed the door and returned to the chaise longue. What had the steward meant?

"It doesn't matter," Penelope told herself. Nottingham would be where they got off.

The Phord Capri screeched to a halt outside the Tower of London, back tyres protesting as the car spun through a hundred and eighty degrees before neatly inserting itself between two other vehicles. "Now that's what I call a piece of parking," Dobie announced smugly from the driver's seat. "What do you think, Ray?"

Boyle was too busy adjusting his mass of brown curls with the aid of an afro comb and a small, hand-held mirror. "Are we there yet?"

"Are we there yet?" Dobie replied in mock indignation. "I cross London in record time and you ask if we're there yet? I swear, my talents are wasted on you, they really are."

"I'd agree, if you had any talents to waste."

"Hark at him! So busy preening, I'm surprised you had time to think up a witty one-liner."

"Some of us are better than others at multi-tasking."

Dobie rolled his eyes. "Can we go and question these idiots? With you being so multi-talented, it shouldn't be a great challenge."

The two men sauntered towards the Tower's main gates, each trying to appear more causal than the other. Dobie bashed his fist against the wooden gates.

Boyle couldn't resist having the last word. "Obviously, I *am* multi-talented, but that wasn't what I said."

The gates swung open to reveal a man mountain of a sentry inside. Dobie flashed some credentials and pushed his way past. "I'm Dobie, he's Ray Boyle. We're bounty hunters, here on official business. We want to see Flatcock and Spatchlint."

"Spatchcock and Flintlock?" the sentry asked.

"Them," Boyle agreed, following Dobie inside. "Hey, do you think Flintlock is any relation to Lord Peter Flintlock, the one who got deported for–"

"Nah, he couldn't be," Dobie replied, shaking his head dismissively. "I doubt he'd ever have the nerve to show his face in the country again."

Dante opened his eyes and groaned. It had not been a bad dream after all, nor some kind of nightmare. He was naked, handcuffed and tied down on a four-poster bed. There was no sign of his captor and no way of calling for help thanks to the panties stuffed into his mouth. His nostrils felt as if they had been scoured with floral acid, thanks to the perfume Penelope had splashed all over his body. Dante's jaws ached from being gagged all night and his bladder was full to bursting. Unsympathetic comments from the Crest were doing little to improve his mood. *Perhaps now you'll listen when I try to warn you about the dangers of dubious women.*

The compartment's outer door opened and a member of the train's staff entered. His eyes widened at what he found inside. "Jings! Where's ye trews?"

Dante tried to answer but could make no more than muffled yelps. The steward ventured closer, sniffing the air suspiciously while stroking his ginger beard. "What a smell? Have ye been torturing a skunk in here?" Another muffled cry from Dante. "Did ye ken you have a pair of lassie's pants in your mouth?"

Penelope entered the compartment in a black version of her habitual catsuit, clutching a small pistol. The steward pulled the lingerie from Dante's mouth, staring at each garment in disbelief. "I was wrong – ye had two pairs of pants in there! Are ye some kind of bampot?" Before Dante could answer, Penelope smashed her pistol down on the steward's head, knocking him unconscious. He fell forward on top of Dante, who groaned at the added pressure on his bladder.

Penelope began stripping off the steward's Highland dress uniform. "You should be grateful. I searched the whole train to find anyone with the same build as you."

"Please," Dante pleaded. "I need the toilet. Now."

"Well, I'm not stopping you."

"No, but these are," Dante said, rattling the handcuffs. "Either you let me free or else I soak the sheets, the mattress and possibly the ceiling. It's your choice."

Penelope paused after removing the steward's kilt. "I see this one's a true Scotsman." She bit her bottom lip while studying her prisoner. "Very well. But one false move and I'll call the Rippers myself to deal with you."

"The Rippers? They've been here?" Dante asked while Penelope untied his numb legs.

"Last night. I used your clothes as a diversion to get them off the train."

"They'll be back."

"Yes, but we'll already be heading for London by then." She undid the cuff from Dante's left wrist, pulled it round the post and then reattached it to his arm. "The bathroom's through there, but leave the door open. I don't want you trying anything stupid."

"I'm stark naked and my legs are stiff from being tied up all night," he protested. "What am I going to do, fly out of here?" He staggered across to the bathroom, both legs weak and wobbly.

"You'd have to, we're still in the air." Penelope finished undressing the steward, then used her discarded silk scarves to tie up the attendant.

She shoved both pairs of saliva-soaked pants into his mouth and rolled him under the bed. The sound of splashing water made her check Dante's progress in the bathroom. "Haven't you finished in there yet?" Penelope found him struggling to throw water at himself while still in handcuffs.

"I'm trying to wash some of this perfume off," he scowled. "I stink like a bitch on heat."

"Get dressed," Penelope said, indicating the clothes she had stolen from the steward.

"What if I refuse?" Dante challenged.

"My orders are to deliver you alive," she replied, aiming her small pistol at his genitals. "That doesn't mean I have to take you back to London unharmed."

Dante arranged his hands across his groin. "Watch where you're pointing that thing!"

"Don't worry, I'd have to be a sharpshooter to hit something that small."

I like her, the Crest announced cheerfully.

"Well, don't get used to having her around," Dante replied.

Penelope glared at him. "What did you say?"

"Nothing – a private conversation."

She smiled. "That's right, the Crest communicates with you telepathically – I read about that in a briefing paper. A remarkable piece of kit."

"It has some uses," Dante conceded.

Like keeping you alive more times than I care to remember.

"Don't let it go to your head," Dante snapped.

Penelope sighed. "Being with you is like sitting next to a surly husband arguing on the phone with his ex-wife about their divorce settlement."

"You should try being inside my head!"

I doubt she'd enjoy the experience, the Crest commented.

"I doubt I'd enjoy the experience," Penelope unwittingly agreed.

"Bojemoi, the two of you even talk alike," Dante lamented. He finished wiping himself with a hand towel and returned to the main cabin. He surveyed the steward's clothes unhappily. "I haven't worn a kilt since visiting the Victoria Falls in Africa. It's not the most reassuring outfit." His eyes lit up after spotting the Sgian Dhub among the accessories. Dante crouched beside the clothes to retrieve the dagger in its elaborately carved sheath.

"I hope you're not planning to stab me with that blade."

"The thought never entered my head," Dante replied. In a single movement he pulled the dagger from the sheath and flung it across the room at Penelope. The blade hit her between the breasts, then bounced away to the floor. She smiled and picked up the ceremonial dagger, bending its blade between her fingers.

"Purely ornamental. This one's made of rubber, it wouldn't hurt a midge."

"I knew that," Dante maintained. "I was simply testing your reflexes."

Penelope rolled her eyes. "Your lying is worse than your snoring. Now, get dressed if you want to eat before we get off the train."

Flintlock's constant complaining had won him a reprieve from being manacled to Spatchcock, but the captives were still sharing a cell. The malodorous runt had retreated to one corner while his aristocratic companion kept to the other, near the door. "We've got visitors," Flintlock announced.

"Female?" Spatchcock asked hopefully. "I was going to ask for a roll in the hay as my final request, before the execution."

"I'm not sure they'll let you have a goat in here, old boy." Flintlock retreated from the door as it was unlocked. A burly sentry let two men into the dank, dismal dungeon, then shut and locked the door once more. The visitors' faces curdled at the stench.

"That guard wasn't kidding about the smell, was he?" one of the newcomers gasped. "I've been to slaughterhouses that weren't this bad."

The other man pinched his nose shut and breathed through his mouth. "Which one of you is Lord Peter Flintlock?"

"He is!" the prisoners replied in unison, pointing at each other.

"Very droll." The curly-haired visitor introduced himself as Ray Boyle, then jerked a thumb towards his nose-pinching associate. "Forgive Dobie's appearance, but he always looks like that."

Dobie looked down at his clothes, a plethora of brown and taupe. "What's wrong with the way I dress?"

"I was talking about your face," Boyle replied with a smirk. He studied the two prisoners before pointing a finger at Flintlock. "You must be his lordship, judging by the white hair and haughty discomfit. I'd have thought the most disgraced man in Britannia would be used to hovels like this by now. You've been in exile long enough – what made you come back?"

"I'd rather not talk about it," Flintlock said primly, folding his arms.

"Have it your own way." Boyle drove a fist into Flintlock's midriff. The prisoner crumpled like a paper bag, gasping for air as he sagged to the stone floor. Spatchcock took a step closer to defend his friend but was stopped by a punch in the head from Dobie. The small man went sprawling, his skull smacking against the nearest wall. He too slumped to the cold floor, blood streaming from a gash on the side of his face. Boyle crouched in front of Flintlock, his cold blue eyes staring into the prisoner's trembling face. "Or you can have it my way. So, which do you prefer? Pain or more pain?"

"What do you want?" Spatchcock asked sourly.

"That's better," Dobie smiled. "See how much easier life can be if you co-operate?"

"Just ask your questions," Spatchcock said.

"All right," Boyle agreed, straightening up again. "Nikolai Dante – where is he?"

"How should we know?" Spatchcock replied. "The last we saw of him was when he jumped out a window at the Palace of London, after the king was shot."

"You haven't seen him since?"

"We were arrested within minutes and brought here. That was at least a day ago, if not longer." Spatchcock gestured at their surroundings. "Not having my social secretary handy, it's a little difficult to be precise about dates."

Boyle used his left knee to give Flintlock a nudge. "What about you? What have you got to say for yourself?"

"Spatch is right," Flintlock whispered between strained breaths. "We don't know where Dante is. He doesn't confide in us."

"So he left you behind to take the rap while he flees London, is that it?" Dobie sneered.

Spatchcock glared at the bounty hunters. "He's left the city?"

"He's betrayed you – both of you."

Spatchcock shook his head. "Not after everything we've been through together. I know Dante, his conscience will get the better of him, sooner or later. He'll come back for us, he'll find a way of getting us out of this place."

Boyle laughed. "I wouldn't count on it." He kicked at Flintlock. "What about it, your lordship? Do you share you foul-smelling friend's faith in Dante?"

"No. If I knew anything useful, I'd tell you," Flintlock said. "I'm no hero."

"But Dante is," Spatchcock maintained. "By now he's busy planning how to free us while sleeping with anything in knickers. You'll see!"

Penelope slapped Dante hard across the face. "Put your hands on me again and I'll chop them off!" They were returning from breakfast in the dining car, where she had kept Dante under control by having her pistol constantly aimed at him beneath the table. But when Penelope tried to unlock her compartment, Dante had been unable to resist fondling her firm buttocks.

"I was checking to see if you have any more concealed weapons," he said.

"Your feeble attempts at seduction couldn't arouse a nymphomaniac." Penelope shoved him into the cabin. "We're due to land at Nottingham within the hour. When we get off, I don't want any trouble. Keep your hands to yourself and you'll keep your hands. Otherwise I'll be forced to disable you – permanently."

"I've been tortured by the best," Dante boasted. "There's nothing you can do to me that hasn't been tried and failed."

"Is that a fact?" Penelope asked, moving closer to him. She ran a hand across Dante's chest, then let it slide down between his legs.

"Absolutely," he affirmed.

"What if I was to seduce you, would that change things?"

Dante shook his head, trying to ignore the sensations her hands were creating. "I possess total self control," he said as Penelope's fingernails dug into his muscular buttocks.

"Total self control?" she asked huskily.

Dante nodded, not trusting himself to speak. Penelope's hands slid up and down, gripping, teasing, taunting him.

Her tongue slid between his lips, exploring him hungrily, her body forcing him back until he slammed into a wall. Penelope pulled her lips away from his. "You don't think I could have you whenever I wanted?"

"Not at all," he whispered, willing her to undo the zip that ran down between her breasts to the catsuit's crotch

"We'll see," Penelope said, smiling broadly. Her hand suddenly clenched around Dante's crown jewels, squeezing with the grip of a vice. He screamed in agony and she kissed him again, momentarily relaxing her hold on his scrotum, then clenching again, harder than before. Dante's face showed every paroxysm of pain stabbing through his body. Just as suddenly she released her iron grip and stepped backwards, letting him sink to the floor, hands nursing his bruised body parts. "So much for total self control. I'll never understand why people call women the weaker sex. One squeeze in the right place and you men keel over like a broken bicycle."

"Urgh," Dante replied weakly.

Penelope retrieved a tiny key from between her breasts and used it to unlock the cuff around Dante's right wrist. She clamped the empty binding around her left wrist and locked it into place, tugging hard at the metal to make sure it was securely fastened. Satisfied with the results, she slapped Dante's face to get his attention. "I am now going to swallow the key for these unique bindings. It is the sole method of opening them. Even if you managed to overpower me, you cannot escape me. Better you know that now and save both of us any further trouble. Penelope stuck the key on her tongue and then swallowed. "By the way, as long as any part of the handcuffs remains in contact with you, neither of your bio-blades will function. You and I are stuck with each other until that key flushes through my body."

You certainly know how to pick them, don't you?

"Oh, shut up," Dante winced.

Dobie and Boyle emerged from the Tower of London to find Rucka sitting on the bonnet of their hover-car. "What a pleasant surprise!" Dobie said sarcastically. "Inspector, that's twice in two days you've been seen with us – people will talk. To what do we owe this dishonour?"

"Spatchcock and Flintlock have no idea where Dante is," Rucka replied.

"That much we found out for ourselves," Boyle remarked.

"But I know where he is," the inspector continued, producing a slip of paper. "On here is written the location where Dante can be found today – if you hurry."

The two bounty hunters exchanged a quizzical look. "Why give that to us?"

"For a start, I'm not giving it to you," Rucka said, standing upright. "I will pass useful facts to you in exchange for a percentage of the reward you claim by finding and killing Dante."

"What kind of percentage?" Bole asked.

"Fifty."

Dobie snorted derisively. "You're joking! The only people we share anything with is each other. How do we even know your information is accurate?"

"You'll have to trust me," Rucka said. "But if you can't trust a policeman, who can you trust?"

"We don't trust anybody," Boyle sneered.

The inspector shrugged and started strolling away. "Have it your own way."

The two bounty hunters watched him go, trying to call his bluff. After a few seconds they caved in, calling him back. Rucka's smile was smugger than ever when he turned round. "Fifty per cent."

"If we don't catch him, that'll be fifty per cent of nothing," Boyle observed.

"Then don't fail. Have we got an agreement?"

The partners nodded reluctantly. The inspector handed Dobie the slip of paper. "Your quarry is on the *Flying*

Scotsman, It should be arriving in Nottingham any minute. He's almost certainly in the custody of a Britannia Intelligence operative called Penelope Goodnight. Your job is to find and kill him, then bring the body back to claim the reward. Don't underestimate Agent Goodnight. She's the best."

Dobie laughed. "With a name like that, how dangerous can she be?"

"Goodnight has lured more men and women to their doom than you've had hot dinners."

"Her feminine charms won't work on us," Boyle said, shaking his head dismissively.

"Why not?" Rucka asked.

"We prefer our lovers a little more butch," Dobie replied. "Don't we, Ray?"

Boyle blew a kiss at his partner.

The inspector sighed. "Nevertheless, Agent Goodnight is a resourceful woman, she could get the better of you two. Kill her and you'll have the entire secret service hunting you to the ends of the earth. But Dante cannot be permitted to return to London alive. He's too dangerous."

"You're the boss," Boyle agreed. "One last question – why us? Why not send your own men after this fugitive?"

"You two may be the scum of the earth, but you're the best," Rucka said. "I've read your files – you've never failed a contract. Don't start now." He consulted his watch. "If I were you, I'd already be en route to Nottingham. Every minute you spend talking with me is a minute wasted, and you don't have time for that. Good day, gentlemen."

Gordonstoun breathed a sigh of relief as the *Flying Scotsman* landed on the tracks outside Nottingham. He had been a crew member for ten years, working his way up from the lowliest position to become head steward. In all that time he had never experienced as many incidents as he had since leaving London on this journey. The shenanigans involving Ms Goodnight and her "husband" were nothing unusual – aristocrats and the rich were perpetually using the train as their love-nest for adulterous interludes. Even the use of handcuffs and other bondage paraphernalia were not unknown among certain passengers. But to have the train boarded by a dozen Rippers, that was exceptional. Gordonstoun did not relish the prospect of preparing a report for head office when the train finally got back to London. Perhaps I can delegate it to one of my assistants, he thought as the *Flying Scotsman* braked to a halt at Nottingham Station.

The head steward banished such musings to concentrate on ensuring the large group of travellers leaving at this station took all their belongings. A typical passenger was a foreign visitor who wished to see Britannia in style, and the *Flying Scotsman* provided that style: sedate, luxurious, old fashioned and yet simultaneously ultra-modern with its innovative use of hover-technology. But this particular party had come from all over Britannia simply to ride the train between London and Nottingham. There were far cheaper and quicker options available to them, but they had willingly paid full price for one night aboard the train. Ours is not to reason why, Gordonstoun reminded himself. Life on board would be a lot less hectic once they were gone.

He moved through each compartment, checking closets and drawers and under the beds for any forgotten possessions. Besides the usual selection of discarded stockings and lonely shoes he also uncovered five sets of handcuffs, several rubber masks and what looked suspiciously like a metre-long double-ended black dildo. "Perverts," Gordonstoun muttered while locking the items away in his personal locker. If nothing else they should make for amusing presents at the crew's Christmas party. Gordonstoun was so busy he missed the news flash broadcast in Nottingham Station as the passengers finished disembarking.

Penelope tugged her left arm, jerking Dante down the stairs on to the platform. The fugitive was still bitterly nursing his testicles and almost lost his footing. "Diavolo, what's your rush? Some of us are still recovering," he protested.

"The only thing I hurt was your pride," she snapped. "Stop touching your groin, it makes you look like a pervert."

"I doubt the handcuffs are making that image any better."

Penelope's face lit up as she spotted an information board beneath a huge holographic display. She dragged Dante towards it, passing three junior stewards in strange garb. Each was acting as a gathering point for the *Flying Scotsman*'s day trips.

"This way all those passengers who want to visit Nottingham's castle!" the first steward shouted, ushering a handful of people towards a waiting bus. He was wearing a jerkin of simulated chainmail and clasping an unwieldy pikestaff.

"Everybody who wants to savour the Robin Hood experience by having lunch in Sherwood Forest, come with me!" cried another steward, clad in ungainly green medieval clothes. Like the first option, this was drawing only a handful of passengers.

"All those bound for the historic country estate of the Fforbes-Lamington family, gather here for transportation," the third steward called out. She was dressed in a pink hunting jacket, light brown jodhpurs and black leather riding boots. An enthusiastic crowd quickly gathered around her, all demanding to be taken to the country estate. "Golly!" she said, somewhat overwhelmed. "I didn't know we would get so many of you today! I'll have to go and arrange for a larger coach to transport everybody." She made urgent signals to another staff member for help.

Dante observed all this with little interest until he saw a familiar figure among the passengers lining up to visit the castle. When the man looked around, Dante could clearly see a goatee beard and mournful expression. "That's him! He's one of people who tried to kill the king," Dante said excitedly, jerking his manacled arm to get Penelope's attention. But by the time she turned to follow his gaze, the man had vanished among the crowds on the platform.

"What is it?" she asked.

"One of the other passengers on the train, he was an accomplice to the assassination attempt on King Henry. That's why I got on the *Flying Scotsman*, I was following him!"

"You're claiming to be innocent?"

"Of trying to kill the king? Yes, of course!"

Penelope did not look impressed. "You would say anything to escape execution."

"Of course, but for once in my life, I'm telling the truth," Dante insisted. "You're not giving me a chance to clear my name!"

"Why should I believe you?"

"Help me catch the real killer and I'll show you."

Penelope shook her head. "This is a ruse to distract me – and not a very good one."

"What have you got to lose by trusting me?"

"My job, my reputation, my chance of promotion – almost everything, in fact."

"Why won't you listen?"

"Because you're a liar, a thief, a conman, a rogue, a brigand and one of the most wanted men in the Empire. If our positions were reversed, would you believe me in such circumstances?"

"No," Dante admitted.

"There, you see–"

"But I'd still give you a chance to prove your innocence."

Penelope shook her head. "Then you would be a sentimental fool."

"Better that than a cold, heartless bitch more interested in furthering her career than discovering the truth. Don't you believe in justice?"

"I believe in what I can see, hear, taste, touch and smell," she snarled. "Everything else is irrelevant. Now, let's get moving." Penelope shoved Dante towards the exit, but they had only a few steps when a woman's voice boomed through the station's public address system.

"We interrupt your regular programming to broadcast this news flash. According to sources within the intelligence community, one of Britannia's own secret service operatives may be a co-conspirator in the attempted assassination of King Henry. A leaked document suggests Agent Penelope Goodnight has links with the fugitive Nikolai Dante, who has already been found guilty of his involvement. It is believed she may be attempted to smuggle Dante out of the country. Police and other law enforcement agencies have already been placed on high alert in the search for Dante. No picture of Agent Goodnight is currently available, but the authorities hope to publish such an image within the next few hours. Thank you for your attention."

"It seems we're partners in crime," Dante observed. "Welcome to my world."

"This isn't right," she protested. "I've done nothing wrong!"

"Now you know how I feel." Dante held open his arms. "Group hug?"

Penelope slapped his face instead. "You did this! Somehow you've dragged me down to your level. I need to find a policeman, tell them they're got it wrong..."

"Oh yeah, that works every time," he said. The smirk on his lips was wiped away when she started waving frantically at a policeman who had wandered on to the platform. Dante grabbed her arm and pulled it back down. "Fuoco, what are you doing?"

"Trying to get his attention."

"You'll get both of us arrested or executed where we stand! Your boss may have wanted me captured alive, but the police have shoot to kill orders – and they know what I look like!"

"You're right. We need to find a place to hide, give ourselves a chance to think." The people waiting to visit the Fforbes-Lamington estate were now being loaded onto coaches nearby. "We'll join the back of that group, lose ourselves amongst them for the rest of the day while I figure out what's gone wrong." She strode towards the queue, dragging Dante along behind.

He pulled the tam-o'-shanter forwards to hide his face as they passed the policeman. "You've changed your tune all of a sudden," Dante commented once they had joined the queue.

"What are you talking about?"

"Five minutes ago I was a liar, a thief, a conman, a rogue and one of the most wanted men in the Empire. You couldn't care less what happened to me, as long as you got the credit for bringing me to justice. Now 'we' need to find a place to hide and figure out what's gone wrong. Since when did we become a team?"

"Since somebody in Britannia Intelligence turned me into a fugitive like you," Penelope said angrily. "Don't make the mistake of thinking I'm happy about this. But you're right – as far as the authorities are concerned, we're partners in crime now." Their queue was diminishing rapidly as the last passengers clambered on to the coach. Dante couldn't help smiling. "What's so funny?" Penelope demanded.

Dante held up his right wrist, the one handcuffed to her left arm. "Bet you're wishing you hadn't swallowed that key now, right?"

"Don't remind me!"

EIGHT

"Many words, little truth."
– Russian proverb

"The Fforbes-Lamington estate is one of Britannia's last remaining examples of a country seat still owned by the landed gentry. Over the past nine hundred years financial strife and mismanagement have bankrupted most of the families that once held feudal rights to vast sections of the countryside. Historic estates were broken up, parcels of land sold off piecemeal to developers and turned into soulless housing dormitories. Happily, the Fforbes-Lamington estate outside Nottingham did not suffer this ignominious fate.

The family has kept hold of its assets and even added to them in recent decades, thanks to adroit acquisitions by the head of the household, Audrey Fforbes-Lamington.

A formidable woman in every sense of the word, her first husband died of a heart condition. She temporarily lost possession of the estate for four years, then married immigrant businessman Dick Revere, who had bought it at auction. He died within a year and Ms Fforbes-Lamington reverted to her maiden name. Few visitors are allowed on the estate, which is said to be guarded by an extensive network of security droids. Once a year Ms Fforbes-Lamington holds a weekend of events for a select few friends. Invitations for this event are among the sought after items on Britannia's social calendar – gatecrashers are certainly *not* welcome."

– Extract from *The Smirnoff Almanac of Fascinating Facts*, 2673 edition

Dante and Penelope were still arguing as they tried to find a seat on the last coach. The hover-bus was filled with passengers Dante recognised from his brief visit to the train's first class lounge the previous night. One of them, a slender man with silver-grey hair and a bushy moustache, stopped the duo as they came down aisle. He grabbed hold of the handcuffs for a closer look. "I say, what an unusual pair of handcuffs! Wherever did you get them?"

"They were a gift from her royal highness," Penelope said archly. "Now, if you'll excuse–"

"You see, I was wondering where I could get a pair," the man persisted. "Mine are almost worn out from years of abuse, so I'm always searching for a good replacement."

"They're a one-off, specially commissioned by the Tsar himself," Penelope snapped.

"Is that a fact? Fascinating!" the passenger enthused. "Well, I'll let you go get changed." He shifted his attention to a leather bag on the seat next to him. "Now, where did I put my cuffs?"

Dante noticed the back row of the hover-bus was empty and led a bemused Penelope to the vacant seats. The two fugitives took shelter in one corner, away from the prying eyes of the other passengers. "I thought you wanted to find a place to hide so we could plan our next move?"

"That wasn't my fault," Penelope said. "I can't help it if some old pervert wants to know where I got these handcuffs, can I?"

"No, but telling him they were a gift from the princess is not what I call keeping a low profile," Dante snapped back. "Diavolo! You've got a lot to learn about being a fugitive."

"And you'd be an expert in that, having been on the run most of your life!"

"Can I help being popular?"

"I didn't realise shoot-to-kill orders were a sign of popularity," Penelope sneered.

Dante, I–

"Not now, Crest! I'm pointing out a few facts to Agent Know-It-All here."

But I've recalled where–

"I said not now!" Dante said, before switching his attention back to Penelope. "I've been the most wanted, most hated, most hunted man on the planet, but few have caught me and nobody has kept me. I trained with James Di Grizov, the greatest escapologist in the *Vorovskoi Mir,* the Thieves' World. You might have lured me into bed, but I would have got away again long before you ever got me back to London. Nobody keeps Nikolai Dante under lock and key for long!"

Penelope applauded him with slow handclaps. "Congratulations."

"Why?"

"Never have I met a man more full of his own self importance than you."

I've remembered where I recognised all those–

Dante smirked. "Crest, I think the lady protests too much."

"What?" Penelope demanded.

"Almost every time a woman says she hates me, it's usually because she hates herself for wanting me. The Tsar's daughter Jena was just the same. She couldn't decide which she wanted most: seeing me dead, or getting me in bed."

"Trust me," Penelope vowed. "My hatred for you is strictly personal."

Dante reached for the hem of his kilt. "Sure you don't want another peek at the goods, see if they change your mind?"

She slapped his hand away. "Please, it's not long since I ate breakfast – don't make me throw it all back up again."

Will you listen to me for once in your miserable, misbegotten life, the Crest raged.

Dante winced in pain from the shouting in his mind. "Fuoco! All right, all right, I'm listening! What's so important I should stop flirting with Penelope here?"

"Flirting?" she spluttered. "You call this flirting?"

"You love it," he replied with a lecherous wink. "Well, Crest?"

I've been trying to tell you I remember where I recognised the other passengers.

"Go on, then, don't keep me in suspense."

Before the war, you went to Venice with one of your Romanov half-sisters, Lulu.

"She's a member of the Cadre Infernale – she wanted me to join," Dante recalled.

Penelope frowned, struggling to make sense of the conversation while only Dante's words. "I've heard of the Cadre. It's a secret society for aristocrats and politicians from across the Empire, allowing them to indulge in decadence and vice without fear of scandal."

The people on the train, the Crest continued, *are all members of the Cadre Infernale.*

"Are you sure?" Dante asked.

Absolutely. It took me this long to identify them because almost everyone you saw at Venice was naked except for their masks.

"So how were you able to recognise them now?" Dante became aware of Penelope tapping him on the shoulder. "Not now, the Crest is trying to tell me something important!

"So am I," she replied. "Look!"

Dante twisted his head round to find the other passengers on the hover-bus gathered around them. All were dressed in rubber and leather bondage garb. Most of their faces were covered by black, studded masks, while male genitals fought to escape from obscene posing pouches and women's breasts dangled from cup-less chain brassieres. Each of the passengers were clutching whips or handcuffs, several also had riding crops and cattle prods in their hands. Dante's face fell as he surveyed the perverts clustered around him and Penelope. "Would it be stating the obvious to say I have a bad feeling about this?"

Boyle was piloting the Phord Capri as it approached the outskirts of Nottingham. He tipped the sleek hover-car over into a banking manoeuvre. Dobie cursed from the passenger seat. "Watch it, Ray! Some of us are trying to pluck our eyebrows."

"You mean clear a path through the undergrowth of your mono-brow?"

"Jealously will get you nowhere. I simply have an excess of testosterone in my system that requires a little more care and attention when it comes to grooming."

"Dobie, you spend so long looking in a mirror, it's a wonder you don't go blind."

"I like looking at beautiful things. Can I help it if I'm one of them?"

Boyle rolled his eyes, but couldn't help smiling too. "Where's this train station then?"

His partner pointed through a gap in the clouds. "At a guess, I'd say where those train tracks all converge."

"From what I hear Dante's a slippery customer – you ready for this?"

Dobie pulled a ludicrously hefty handgun from a holster in his left armpit. "You knew me, Ray – I was born ready."

Dante and Penelope were rigorously searched by the other passengers during their journey to the Fforbes-Lamington estate. Dante had nothing to lose since he was already in borrowed clothes, but an unhappy Penelope was forced to surrender a small pistol, her boots and wristwatch as the coach landed outside a pair of ornate, wrought iron gates. Silver security droids took custody of the two unwanted guests. Dante and Penelope were frog-marched from the vehicle by the two-metre tall mechanoids. Once the bus had entered the estate, the droids shoved their prisoners inside before the gates slid shut. A sky-sled appeared overhead, slicing through the air like a metallic magic carpet. The sole augmentation to its utilitarian design was a handrail above the outer edge at waist height. The sled dropped from the sky and the mute droids stepped up, dragging Dante and Penelope behind them. The words "HOLD ON" flashed on the floor twice.

"Is that telling us to wait?" Dante asked.

The message is probably more literal, the Crest replied. *The sled's hover-engines are preparing for take-off. I'd advise you to get a grip on something solid.*

Penelope had already grabbed the nearest handrail, but Dante was not so quick. Suddenly the sled flung itself back into the sky, throwing him off his feet. Only the handcuffs binding him to Penelope saved Dante from flying off the sled and tumbling to his death. One of the droids pushed Dante across to the nearest handrail, which he gratefully gasped. "Bojemoi!" he gasped after finding his footing again. "You don't get much warning on this thing, do you?"

Penelope glared at him. "It's a wonder you've stayed alive as long as you have, considering how little intelligence you display."

If only she knew how right she is, the Crest sighed.

"I like to lull my enemies into a false sense of security," Dante replied.

"Try not to lose yourself in the role," Penelope advised.

The sky-sled skimmed over a glorious patchwork of fields and hedgerows, streams and thickets. It was still mid-morning, but the sun was already baking the countryside below. A stately home appeared in the distance, rapidly getting closer.

That must be Fforbes-Lamington House, the Crest observed. *A most remarkable building, the last great example of rococo architecture in Britannia. The marble interiors were imported from Italy, while each pane of glass was ground by hand to match the prescription of the Fforbes-Lamington patriarch, so he wouldn't have to wear glasses indoors. The entire structure was relocated here seven hundred years ago to avoid demolition work for a bypass. The task took a thousand craftsmen more than twenty-seven months.*

Dante frowned as the sky-sled landed outside the front entrance on the gravel courtyard. "Looks like the world's ugliest wedding cake to me."

Must you always act the philistine?

"Who said I was acting?"

Penelope sighed theatrically to the security droids. "You see what I have to put up with? This fool talks to himself constantly. He took me captive, forced me on board that coach."

Dante arched an eyebrow at her. "What are you doing?"

"Don't listen to a word he says," she continued. "He claims I'm his accomplice, but I had never seen him before he abducted me yesterday." The mechanoids stepped off the sky-sled, dragging Penelope and Dante with them towards the stately home's huge double doors.

"They're not buying your little Miss Innocent act," Dante commented. "I guess your powers of seduction only work on creatures of flesh and blood."

"Actually, no," another voice replied. "Ms Goodnight has had some success with robots that possess emotion circuits. Alas, my security droids do not, so her charms are lost on them."

Penelope looked at the woman who had emerged from the double doors. "You! *You're* Audrey Fforbes-Lamington?"

The mistress of the estate laughed. "But of course! Who were you expecting?" The middle-aged woman was dressed in a dowdy tweed skirt and cream woollen top.

Her face was haughty and severe, framed by sandy brown hair cut in an unforgiving bob. Everything about her screamed asexual harridan to Dante.

"I'm guessing you two know each other," he quipped, trying to lighten the mood.

"Quite so," Fforbes-Lamington replied. "But young Penelope here knows me by another name. Within Britannia Intelligence I am simply called F. I am Agent Goodnight's commander."

"That explains the perverts!" Dante exclaimed.

"Sorry?" Penelope and F said in unison.

"It's traditional for the head of Britannia Intelligence also to be leader of the Cadre's Britannia chapter. That's why you had a coach-load of sex freaks coming to visit. You're holding the annual Sabbat here."

F applauded his powers of deduction. "Precisely. Now, since you've so kindly presented yourselves at my door, why don't you come inside – if you'll pardon the expression."

After they parked the Capri, Dobie and Boyle sauntered into Nottingham's train station. All looked normal except the entrance to Platform Five. A dozen men in black cloaks and top hats were guarding the gate, while the sound of frenzied activity was audible beyond them. "Do you see what I see?" Boyle asked his partner quietly.

Dobie nodded. "Rippers. The *Flying Scotsman* must be on that platform. Sounds like they're going over it with a fine tooth comb."

"Being Rippers, they're probably using a stiletto – but the principle's the same. Know what I like most about the Rippers?"

"Not their fashion sense. Don't they know black is out this season?"

"No," Boyle said impatiently. "Their lack of imagination. Somebody told them Dante is on that train, so they'll keep searching till they find him."

"But if he isn't on the train…"

"He must be nearby."

Dobie smiled. "Time to find some answers. Meet you back here in ten minutes?"

His partner nodded. "See you soon." The pair strolled away in opposite directions.

F escorted Penelope and Dante through her stately home to a huge, empty room facing the back of the estate. The floor was a checkerboard of black and white marble, while tall picture windows afforded a magnificent view of sculpted gardens outside. The other walls were given over to row upon row of bookshelves, all of them barren of volumes. There were only three pieces of furniture in the cavernous space – an elaborate throne of silver and blue, and a pair of old dentist's chairs. Each of these was augmented with several leather restraint straps and both stood on a dais of thick, black rubber.

"This was the library for several centuries," F said grandly, "but I sold all the old books to the Britannia National Library. Nobody ever read the bloody things, they were a nightmare to dust and the money paid to restore the house to its former glory after my second husband's timely demise." She gestured towards the dentist chairs. "Would you like to take a seat?"

"I prefer to stand," Penelope replied tersely.

"Perhaps I did not make myself clear," F said. She gestured to the four corners of the ceiling, where small laser cannons appeared among the rococo ornamentation, their terse snouts taking aim at her guests. "Take a seat, both of you, or else my interior security system will incinerate you. It's a simple choice."

"Well, since you put it like that," Dante smiled and jumped into the nearest chair. "Penelope, come and join me."

"First, use the leather restraints to tie him down," F commanded. "I want to avoid any unpleasantness. Young

Nikolai does have quite a reputation for causing mayhem and chaos."

"Vastly exaggerated," he said as Penelope bound him in place, strapped his arms and legs into position. She sat in the other dentist's chair, securing both her legs and an arm in place.

"That will do," F said, easing herself into the imposing throne opposite them. "I think we can trust the laser cannons to dissuade you from taking any direct action. Unlike Dante, you do not have the advantage of enhanced healing abilities." F smiled at her guests. "I must say it's quite a coincidence, you two appearing at my door! If I believed in such nonsense, I might call it fate."

"Bad luck would be a better description," Penelope said sourly.

"Whichever makes you feel better, my dear. Tell me, how did you evade the Rippers?"

"You sent them! I should have known... Why?"

"My code breakers intercepted a transmission between you and Princess Marie-Anne. It was obvious she had turned you in, no doubt with some lofty promise to appeal to your vanity and ambition. Did she offer you my job, perhaps?" Penelope did not answer, but her silence was eloquent enough. F nodded. "I thought as much. Beware her royal highness, Agent Goodnight – she cares for nobody but herself, as I'm sure Dante here can confirm."

"That bitch and I have had our moments," he conceded.

"Twice you've succeeded in thwarting her plans and having the princess confined to a cell inside the Tower of London. I'm surprised you're still alive, frankly."

"I'm too cool to kill."

"Take care," F warned him. "One day that could become your epitaph."

"Not if I can help it," he replied. "My half-sister Lulu is leader of the Cadre Infernale. That makes you her underling. Shouldn't you check with her first before engineering my execution?"

"I've always hated that bitch," F snapped. "She uses our members for her own twisted ends, to further her crusade against the Tsar. She abuses her rank and its privileges!"

"I thought that was the whole point of your little perverts' club: twisting members and acting the bitch. You're like the Freemasons, but with more ball gags and fewer aprons."

"The Cadre Infernale is a sexual release for its membership, not a political powerbase. Yes, if one of us needs help when in trouble, we do what we can for them. The acquisition and retention of power is not what drives the Cadre, what puts fire in our bellies or a thrill in our loins. We value perversity, in all forms, above everything else. Nothing is more important to us."

"So, you're just a bunch of sick, sex-obsessed losers trying to get your rocks off?" Dante asked. "In that case I'm glad I never accepted Lulu's offer to join – I get all the action I want without having to dress in rubber or beg for a spanking."

"You're not a begging man?" F asked. When Dante nodded, she pressed a button built into the left arm of her throne. The effect was startling. Electricity surged through the two dentist chairs, passing back and forth across the prisoners' bodies, making them jerk and thrash like rag dolls in the grip of an angry child. Dante and Penelope screamed in agony, blue sparks escaping from their chattering teeth. After a full five seconds of this treatment, F removed her finger from the button and the electrocution ceased. She waited until they had recovered before speaking. "Now, what were you saying?"

A few bribes, some vague threats and careful questions soon secured Boyle and Dobie all the facts they needed. Dante and Penelope were last seen boarding a hover-bus bound for the Forbes-Lamington estate on the outskirts of Nottingham, with a bus full of sexual deviants. Dobie smiled to himself. "Sounds like our kind of party, Ray."

"That's what I was thinking." Boyle looked down at his taut jeans, knit shirt and plaid bomber jacket. "But I feel overdressed for a weekend of bondage and discipline."

"Well, let's find something more suitable for the occasion. I'm sure we can always whip ourselves into shape in no time."

The Capri was gone in sixty seconds, a puff of blue smoke and rubber burn marks on the roadside the only signs it had even been there.

F took her finger off the button, having administered a third, brutal dose of shock treatment to her prisoners. Dante gasped for air while Penelope spat a mouthful of abuse at her commander. "Such language!" F replied haughtily. "Not very ladylike, I must say – not very ladylike at all." She gave both of them another jolt, letting her finger linger on the button slightly longer this time. When she had finished, Dante gave a low, throaty chuckle. "May I ask what is so amusing?"

"You are."

"Please elucidate," F prompted but got no reply.

She wants you to explain, the Crest told Dante.

"Oh. Right. I knew that," he muttered. "I was laughing because I've met your kind before. You get your kicks by hurting and tormenting others – not from their actual pain, but from wielding the sort of power you have over us at present."

"Is that a fact?"

"He's right," Penelope agreed. "I've seen how you operate at headquarters, the way you deliberately humiliate the operatives – your hands start to quiver with excitement. You start sweating too, the skin between your nose and your top lip gets all moist. It's disgusting."

"It's probably not the only area getting moist," Dante added.

Another stab at the button, and a fresh jolt of electricity shot across the prisoners' torsos. F let them dance about inside their restraints for a full minute before stopping the torture.

"I'll bet every time you touch that button, we're not the only ones getting the juice," Dante snarled, his lips pulled back from his teeth in an animal grimace of pain. F sent another jolt of power through them, then another and another. When she finally sat back in her chair, the head of Britannia Intelligence could not disguise her lustful panting.

"You sick, twisted bitch," Penelope said, shaking her head.

"Yes, I am," F agreed, "but you don't become mistress of the Cadre Infernale without having a few kinks in your system. Now that I've enjoyed myself, it's time for you to answer a few questions. Dante, why did you try to assassinate the king? Before this visit you were his greatest supporter. Why turn on him when he needed you most?"

"Bojemoi, when will somebody believe me?" Dante protested. "I had nothing to do with the attack on the king, nor the murder of his mother. Henry brought me here to protect him from an assassination attempt. All I feel guilty about is failing to stop the hit happening."

F pondered this. "That would fit with your previous pattern of behaviour–"

"At last! Somebody who can see the truth!" he rejoiced.

"But your reputation as a liar and a scoundrel makes anything you say difficult to trust," F concluded with a small smile. "Convince me. If you weren't responsible, who was?"

"I don't know," Dante conceded. "Why? Could you intervene on my behalf?"

"I could, but I'm not going to," she said. "You make a convenient scapegoat. The attack on the king's life is a useful catalyst for change. Had someone else not perpetrated this crime, I might have been forced to commission it myself."

"How can you play god with people's lives like this?" Penelope demanded.

"Please, don't lecture me on morality, Agent Goodnight. You've destroyed plenty of lives with your bedroom antics for Britannia. I've never noticed any qualms from you in the past."

"That was different. I was doing my job."

"Just following orders, is that your defence?" Penelope spat more curses at her commander. "You've been spending too long with Dante," F said, "judging by your vocabulary's rapid descent into the gutter. I'd expect such obscenities from a low-born wretch like him, but not a cultured, highly trained agent of Britannia Intelligence."

"Who are you calling a wretch?" Dante protested, but F ignored him.

"I know Princess Marie-Anne wanted young Nikolai delivered to her alive but, alas, I cannot permit that to happen. Far better for him to die a guilty man than survive and prove his innocence – assuming, of course, he is innocent. As for your duplicity, Agent Goodnight, I'm afraid there can be but one punishment for such a blatant show of insubordination to my direct orders."

"Let me guess," Dante interjected. "You're giving her a severe reprimand and a bare bottom spanking. I'd be happy to administer the second half of that punishment if you'd like."

"Silence!" F snapped, her voice echoing around the empty library. "Since my Rippers singularly failed to do their job, I've decided to let my associates in the Cadre Infernale have that rare pleasure instead. You will be taken from this place by my security droids and released on the grounds of the estate. Ten minutes later my all too eager members will be let loose with orders to hunt both of you down like dogs. Who ever catches you first has permission to perform whatever acts of depravity upon you they see fit. Afterwards, when you are begging to be released from this purgatory of punishment and perversity, I may deign to grant your wish. I advise against attempting to leave the estate – my automated security system is quite ruthless. Any questions?"

"Are you sure we can't go with Dante's suggestion?" Penelope asked.

F gave them a last dose of shock treatment as retaliation for that comment. When both prisoners had lost consciousness completely, she released the button and summoned her security droids. "Put homing beacons on them," she commanded brusquely. "We don't want the hunt dragging on all day, do we?"

NINE

"What is born a wolf cannot become a fox."
– Russian proverb

"Blood sports such as hunting have been a countryside tradition in Britannia for more than a millennium. An attempt was made to outlaw hunting with hounds in the early Twenty-First century on the grounds of animal cruelty, but ultimately this failed due to the royal family's continued support for the sport. To this day gangs of aristocrats can be seen racing across the countryside in hunting pink jackets – a curious name since the garment in question is actually warm red in colour. In the past such events were held on horseback, but the equine plague of 2626 put paid to that."
– Extract from *The Smirnoff Almanac of Fascinating Facts*, 2673 edition

Having been incarcerated, manacled and interrogated, Spatchcock and Flintlock were beginning to give up hope. Shortly after midday the two prisoners were marched from their basement cell to the open courtyard in the centre of the Tower of London. Flintlock was convinced their execution had been brought forward, a fear that grew worse when he and Spatchcock were shoved against a wall, facing a line of armed guards. The prisoners' hands were tied behind their backs and both men were offered blindfolds, which they refused.

"Spatch, old boy, I think this is it for us," Flintlock whispered.

"So much for waiting until next week," the rancid runt complained. "What about our final requests? Even a last meal for the condemned men would have been nice. I don't want to die on an empty stomach, I'll be all grumpy when I get to the next life."

"You believe there *is* a life after this one?"

"I bloody hope so," Spatchcock grumbled. "I'd have made more of an effort otherwise."

Flintlock wept quietly, his bottom lip wobbling as tears spilled down his face. "I never believed in anything, except looking out for myself. Now I wish I'd paid attention in chapel Eton. I don't even know any prayers I can say."

"What happened to people from Britannia having a stiff upper lip?"

Flintlock managed a smile. "I prefer to save stiffness for another part of my anatomy."

"You dirty dog," Spatchcock said approvingly. Still the guards remained opposite them, keeping watch but making no attempt to carry out the execution. Eventually the foul-smelling thief lost patience with the situation. "Well, are you going to shoot us or not?" He demanded. But the guards gave no reply, continuing to stare resolutely at the prisoners. "Perhaps they think we'll die of starvation soon, save them the cost of a few bullets?"

"At least we got to feel the sun on our faces one last time," Flintlock replied wistfully, tilting his head up towards the blue, cloudless sky.

"Since we've got a few minutes to spare, your lordship, tell me what it was you did that got you deported. What could be so bad, so depraved, it got you kicked out of your own country?"

But Flintlock ignored his associate's question, preferring to keep his attention on the sky overhead. "I say, is that a skimmer coming in to land?"

Spatchcock followed his friend's gaze. "Looks like it. Quick, while we've still got time, tell me what you did. I'm dying to know!"

"Rather a poor choice of words in the circumstances, don't you think?"

"Yeah, but–"

"Attention!" The scream of a military voice cut off Spatchcock. Another sentry marched into the courtyard, three strips on his epaulets indicating he held the rank of sergeant. A single bellow from him dismissed the line of men that had guarded the two prisoners. Three new sentries replaced them, two unreeling a fire hose while the third carried a toy bucket and spade.

"Now what?" Flintlock wondered. "Are we going to make a sand castle?"

"Strip!" the sergeant bellowed.

"Do you think he means us?" Spatchcock asked blithely. "But we hardly know you."

"I said strip!"

"Rather difficult in the circumstances," Flintlock said, twisting sideways to show his hands were bound behind his back. One of the guards hurried forward and undid the shackles.

"I won't ask again," the sergeant warned. The prisoners quickly stripped, creating two untidy piles of discarded clothes at their feet. "Kick those away from you!" Spatchcock and Flintlock did as they were told. "Commence hosing – now!" The two guards holding the hose unleashed a torrent of ice cold water over the prisoners, pinning both of them against the stone wall. "Cease hosing!" The deluge stopped abruptly, giving the captives a chance to gasp for air and dry their eyes. "Administer delousing powder – now!" The third guard marched across to Spatchcock and Flintlock, then used his plastic spade to coat them with grey powder from inside the bucket. It stung their skin and burned their eyes, the stench violating their nostrils. "Prisoners – turn around!"

The unhappy duo did as they were told, receiving another heavy dusting across their backs, buttocks and legs. Then the hosing resumed, blasting the powder off the bodies of the weeping, choking captives. By the time this scouring procedure was complete, both men were close to collapse. The sergeant dismissed his men, calling for replacement clothes to be brought out. Spatchcock and Flintlock were handed silver boiler suits and told to put them on. Once dressed, the prisoners were led to a ground floor room that faced out on the courtyard. Another guard passed them, wielding a lit flamethrower. They watched with bemusement as he burned their discarded clothes.

The sergeant noticed his prisoners dawdling and raced across the courtyard towards them. "Move, you worthless maggots! Her royal highness Princess Marie-Anne is due any minute!" He shoved both of them into the small, featureless room, his nostrils flaring like bellows. A metal ring was set into one wall, two manacles at either end of a chain suspended from the ring.

The sergeant locked Spatchcock and Flintlock into the manacles, then pocketed the key. "The princess has said she wants to meet you vile worms. But say one word out of turn, make one obscene remark to her royal highness, and I will make certain your few remaining days, hours and minutes on this earth are filled with pain, misery and anguish. Do I make myself clear?"

"Not quite," Flintlock replied, tipping his head over to one side and shaking it. "I think I've still got water in my ears. Could you shout a bit louder?"

"Silence!" the sergeant bellowed. "You will speak only when spoken to and maintain a respectful decorum at all times!"

"You mean brown nose her like you do?" Spatchcock smirked. "Talk about changing your tune – a few days ago she was your prisoner, now you're treating her like…"

"Royalty?" Flintlock chipped in.

"Oh yeah," Spatchcock conceded. "I guess it does make some sort of sense." He smirked. "Well, bring the prissy cow in here, I'll show her a good time."

"Why, you–" But the sergeant's response was cut short by the royal skimmer landing in the courtyard. Once its engine noise had died away, he leaned closer to Spatchcock. "You'll pay for what you've done, you little shit," he snarled before storming out of the room.

"I think you've made a friend there, Spatch," Flintlock observed dryly. The prisoners watched from their limited vantage point as a door appeared in the side of the skimmer and a set of stairs unfolded, disgorging a dozen security guards into the courtyard. Princess Marie-Anne emerged from inside the skimmer, sniffing the air disdainfully. "Oh good. The bitch is back."

"If you tell me what you're looking for, I'd be more than happy to help find it," Dante offered. He had regained his senses in the middle of a small, flat field, surrounded by tall grass baked yellow by the sun. The warm, pleasant smell of hay-making hung in the air. Penelope was crouched beside with her hand buried deep inside his sporran, groping and grasping at the small pouch's lining. Eventually her face lit up with a smile of triumph. Dante noticed she had a smattering of freckles across her nose and cheeks. He had always found freckles curiously attractive, so he leaned closer to kiss her sensuous mouth. Penelope responded by slapping him hard across the cheek. "Diavolo!" he protested. "What was that for?"

"Why were you trying to kiss me?"

"I thought you wanted me to! You were feeling around my groin and smiling, so I–"

"You thought I had finally fallen for your roguish charms?"

"Well... yes."

Penelope removed her hand from inside his sporran to reveal a tiny pistol. "I hid this earlier, in case of emergencies.

I knew you'd never have the wit to look inside and I doubted anyone else would want to search the area near your genitals too closely."

"I'm famous as a great lover across most of the Empire," Dante replied.

A great liar, more like.

"Crest, keep quiet if you haven't got anything useful to add!"

I wanted to get your attention and uncomfortable truths usually have that effect. There's rather a large group of people coming this way.

"How many?" Dante asked, getting to his knees to peer over the tall grass.

More than thirty, approaching from the east. Most are on foot but a few seem to be mounted. They are being led by a pack of hounds. As the Crest finished speaking the distant barking of dogs became audible over the cries of black crows in nearby trees. *I estimate you have three minutes before your hunters reach this location.*

Penelope was already crawling away in the opposite direction, but the black handcuffs held her back. "Come on," she said, jerking her left arm to pull Dante after her. "We need to get under cover." The two fugitives got to their feet and ran towards a nearby thicket, crouching low to avoid being seen. They reached the trees, sweat already dripping down their faces. The sun was directly overhead, its scorching heat offering little respite, even in the shade.

Dante scanned the horizon for a sight of their hunters. "I can't see them yet..."

"There they are!" Penelope whispered, pointing at the far side of the field. A crowd of nearly naked people was spilling through a wooden gate, their pale white skin almost aglow in the blazing sunshine. Black lines were visible across their bodies and many faces were hidden behind black masks. A few were clad in shiny PVC bodysuits fashioned in the style of hunting garb. Most bizarre in appearance were the horses several of the men were riding. "Those sick perverts," Penelope muttered. "They're using pony girls."

"Pony girls?" Dante asked, unfamiliar with this jargon. "Crest?"

One of the more unlikely sexual fetishes is the urge to be treated like a horse. Men and women are stripped naked, then strapped into custom-made replicas of a horse's bridle and riding tackle – buckled leather restraints around the head and body, a mouthpiece, even reins, so the beast can be controlled. For added verisimilitude the equine imitator will sometimes have a probe inserted so a horse-hair tail protrudes from between their buttocks. In extreme cases, these steeds are ridden as if they are real horses, with one rider mounted on two horses simultaneously. When younger women submit to this treatment, they are known as "pony girls". The things you humans do to get your thrills never ceases to amaze.

"And people do this willingly – for pleasure?"

They have done for centuries, particularly here in Britannia.

Dante shook his head. "Well, if we can't outrun them we deserve to be caught."

"Sunstroke and exhaustion will eventually eliminate most of our hunters," Penelope agreed. "But the hounds are bred to run for hours without tiring. They're our biggest problem. Come on!" She dragged Dante through a thicket and out into a neighbouring field of ploughed earth. He lost both his borrowed brogues within a few minutes, each shoe buried in a clump of glutinous, rapidly drying mud. The two fugitives were still crossing the open ground when the first hounds emerged from the thicket behind them, yelping excitedly.

"Diavolo, they've spotted us!" Dante said, putting on a burst of speed.

Princess Marie-Anne was enjoying her visit to the Tower of London. Having been held prisoner there for far too long, she was savouring the chance to torment her former captors, making the guards run ludicrous errands and perform endless drills in the courtyard beneath the blistering midday sun. For once the familiar aroma of raven droppings and brass polish did not turn her stomach as it had done every day she was kept incarcerated here. Eventually she tired of watching the sentries wilt and summoned their leader to her side. He was a big, blustering man with a bristling brown moustache and a knack for shouting. "Sergeant Barnes, isn't it?"

"Yes, Your Highness," he snapped, unable to keep the military training from his voice.

"I think I've seen enough of the guards' precision for now."

"Very good, ma'am," Barnes agreed. "It is quite hot, the men will be glad of a rest."

"You misunderstand me," she responded with a sadistic smile. "I merely said I had seen enough. Your men can keep at it until I am ready to depart."

"Oh, right. If you say so, ma'am."

"I do. In fact, why don't you go and join them in a few minutes? I always feel those in positions of power – however humble, like yours – should lead by example. Don't you?"

"Yes, ma'am. Absolutely."

"Very good. But first I'd like to see the prisoners."

Barnes nodded his assent. "This way, ma'am, if you please." He led her to the room where Spatchcock and Flintlock were chained to the wall. The princess paled at the powerful body odours emanating from the two men. "My apologies for the smell, your royal highness. We did have both prisoners deloused before your arrival, but even that could not counteract their stench."

She nodded hurriedly, clutching a white linen handkerchief over her nose and mouth as a shield from the noxious vapours filing the room. "Stand to attention!" Barnes bellowed.

"Shove it up your arse," Spatchcock replied cheerfully.

"I can have them thrashed for that display of impudence," the sergeant offered, but the princess waved him away. She waited until he had left before approaching the prisoners.

"Enjoying the accommodation?" she asked icily.

"We've had worse," Flintlock replied lightly.

Spatchcock nodded. "After you've been held prisoner by the Imperial Black, a few days in the Tower of London is more like a holiday resort."

"How distressing," the princess agreed. "I'll ask the sergeant to institute a regime of hourly punishments for you, perhaps some extra torture sessions too. We don't want you thinking the people of Britannia are soft on crime, do we?"

"Heaven forefend," Flintlock said, rolling his eyes.

"Did you have a reason for asking to see us? Or was this purely a social call – a spot of gloating before returning to the palace?" Spatchcock asked.

"A little of both," she replied happily. "I have good news and bad news. Which would you prefer to hear first?"

"The good news," both men said simultaneously.

"Very well – although our definitions of good and bad may differ," she warned. "The good news is your troublesome friend Nikolai Dante remains stubbornly alive." Spatchcock began to give a small cheer but an icy glare from the princess made it die in his throat. "The bad news for you is that my father's condition is improving, however slightly."

"Why is that bad news?" Flintlock asked.

"If he survives, the king may decide to send her back here," Spatchcock said.

"Precisely," she agreed, "and I can't allow that to happen. Too much of my life has already been wasted in this hellhole. I do not intend to spend another day here! So, once the excitement from your execution has died down, my father will suffer a terrible relapse and pass away."

"Why tell us any of this?" Spatchcock asked.

"To see the reaction on your repellent, smug faces. Since my agent has failed to bring Dante to me as I wished, I've decided to use you two as bait for a trap. I've arranged for your executions to be brought forward to this Saturday."

"But that's only two days away," Flintlock protested. "I'm not ready to die yet!"

"That matters little to me," she said with a broad smile. "Dante will not be able to resist an attempt to rescue you from the executioner's blade or the hangman's noose – to be honest, I haven't yet decided which way you should die. Regardless of that, your foolhardy friend cannot turn down the chance to save his accomplices while humiliating me. That will cost his life."

"And ours," Spatchcock noted. "The agent you sent to catch Dante – male or female?"

"Her name is Penelope Goodnight, not that it's any of your business. Why?"

"Knowing Nikolai, he's probably making love to her right now," Flintlock replied.

"Shagging her senseless, you mean," Spatchcock corrected. "They'll be too busy having a good time to even notice we're being executed."

"You know how to show a girl a good time, don't you?" Penelope asked accusingly. She and Dante were crouched on the bank of a small lake, hiding from the hunting party of perverts. The hounds had temporarily lost the fugitives' scent after Dante and Penelope had run through a lavender field, but the dogs would soon be closing in on them again.

"It wasn't my idea to come here," he said. "We need to find a place to hide, you said, give ourselves a chance to think – we can lose ourselves here for the rest of the day."

"How I was to know the hover-bus would be full of sexual deviants?"

"I'd have thought you could spot them in seconds, considering your line of work," Dante said. "We should get going. The longer we stay in one spot, the more likely they are to find us. Trust me, I've spent most of my life on the run, one way or another."

"Then it's amazing you're still alive," Penelope observed. "Trapping you was one of the easiest assignments I've ever had."

"That's been bugging me," Dante admitted. "How did you know I'd go to that train station? I could have decided to hide anywhere in London."

"Fugitives run," she said. "There was a better than average chance you'd try to get out of the city. Once I knew the location of your Black Maria, I headed for the nearest major terminus. Luckily for me, the *Flying Scotsman* was the only train still running, so I put on my best damsel in distress act and let your rampant libido do the rest. It was child's play." An excited yelp from a nearby hound signalled the fugitives' scent had been sniffed out again.

"I don't understand how they keep finding us," Penelope muttered under her breath. "Unless…" She leaned closer to Dante and inhaled deeply from his body. "You stink of *Bitch*!"

"Charming! You're not exactly covered in rose petal aromas either, you know!"

"No, I meant *Bitch* – the perfume I sprayed over you last night to throw the Rippers off your scent. You obviously didn't wash it all off. The perfume must be attracting the hounds – they don't call it *Bitch* without good reason." She dived into the lake, pulling Dante in with her. Together they swam underwater as far as they could, before surfacing halfway across the lake. The duo took shelter beneath a selection of lily pads, watching the water's edge where they had been hiding. A stream of hunters appeared along the bank, searching the shallows for their quarry.

An obese pervert spotted the swimmers and pointed at them, his breasts wobbling above an obscenely large belly, his puny genitals dangling limply in the shadow of his massive stomach. "There they are!" he cried, the sun glinting off his bald, sunburnt scalp. "All you riders, take your pony girls round to the left! Everybody else, follow me!"

Dante and Penelope were already swimming towards the far side of the lake, their movements hampered by the handcuffs. "Our hunters don't seem to have any weapons except the dogs," Dante observed, between strokes. "How many shots have you got in that pistol?"

"Six – not nearly enough to deal with all of them," Penelope said between gasps as they reached the water's edge. "I'm saving those for F, if we make it back to the house." She scrambled up the muddy bank, dragging Dante out of the water. "Come on, move it!"

He stumbled after her, the sodden kilt slowing him down. "I'm doing my best!" he shouted.

F watched the twin homing beacon signals on a holographic display screen in her private office. As head of Britannia Intelligence she was expected to have a state of the art communications centre at her private residence, to ensure she was never out of touch with events. Happily, the cost of this equipment and its installation was borne by Britannia's taxpayers, so F had arranged for the conversion of a small space adjoining the library into her comms centre. In centuries past the chamber had been a panic room for Fforbes-Lamington family members paranoid about home security. Before that it had been a priest hole, a hiding place for clerics on the run from religious oppression. Now the room gave F an armchair view of the world.

An entire wall was devoted to a hundred holographic displays set in a ten-by-ten grid that reached up to the ceiling. In front of them was a control desk and black leather swivel chair. F sat forward in her chair, manipulating the security cameras carefully placed around the grounds. Alas, having such a sprawling estate made total coverage impossible. Dante and Agent Goodnight had fled into an area that defied F's eager gaze, but she could still monitor their progress thanks to the homing beacons hidden on their bodies.

F activated the microphone on the control desk and barked an order to the hunt leader, an ageing cabinet minister fond of wearing women's lingerie and being sexually misused while sucking a satsuma. "McClory! Your targets are headed due west, away from the lake. They have half a mile head start, but you should be able to see them once you clear the next hedgerow."

"Understood, ma'am," a wheezing, groaning voice responded.

F sat back in her chair and smiled. She would dearly love to be leading the hunt personally, but her status as queen bitch of the Cadre Infernale in Britannia forbade her from mingling with members of a lesser rank. She must appear imperious and aloof at all times, otherwise her air of mystique would be forever tainted. F let her fingers wander between her legs, searching for a distraction. Vicarious enjoyment was all very well, but hands-on action was better.

They ran away from the lake, crossed a field of golden grass and scrambled through a hedgerow of box and hawthorn. The duo emerged from the other side, their skin and clothes covered in tiny rips and tears from the thorn-laden hedge. The sound of yapping hounds still rang loud in their ears, so Dante and Penelope kept running. They reached the far side of a cornfield and took shelter in a hedgerow before their stalkers came into view. Despite the fact both fugitives were well hidden, the perverts continued to unerringly follow their path, as if they already knew what direction to take. "So much for your *Bitch* theory," Dante observed.

Penelope frowned. "I was sure they must be..." Her words trailed off, realisation lighting up her features. "Stupid, stupid!" Penelope began patting herself down, examining her body through the catsuit's torn and tattered fabric.

"I like to watch a woman enjoying herself if you know what I mean," Dante commented, "but I'm not sure this is the time or the place."

Penelope's fingers paused over her belly button. "There!" she said excitedly and tore down the zipper holding her catsuit together. paying no attention as her breasts spilled out.

"I see you've got freckles in all sorts of places," Dante said appreciatively.

Penelope extracted a small silver disc from her belly button, then did the catsuit back up. "If I've got one, you probably have as well," she said.

"Got one what?" Dante wondered.

Penelope tore his shirt apart and pointed at a silver disc hidden inside Dante's belly button. She plucked it out, removing several black, curly hairs at the same time. "Bojemoi," he protested. "Watch what you're doing!"

She showed him the identical discs. "Homing beacons. No doubt F had them put on us before we were released out. She's been helping the hunters track us."

"And you said I stank of *Bitch*?"

"Not as bad as her," Penelope conceded. She drew back her arm, ready to fling the beacons away, but Dante stopped her.

"I have a better destination in mind for those."

I'm getting too old to be a pony girl, Muriel told herself. Getting dressed in the beastly equipment had been exciting once upon a time, while letting herself be groomed by several breathless young women was joy unconfined. Even galloping around courtyards or acting as willing steed for some burly, sweaty man had been acceptable, no matter how foolish it made her feel, because she could look forward to a treat at the end of the day. Perhaps some frolicking with the other pony girls amongst the hay bales in the stables, or being pleasured with the specially tailored end of a riding crop. Pain and humiliation, they went hand in hand with pleasure and desire for Muriel.

But today's hunting, it was hard work and nothing more. Chasing some unseen quarry across fields and streams, that was all very well for the riders – but what about the pony girls? Muriel was used to carrying someone on her back for a few minutes, not a few hours. It was when they reached the first fence after skirting the lake that Muriel refused to go any further. Her rider, an ugly brute from the Inland Revenue with a fondness for the whip, was unceremoniously unseated and Muriel couldn't have cared less. Good riddance to bad rubbish. He was no kind of master for a fine mount like me, she told herself. Besides, I'm pink with sunburn, my knees and hands are rubbed raw and my back hurts. Enough is enough!

So, while the rest of the hunters hurried onwards, Muriel sat down under a tree to peel off her pony girl harness and bridle. She heard a twig snap behind her and found a pistol pointing at her face. Beyond it were the two fugitives, a woman in a battered black catsuit and a bare-chested man in a kilt. He looked at her thoughtfully, making Muriel blush with embarrassment.

"I've seen you somewhere before," the man said, then cocked his head slightly to one side, as if someone was whispering in his ear. "Of course – the customs official at Dover!"

At that moment Muriel wished the ground would swallow her whole. "Yes," she whispered. "Please don't tell anyone you saw me like this, they'd never understand."

The female fugitive produced a pair of small, silver discs. "We won't talk if you'll do us a favour or two in return. First of all, what's the quickest route from here back to the main house?" Muriel pointed north, her upper arm wobbling slightly. "Very good. The second favour is of a more... intimate nature. Turn around." Muriel did as she was commanded. "Touch your toes." Again, she followed the woman's orders, straining to reach past her knees. "That'll do," the fugitive commanded. "Now, brace yourself, while I find a suitable repository for these homing beacons."

Boyle brought the Capri in low over the boundary wall of the Fforbes-Lamington estate. He was too busy admiring the leather posing pouch, PVC corset and black peaked cap worn by his partner to notice the laser cannon emplacements in the wall's ancient stonework. "You should wear that sort of thing more often," he said. "Think of the work we could pick up around Brighton."

"That's not all we'd pick up," Dobie agreed, gesturing toward Boyle's black rubber body stocking. "Think of all the tight young–"

Suddenly a beam of light lanced through the vehicle's bonnet, slicing the engine in two and turning the rest of the flying car into a hunk of tumbling metal and glass. Boyle had time to scream before the remains of the Capri plunged into ground, gouging a mighty divot from the earth before the vehicle flung itself end over end over end. On and on it rolled, before finally coming to rest upside down by a scarecrow in a field of brutalised corn.

Four dull thuds were audible inside the car as both bounty hunters used their handguns to deflate the Capri's airbags. They smashed out the side windows and crawled from the wreckage, each leaving a trail of blood on the ground. Neither had got more than a few metres when the car exploded in a fireball, setting ablaze the surrounding corn.

"What the hell was that?" Dante wondered. He and Penelope watched a fireball curling into the sky from several fields away, followed by a mushroom cloud of black smoke.

"I don't know and I don't care," she said, tugging at his arm. "I need to find F. She can clear my name, tell the authorities I had nothing to do with the assassination attempt."

"How do you know she wasn't the person who implicated you?"

"She probably was, the vindictive old cow," Penelope conceded, pausing to check her small pistol was ready. "I'm going to convince her that was a mistake."

Muriel was running from the hounds when she saw the car fall out of the sky. The rest of the Cadre Infernale had been unwittingly hunting her across field after field of head-high grass and corn, ravenous dogs leading the pack of perverts ever closer. Muriel considered stopping to explain her predicament, but the savage barking of the hounds terrified her too much. Now, as her last reserves of energy were close to exhaustion, she saw a Phord Capri tumbling from the sky at her. Muriel dived amidst the corn and prayed for mercy as the metal meteor shrieked by.

Dobie and Boyle found each other ten minutes after their vehicle exploded. Both men were singed, but otherwise unhurt. The aroma of barbequed corn on the cob mixed with scorched rubber and gasoline in the air. The bruised and bloody bounty hunters surveyed the charred wreckage of their Capri with fond sadness. "We've been through a lot in that car," Dobie said wistfully. "Killed our first target in the back seat."

"Had our first kiss in the front seat," Boyle recalled.

Dobie smiled at the memory, before frowning again. "What the hell hit us?"

"The estate must have the mother of all security systems round its perimeter. We're lucky to have got out of that alive." He brushed broken glass out of his curly hair, then adjusted Dobie's peaked cap to a jauntier angle. "Our normal clothes were in the boot, you know."

"Yeah, and all our other guns. I've got this pistol and five clips of ammo."

Boyle checked his handgun. "I've only got this, but I'm nearly out of bullets. You better give me two of your clips."

"Get your own ammunition, you lazy sod!"

"From where? In case you hadn't noticed, we're in the middle of a burning cornfield on a country estate. I doubt there's many dum-dum stockists around here."

"Moan, moan, moan – that's all you ever do, Raymond."

"I've told you before, don't call me Raymond. My father called me Raymond and I bloody hated him for it, amongst other things."

"You know I only do it to wind you up," Dobie said.

"Well, don't, okay?"

"Okay, Raymond."

"That's it!" Boyle exploded. "I have had a gut full of your sly innuendoes and little digs."

"Well, you know my policy – innuendo and out the other," Dobie quipped.

"Hey, you there!" An aristocratic voice interrupted the bounty hunters' bickering. They quickly concealed their weapons, then swivelled round to see a cluster of perverts in leather and rubber marching towards them. "What the dickens do you think you're doing on this estate? This is a Sabbat of the Cadre Infernale, not a come-as-you-are party for any passing rough trade!"

"Rough trade?" Dobie snorted derisively. "Look who's talking!"

"Come as you are?" Boyle added. "You think we dress like this normally?"

"I don't care how you dress," the leader of the pack replied sternly. He was over sixty, flat-chested and wearing a selection of frilly pink lingerie. His right hand was clenched around the butt of a black leather whip, tapping it against his stocking-clad thigh. "Clear off, or else we'll be forced to give both of you a short, sharp shock – the more shocking the better!"

The bounty hunters exchanged a glance. "Oh, piss off, grandad," Boyle warned.

The old man's face quivered with rage. "Why, you little swine! Right, you asked for this – now you're going to get it. Brothers! Sisters! Let's show these gatecrashers they're not welcome!"

The perverts advanced as one towards Dobie and Boyle, pushing their way through the blackened heads of corn. Boyle looked at his partner. "Do you want to sort this, or shall I?"

"Let's do it together," Dobie suggested with a smile. The bounty hunters opened fire.

F was surprised to hear gunfire drifting in through the library doors from outside. "Oh, for heaven's sake! I specifically forbade anyone from taking sidearms on the hunt to avoid exactly this sort of incident," she muttered. The head of Britannia Intelligence wandered outside onto the balcony to see if she could spot the culprit and remonstrate with them. Instead she felt the barrel of a small pistol pressing against one side of her head.

"I guess somebody didn't get the memo," Penelope commented. "Call for help and I redecorate these doors with your brains. Nod if you understand." F quickly indicated her obedience. "Good. Let's go back inside – you first."

F returned indoors, followed by Penelope and Dante. "You'll never get off this estate alive," the mistress of the house said in a matter of fact voice. "My droids conduct a random sweep of the building every few minutes, so they're bound to discover you sooner or later."

"Not if you disable the security system," Dante pointed out.

"I can't, it's controlled from another location," F insisted.

"Liar!" Penelope snapped.

"Can you be sure of that?" her boss replied. The sound of mechanoids moving nearby was audible and getting louder. "As you can hear, my droids are close by – they could come in here any minute. You have me at gunpoint, but you're the ones trapped – we are at an impasse."

"Crest, can you hack the security system, take it out of action?" Dante asked.

Not while you wear those cuffs. Most of my functionality is disabled by their influence.

"Well?" Penelope asked hopefully, but Dante simply shook his head.

F smiled. "Let me offer you a solution. I must insist upon Dante's execution going ahead as planned, but there's no need for you to sudden the same fate, Agent Goodnight."

"That's not what I call a solution," Dante said.

"Keep talking," Penelope told her commander.

"Hey!" Dante protested. "I thought you were on my side!"

"Since when?" she replied tersely. "Just because we're handcuffed together, that doesn't mean I believe a word you've told me. We've been forced to work together to stay alive, but that's as far as loyalty to you stretches, Dante. I couldn't care less whether you live or die, and I have no interest in ever knowing you better. Get that through your thick skull!"

Oh yes, you're definitely winning her over, the Crest observed tactfully.

"What's your solution?" Penelope asked F.

"It seems her royal highness is getting impatient. She's brought forward the execution of Dante's two accomplices to Saturday afternoon. No doubt she is hoping this Russian renegade will be foolish enough to attempt a rescue mission."

"I wouldn't put it past him," Penelope said. "So?"

"As I said, Dante must die. But your fate need not be so... fatal." F took a step closer to her operative, one hand reaching forwards to stroke the side of Penelope's face. "Submit yourself to me for a year and I will quash all suggestions that you were any way associated with the assassination attempt. I can guarantee you a handsome promotion, your pick of future assignments at Britannia Intelligence and a lifestyle any sane woman would envy."

"What do you mean by the word 'submission'?"

"Exactly what I say. You will become my slave for the next twelve months, giving yourself over to my will, doing whatever I command without question. At the end of that time you will be a free woman, considerably richer and with a much broader experience of all life can offer." As F spoke she let her hand slide down from Penelope's face, passing off the secret agent's right breast and abdomen, before coming to rest between her legs. "Give yourself to me and I promise a sexual education that will make your hair curl."

"Don't do it," Dante urged. "You said it yourself, this bitch can't be trusted!"

"If I ever break my word to you," F told Penelope, "you have my permission to shoot me."

"All right," the secret agent replied, pressing herself against F's hand. "I'll do it."

"How delightful!" F said, giving a tiny squeak of pleasure. "I can't wait to get started."

Penelope shook her head. "You misunderstand me." She aimed her pistol between F's lips, a finger reaching for the trigger.

"No, don't, I–"

But F never finished her sentence, the words ripped away along with the back of her skull and much of her brain. The middle-aged woman's body tipped over backwards, the remains of her head hitting the marble floor like a wet flannel. Penelope spat on the corpse.

"I'm nobody's slave, bitch!" she snarled at the dead commander.

Dante rubbed the back of his neck. "You could have told me you were going to do that! You really had me going with all those lies about not caring if I lived or died."

Penelope's eyes narrowed. "What makes you think I was lying?"

"Oh. Right." He looked round the empty library. "So, how do we get out of here without setting off the security system? We outwitted the perverts, but I doubt the droids are that gullible."

Penelope crouched beside F's corpse. "When she escorted us through the house, I noticed F was using an old fashioned retinal scanner to confirm her identity. So, all we need do is borrow a little something from her and then we can walk out of here unscathed." She glanced at Dante. "Which eye should I pluck out? The left or the right?"

TEN

"The day is over and death is nearer."
– Russian proverb

"It goes without saying that Dante became a far more formidable opponent after he was bonded with his Romanov Weapons Crest. But an examination of his earlier career as a thief, adventurer and brigand proves he was no slouch in unarmed combat before his unexpected augmentation. For example, Dante's first encounter with the Tsar came after the renegade was charged with fighting and besting an entire squad of the highly trained hussars. His skills as a fighter should never be doubted or downgraded. Nikolai Dante is a worthy adversary for any man."
– Extract from *Nikolai Dante: Hellraiser Extraordinaire*, Maria Beria

Penelope and Dante used their grisly acquisition to contrive a way through the stately home's internal security system, flashing the eyeball at anything that questioned their presence. Within minutes they were out on the gravel courtyard in front of the house. "Now what?" Dante asked

"I don't know," Penelope admitted. "I probably shouldn't have killed F, but she was going too far. Bad enough to be labelled as your accomplice, but I won't be anybody's sex toy."

"Crest, what time is the *Flying Scotsman* due to leave for its next destination?"

Shortly after six. You've less than two hours.

"We can't go back to the train," Penelope insisted.

"Why not?"

"When we arrived here F was complaining the Rippers hadn't killed you. She must have sent another squad to the train after the first team failed. They've probably spent the day tearing it apart, looking for you. Plus we left a naked steward underneath my bed. The other staff will have found him by now. I doubt they'll welcome us back on board with open arms."

"I'm sure you can talk them round, since you're such a great seducer," Dante countered. "We have to get back on that train before it leaves. The real assassin is going to Peebles on the *Flying Scotsman*. He's the only person who can prove our innocence, especially now you've killed the one woman who could have cleared your name!" He folded his arms and glared at Penelope.

She blinked at this accusation. "God, you're right. What have I done?"

"Nothing anybody else in the same position wouldn't do."

"I've murdered my boss. Even if I can prove I had nothing to do with the attack on the king, I'm still guilty of slaughtering the head of Britannia Intelligence!"

Dante waved her concerns away. "You were defending yourself against a sexual predator. She's probably groped every woman who ever worked under her at the secret service."

"And a few others besides," Penelope agreed.

"Then you don't need to shed any tears for her." Dante studied their surroundings. "Crest, how far are we from the nearest estate boundary?"

More than twenty kilometres.

"Then we haven't time to get out of here on foot. We need a hover-car of some sort."

Penelope pointed to her right. "Or something larger?" The end of the bus that had brought them from Nottingham Station was visible beyond the house's eastern wing. "That must have pre-programmed safety clearance, otherwise it would never have got through the gates."

Dante smiled. "Do you want to drive, or shall I?"

Boyle and Dobie reached the rear of the stately home sixty seconds later, having slaughtered most of the Cadre Infernale's hapless members and sent the rest fleeing into the undergrowth. The bounty hunters found a trail through the long grass that led directly to the imposing house. The duo heard the roaring noise of a hover-bus taking off nearby and took cover beside the doors to the library. They relaxed as the sound faded into the distance, removing any threat to them.

Dobie sniffed the air. "You smell what I do?"

Boyle's nose wrinkled disdainfully. "Cordite and faeces. That means one thing–"

"Somebody's been shot and killed," Dobie agreed. "I'm going in – cover me!" He burst through the double doors, throwing himself into a forward roll and coming up with his gun drawn, ready to fire. Moments later Boyle followed him in, pistol ready, eyes scanning the empty shelves and empty corners for any sign of movement. Once they had confirmed the room was devoid of life, the pair straightened up again, letting themselves relax. Dobie sauntered over to the female body on the floor. A crimson pool had spread out around her head, while a puddle of yellow and brown had spilled from between her legs. "That's something I'll never get used to, Ray."

"What?" His partner looked around the room for anything that might identify the corpse.

"The way a human body purges itself after death."

Boyle shrugged. "The muscles naturally relax. It's not purging, more like spillage."

"Yeah, well, remind me to get an enema before I die. Or wear rubber underpants."

"You better not get killed in that posing pouch then. Not much dignity to be had in there."

Dobie nodded, still studying what remained of the corpse's face. "I've seen her before somewhere. The state opening of Parliament, maybe?"

Boyle joined him, crouching down for a closer look at the body. "Hard to tell with one eye and the back of her head missing... But you're right. We've met her before somewhere."

"Not a target or else we'd have killed her, not somebody else."

"A client?"

"Of course!" Dobie said, snapping his fingers. "Ray Boyle, allow me to introduce you to F – the head of Britannia Intelligence. Or what's left of her."

"You're right! She hired us to finish the career of that cabinet minister who wanted to cut her budget. A very dangerous lady, I seem to recall." Boyle studied her remains with fresh interest. "Maybe we've underestimated Nikolai Dante. He must be pretty resourceful to take out a woman like F. Single shot, as well – up close and personal. This guy is not to be taken lightly."

"But why did he take her eyeball? Some kind of trophy?" Before Boyle could reply, two security droids burst into the library, their weapons raised and ready for action. The bounty hunters dived in opposite directions, emptying their handguns at the menacing mechanoids.

The hover-bus swerved drunkenly around a clock tower above central Nottingham, narrowly avoiding a mid-air collision. As Dante piloted his way past the erection, Penelope pointed out the time on display. "It's nearly six! We'll miss the train if you don't land soon."

"I'm trying, I'm trying," he protested.

"You said you could fly this thing!"

"I said I'd give it a try. Here!" Dante let go of the steering wheel and the bus plunged towards a crowded pedestrian plaza. "You think you can do better, you take over!"

"Just get us down near the station, okay?" she pleaded.

"Okay!" Dante took hold of the controls again but they did not respond. If anything, the bus accelerated its rapid descent. "Ahh – Nottingham, we have a problem."

"What kind of problem?" Penelope said angrily.

"The kind of problem that involves crashing, burning and large amounts of pain," he replied. "I mean, I'm guessing, but it's an educated guess..."

"Look out!" she screamed as the pedestrian zone filled the hover-bus's front windscreen, residents diving out of the way. At the last possible moment the vehicle wrenched itself sideways, then straightened out until it was running parallel to the ground. Penelope opened her eyes again. "You did it!" she cried happily. "I can't believe you did it!"

"Neither can I," Dante said, pointing at the steering wheel. The bus was moving of its own volition, the wheel twisting from side to side as it drove along the city streets. Signs for the railway station became increasingly frequent. "Guess this thing has some sort of automatic pilot for the last part of its programmed journey. Look, the station's up ahead."

The bus glided to a halt by the entrance, front doors sliding back gracefully. Penelope and Dante hurled themselves out of the vehicle and sprinted into the station. "How long, Crest?"

Thirty seconds and counting.

"Bojemoi, why do I always cut things so fine?"

You crave excitement, deliberately creating situations that push you to your limits and beyond, probably in an attempt to distract yourself from the ultimate futility of your life.

"I wasn't actually asking for your opinion!" Dante shouted as he and Penelope ran to the platform where the

Flying Scotsman had been that morning. But the tracks were empty. "Diavolo, we're too late!"

Penelope pointed at another platform close by where their train was waiting. "No, look – it's over there! They must have shifted platforms during the day. I don't see any sign of the Rippers. They must have been and gone."

The station tannoy crackled into life. "The train now leaving from Platform eleven is the *Flying Scotsman* tourist service, calling at Peebles, Edinburgh and Orkney. Stand away from the doors now, please, this train is ready to depart. Stand away from the doors!"

Penelope raced towards Platform eleven, dragging Dante after her. As they reached it the train was already rolling away from them, gathering acceleration in preparation for take-off. "Come on!" Penelope screamed, quickening her speed. She reached the back door and pulled it open, Dante running as fast as he could to keep up with her. Penelope pulled herself into the rear carriage, then reached back to help Dante on board. The train gave a sideways lurch as it left the tracks and rose into the air, tipping Penelope towards the open doorway. She fell over, Dante's weight dragging her back outside. Penelope jammed her legs against the door frame, wedging herself in place. "Hold on!" she screamed at him.

"I'm holding, I'm holding!" he shouted back, dangling in the air beneath the train.

Dante, evasive action!

He looked round in time to see the same clock tower the bus had narrowly avoided earlier now looming towards him. Dante swung his legs up in the air and the tower scraped beneath him, ripping through the fabric of his kilt. The tartan fabric was wrenched from his body, wrapping itself around the weather vane on top of the clock tower. The cool evening air whistled past Dante's naked body as he hung from Penelope's grasp, only the handcuffs keeping the two of them together. "I can't hold on much longer!" she warned. "My legs are giving way!"

Dante nodded, painfully aware of the precariousness of their situation and the ever increasing strain upon both their bodies. "I'm going to try and swing myself upwards," he shouted, raising his voice to be heard above the whistling wind.

"Whatever you're going to do, make it quick!" she called back.

Dante kicked both his legs back, then swung them forwards, repeating the motion over and over until the tendons in his shoulder were screaming in pain. Finally, keeping time with the pendulum swing of his body, Dante flung himself into a backwards somersault up into the air. His upside-down body smacked into the side of the carriage, but he managed to grab hold of the door frame. As his battered and bruised back slid down the woodwork, Dante pulled himself into the open door and collapsed. The two of them lay there for more than a minute, gasping for breath and moaning in pain, Dante's naked body splayed out on top of Penelope.

A polite cough from the corridor eventually got their attention. "While I applaud your obvious gymnastic abilities," Gordonstoun said icily, "may I suggest that in future you leave sufficient time for your return journey from any of our scheduled day trips?"

"Whatever you say," Penelope whispered.

"Also, I must ask you to refrain from involving my staff in your sexual shenanigans. The man you left bound and gagged under the bed is still in Nottingham, receiving counselling." The head steward stepped past them and closed the back door of the carriage. "Dinner will be served in the dining car from seven," he said brusquely. "While evening dress is usually considered optional, we do ask our guests to show some slight measure of decorum."

"Don't worry, I'll make sure she changes out of her catsuit," Dante replied cheerfully.

"I was referring to your current attire, sir – or lack of it." Gordonstoun's withering gaze lingered on Dante's groin.

"My, there must be quite a chilling wind out this evening." He strode away along the corridor, muttering under his breath.

Penelope got up with a groan, rubbing her left shoulder. "I swear, this arm is going to be half a metre longer than the other before this is over."

Dante grimaced. "At least you've still got your own clothes. I've just given half of Nottingham a worm's eye view of my genitals!"

"At least the other half didn't miss much," she replied. "Let's go back to my compartment, see if we can't find you something to wear. Then I need to eat."

"Food can wait," he said as they strode along the corridor. "Ever since the attempt on the king's life I've been arrested, beaten, interrogated, stripped naked – twice! – and hunted by a pack of sexual deviants. All I want now is some answers. I vote we search every cabin and carriage on this train until we find the real assassin."

"Assuming he's still on the train."

"He has to be," Dante insisted. "Otherwise…"

Penelope paused outside the door to her compartment. "Otherwise what?"

He shrugged. "I don't know. I'm out of my depth and the Crest is next to useless while I've still got these damned handcuffs on."

Don't blame me for your current predicament!

"I wasn't," Dante said. "I guess I've come to depend upon the Crest, it gets me out of so many tight spots. It's only now I haven't got that help that I'm learning to appreciate it."

I hope you'll remember that in future.

"Look, this is all very touching," Penelope said, "but I've seen enough of your genitals to last me a lifetime. I need a change of clothes and some food. After that I'll be more than happy to help you find this elusive mystery man, okay?"

"Okay."

"Besides, I've only got five shots left in my pistol," Penelope said, producing the tiny handgun from inside her catsuit. "If this person is part of a conspiracy to kill the king, we'll need more firepower than I'm carrying at the moment."

"I said okay," Dante replied, opening the compartment door. Inside were four expectant Rippers, all of them clutching a stiletto in each hand, malevolent grins spread across each face. Dante slammed the door shut again and smiled. "However, a slight change of plan might be wise."

Dobie and Boyle disabled the first pair of security droids with ease and despatched the next set of mechanoids to approach the library, but both men knew their limited ammunition supply would not be sufficient to see off any further attacks. It was Boyle who first grasped the significance of the missing eyeball. "Of course! This place must use retina scanning as a security override. Dobie, keep watch at the door while I get her other eyeball out."

"Why I do always get guard duty?" his partner said.

"Because you're a better shot than me."

"You're saying that to butter me up."

Boyle grinned. "Save that idea for later, lover boy." Unable to prise the eyeball free from the front, he tipped the corpse over and shoved his fingers through the exit wound. Within moments the eyeball popped out and rolled across the floor like a marble.

"We've got company, Ray – time to get moving!" Dobie spun away from the door and inadvertently stood on the eyeball. It squashed beneath his weight with a wet popping sound.

"Brilliant! That's brilliant! Our one chance of getting out of here alive and you stand on it!" Boyle raged, getting to his feet. "What are we supposed to do now?"

His partner glanced back at the cluster of security droids gathering outside. "Run!"

The duo raced to the external doors but another group of mechanoids was also blocking that exit. "We're trapped!" Boyle said.

Dobie pointed to a corner of the library. "What's that?" One of the bookshelves jutted out slightly from the wall, a glimmer of light spilling out through the gap.

The duo sprinted across to the corner and tugged at the bookshelf, until it moved far enough for both of them to squeeze through. Once they were on the other side, a mechanical warning sounded and a solid steel barrier slammed down to block the only exit. Dobie spun round, his eyes urgently scanning their surroundings. "If we weren't trapped before, we are now!"

"Not exactly," Boyle said. They were standing inside a cube-shaped room. An entire wall was covered in holographic display screens showing a hundred different scenes. Most were images from security cameras around the estate, but there were also feeds from the main news channels, communications channels and entertainment networks. "This must be the dead woman's private office. From here we can contact anyone in the world."

"So we're safe?"

"Yeah."

"But we can't get out?"

"Not until we call in a favour or two." Boyle sat in the swivel chair facing the display units, studying the range of switches and controls in front of him. "If our hostess was head of Britannia Intelligence, she'll have a direct line to Scotland Yard. Ahh, here we go: the police." He smiled over his shoulder at Dobie. "I think it's time we gave a progress report to Inspector Rucka, don't you? No doubt he's been wondering how we're getting on..."

Penelope killed the first Ripper to open the compartment door, blowing the back of his head clean off. Her second shot only wounded the next in line and her third shot jammed inside the pistol. "Misfire!" she shouted to Dante, shaking the tiny pistol in frustration. "Run!" The pair bolted along the corridor, only to find two more Rippers waiting for them at the far end.

Dante – evasive action!

"No kidding!" he replied, ducking beneath a stiletto as it sliced through the air. Dante thrust his knee into the Ripper's gut so the black-cloaked figure folded forwards, then smashed the base of his left hand into the Ripper's nose. Bone was punched backwards into the Ripper's brain and the murderous invader was dead within moments, crimson spraying from his face.

"You don't get rid of us that easy, sunshine!" the second Ripper in the corridor boasted, climbing over the crumpled body of his colleague.

"We'll see about that," Penelope snarled, cracking him across the face with the butt of her pistol. The weapon fired, its bullet ricocheting off a brass fitting before lodging in the Ripper's brain. He collapsed on top of Dante, who was crouched on the floor, searching for a knife.

"Lucky shot," Dante said, finding a discarded stiletto among the corpses.

"I'll take any luck I can get," Penelope replied. "I've only got two shots left."

"Then you'd better make them count – here come the others!" The rest of the Rippers were pushing past their dead brother to get out of Penelope's compartment. Dante charged at them, roaring at the top of his voice, but was abruptly jerked back again by the handcuffs. His feet flew up into the air, a look of comical bewilderment crossing his face before he fell to the floor with a heavy thud. "Bojemoi," he gasped. "I forgot."

The Ripper with the gunshot wound sneered at Dante's naked body. "Well, well, well. What 'ave we 'ere? Looks like this one's been a naughty boy!"

"He needs to be punished," the next Ripper agreed.

"We'll cut out his lights and giblets," the Ripper cackled. "We'll feast on his sweetmeats for our dinner, eh lads?" A flying stiletto impaled itself in his left eyeball, the tip stabbing deep into the Ripper's brain. He was dead before his body hit the floor.

"I don't share my sweetmeats with any man," Dante said smugly, smiling at the accuracy of his knife-throwing skills. "Now, if you were female, things might be rather different."

The remaining two Rippers launched themselves at Dante, lunging at him with blades in both hands. "Look out behind!" Dante shouted, pulling his feet up to propel the first Ripper over his head. Penelope dropped to one knee and shot the Ripper as he flew past her in the air. When the murderous creature hit the floor, already twisting round for another attack, she used her final shot to remove his lower jaw. He stayed down after that. But the last Ripper landed right on top of Dante, twin stilettos gouging into the floor on either side of his face. Dante responded with a head butt, smacking his forehead into the Ripper's nose. Both of them screamed in agony, blood streaming down their faces. "Diavolo, that hurts!" Dante cried out.

"Not as much as this will, my pretty," the Ripper promised, ripping a dagger out of the floor and pulling it back into the air, ready to plunge the blade through his enemy's heart. Dante yanked the other stiletto free and stabbed it into the Ripper's chest. He twisted the knife, making the blade squirm around in the wound. The Ripper vomited blood into Dante's face before collapsing on top of him, the knife falling safely to one side.

Penelope rolled the Ripper away, moving closer to look at Dante. "Nikolai! Nikolai, are you all right? Speak to me, damn you!"

His face split into a smile. "That's the first time you've ever called me Nikolai."

"I thought you were–"

"Dead?" Dante coughed up a mouthful of blood, spitting it onto the Ripper's corpse. "Not yet. It takes worse than that to kill me, even without my enhanced healing abilities." He sat up, crimson-flecked phlegm dripping from his face. "Is that all of them?"

"Probably," Penelope said. "Rippers travel in squads of six or twelve. Count yourself lucky there were only half a dozen this time." She helped him up, wiping the scarlet mucus from his face. "Let's get you clean and find some fresh clothes. Then I must eat, or else *I'll* kill someone."

Dante nodded at the corpses in the corridor. "What about this lot?"

"Okay, I need to eat before I kill someone else."

"No, I meant – shouldn't we dispose of them first?"

Penelope sighed heavily. "I suppose you're right. The train will be spending the night over the Lake District. We'll put these carcasses into an empty compartment for now, then throw them out when we're above Lake Windermere."

"You know," Dante said as they dragged the Rippers out of sight, "fighting these freaks would have been easier if we weren't cuffed together. Are you any closer to passing that key?"

"Not yet," Penelope admitted. "That's another reason for eating soon. A little extra roughage in my system would help speed the key's progress." She pushed one Ripper into a vacant berth, then went back to collect another corpse. Right now I'm so hungry I'll eat anything they put in front of me." Her gaze caught sight of Dante's exposed genitals as the duo continued their grisly task. "Anything except sausages."

ELEVEN

"Women's tears are nets, not water."
– Russian proverb

"Traditional games of strength and agility have been practised in the Highlands for many, many centuries. These annual gatherings became formalised around 1820 as part of a national revival of tartan culture. With Caledonia now principally a tourist destination, the Highland Games are more popular than ever. Travellers from across the Empire come to witness such arcane sports as putting the shot, tossing the caber and throwing the weight. Highland dancing is an essential part of any Games, as is the inevitable skirl of the bagpipes. So, put on your kilt, strap down your sporran and get ready for a sporting event unlike any other!"
– Extract from *The Duffer's Guide to Britannia*, 2670 edition

Dante and Penelope spent an uncomfortable night on her bed, thanks to Penelope's insistence on keeping a row of pillows between them as a divider. "We may be handcuffed together, but that doesn't give you any claim over my body," she warned.

"Don't flatter yourself," Dante replied. "Besides, I've seen how you treat uninvited sexual overtures. I'd like to keep my brains intact."

Despite that, the two of them still ended up in each other's arms the next morning. Dante opening his eyes on Friday to find Penelope snuggling into his back. "I knew you couldn't resist me forever," he whispered huskily. Her scream of dismay when she woke quickly shattered that illusion. Both of them bounded off the bed in opposite directions, then were jerked back together by their handcuffs. A string of obscenities filled the air as their heads collided with a crack.

Early morning ablutions proved just as problematic, Dante leaning out the bathroom door whistling loudly while Penelope emptied her bladder. She was considerably less squeamish, offering a stream of unwelcome observations as he tried to urinate. "We haven't got all day, you know. They stop serving breakfast in half an hour."

"I am trying to concentrate," he replied through gritted teeth.

"Well, it doesn't seem to be working."

"Look, I find this difficult with anyone watching, let alone offering a running commentary!"

"What about having the Crest in your head?" Penelope asked. "How does that work?"

"We have an understanding. It allows me a little privacy when I need it most – like now."

"How about when you're making love?" Penelope asked. "I imagine having an alien battle computer offering advice on your technique must be quite distracting."

"Please," he said quietly. "Could you give me a minute's peace, okay? Just give me one minute of silence and then we can go and have breakfast, all right?"

"One minute?"

"Yes!"

"Fine by me," Penelope said. Seven seconds of agonising silence followed, unbroken by the sound of any liquid splashing into the toilet bowl. "I mean, I have absolutely no problems with keeping quiet for that long. I–"

"Oh, forget it!" Dante snapped, flushing the toilet and stomping out of the bathroom. "We'll go and eat. With any luck breakfast will shift the key from your vice-like bowels, putting an end to this nightmare for both of us. Then I might be able take a piss in peace and quiet!"

Henry Windsor McKray blinked. "I think he's coming round," a voice whispered. The king breathed deeply, the smell of frying bacon drifting into his nostrils and awakening his taste buds. He opened his eyes to find himself in a small, pale green room filled with doctors, nurses, a camera crew and a chef. The last of these was clutching a sizzling skillet with seven rashers of bacon cooking on it, each segment cheerfully spitting pork fat into the air.

"I say," the king murmured sleepily. "Is it breakfast already?" The doctors and nurses burst into spontaneous applause, laughing profusely at his first words in three days. "That bacon smells wonderful. Any chance of someone slapping it inside a roll with brown sauce for me?"

"King Henry!" shouted a rat-faced reporter in a suit and tie, waving from behind the cameraman. "King Henry, how do you feel?"

"Quite hungry," he replied, smiling weakly. "Positively ravenous in fact." A shrieking female voice became audible, getting louder by the moment. "Has someone let a banshee loose in here?"

"Where is he?" the woman demanded from outside Henry's room, her aristocratic voice akin to hawk talons clawing a blackboard. "He's my bloody father! You will let me see him and you will let me see him right bloody now!"

"Oh dear," the king lamented. "I thought my daughter was still in prison."

Princess Marie-Anne burst into the hospital room, ruthlessly shoving doctors and nurses out of the way to reach the king. Seeing his frail body on the bed, she began sobbing theatrically and collapsed beside him. "Father, my dear papa! Speak to me! Say something – if you're able!"

"Hello. What are you doing here?"

The princess looked up abruptly, surprise etched into her features. "You're conscious!"

"Yes, that's right," Henry said brightly.

"You're talking!"

"Right again, daughter."

"But… the doctors… they didn't think you'd make it!"

"Well, here I am, on the mend."

She glared at the doctors, her voice a venomous hiss. "You said he wouldn't make it!"

The nearest surgeon shrugged, hands buried in the pockets of her white coat. "The king apparently possesses remarkable powers of recovery, your royal highness."

"What's your name?"

"Bhamra, ma'am. Doctor Parminder Bhamra."

"You told me he had a one in ten chance of surviving his wounds – at best."

"What can I say? He beat the odds."

"He beat the odds," the princess repeated slowly, her gaze slowly taking in the camera crew filming everything in the room. "He beat the odds! What a blessing for us all!" The princess removed herself from the floor, adjusting her clothes and trying to recover some dignity. "Tell me, what was it that brought him back from the brink of seemingly not so certain death?"

Doctor Bhamra pointed out the trembling cook in the corner. "Your royal chef, Ramsey, told us the king could never resist the aroma of frying bacon. We had tried everything else, so we decided to make an appeal to his sense of smell – and it worked! Quite remarkable."

Marie-Anne raised an eyebrow at the chef. "I couldn't have put it better myself. Ramsey, remind me to give a special reward for the service you have done us all by reviving my father."

"Y-Yes, y-your royal highness," the chef stammered fearfully.

The king raised his left hand, trying to get some attention.

"Yes, your majesty?" a nurse asked.

"So, do I get a bacon sandwich or not?"

Everyone in the room burst out laughing again, the princess laughing louder and harder than the others at her father's unwitting jest. "Oh, papa, what a joy it is to see you alive and on the way to recovery. Some days I think you'll out last us all!"

"Well, you never know," he agreed.

Marie-Anne leaned down to hiss in his ear. "I wouldn't count on it, you old goat!"

Henry pinched her cheek, an affectionate gesture but for the force of his grasp. "You'll rot in hell before you sit in my throne, you poisonous little harridan," he whispered back at her.

The princess dug her fingernails into his wrist, forcing him to let go, then stood upright again. "Well, I'll come back this afternoon to update you on all the important matters of state," she announced for the camera crew's benefit. "Two of the men responsible for your wounds and for murdering the Queen Mother are awaiting execution, while a third is being hunted down."

"Babs is dead? I didn't know. That is sad news." The king's face fell, but he quickly rallied. "Still, she had a good innings, the old girl, you can't deny that."

Marie-Anne rested a consoling hand on her father's arm. "Yes, the Queen Mother was an example to us all, with her youthful exuberance and playful attitude to life, Sadly, she was slain by three cowardly assassins. The worst part is you invited them into the palace."

"Did I?"

"Don't you remember, father? The man who murdered my beloved grandmamma was that vicious Russian renegade, Nikolai Dante."

"Nicola? She would never–" Henry protested, but his daughter hushed him to silence.

"Poor father, you're still confused by what's happened. I said Nikolai, not Nicola." Marie-Anne glared into the camera lens. "If you're watching, Nikolai Dante, I want you to know I will never rest until you pay for what you've done to my family!" In an instant her expression switched to a gracious smile as she addressed the doctors and nurses. "Would you all be kind enough to leave the room? I'd like to say a prayer of thanks at my father's bedside before I leave..."

Doctor Bhamra nodded hurriedly. "Of course, your royal highness." She ushered all the others out, then bowed low before leaving, shutting the door after herself.

Once father and daughter were alone, they dropped any pretence of liking each other. "You old fool!" Marie-Anne snarled. "Why couldn't you die like grandmamma?"

"Some of us are made of sterner stuff," he snapped. "I have few illusions about your feelings for me, but having your own grandmother killed – isn't that beneath even you, dear?"

"I didn't hire the assassins!" the princess protested. "If I had you wouldn't still be here."

"Nicola will discover the truth," Henry insisted. "My betrothed never lets me down."

"You really are madder than a gift box of badgers, aren't you? His name is Nikolai, not Nicola, and he fled London like the coward he is, leaving his two accomplices to die for him. Every policeman, every secret service operative and every bounty hunter in the country is stalking that pernicious piece of filth."

The king smiled. "Most of our constables couldn't find their way out of a wet paper bag with a sharp pencil. Lovely uniforms but not a brain between them. As for the secret service – if you didn't hire the assassins, they probably did. I doubt they'll find young Nicola. Besides, she is a wonderfully resourceful woman. I've seen her get out of all manner of scrapes."

"*Nikolai* Dante is as good as dead," the princess snarled. "That's if he isn't dead already!"

■ ■ ■

"I wouldn't be seen dead eating some of this," Dante said, disdainfully studying the breakfast menu in the *Flying Scotsman*'s dining car.

"Take this one: porridge. What is porridge?"

A traditional Scottish delicacy, made of oats stewed in milk or water. It is usually served with salt or sugar and milk, the Crest replied. *According to legend, families would store it inside a drawer, cutting off a slice whenever they were hungry.*

"Sounds disgusting!"

If you think that sounds disgusting, I won't tell you what is used to make a haggis.

"Good." Dante lowered his breakfast menu to look at Penelope. "What are you having?"

She smiled. "Definitely porridge, and possibly kippers to follow."

"Kippers?"

"Yes, a pair of kippers would be lovely. I haven't had kippers in years."

"Crest?"

A kipper is a fish which has been split from tail to head, eviscerated–

"Enough, enough, I've heard enough," Dante replied hastily. "I'll stick with what I know. Last time I was in this country the hotel served something called a full Britannia breakfast. It included this delicious thing called a black pudding. It was round and had been–"

Made out of suet, breadcrumbs, oatmeal and pig's blood.

Dante swallowed hard. "Pig's blood? I ate a sausage made out of pig's blood?"

Plus suet, bread crumbs and oatmeal, the Crest confirmed. *You said it was delicious.*

"That was before I knew what was in it." He glared at Penelope. "I thought this was a cultured country, but you people eat the most obscene… Words fail me."

If only.

"I'll stick to toast," Dante decided. "You don't do anything strange to that, do you?"

Penelope smiled. "Not unless you count spreading marmalade all over it."

One of the stewards approached them, doing his best not to stare at Dante's clothes.

Gordonstoun could only produce a spare kilt, so Dante was forced to wear that with a frilly white blouse borrowed from Penelope. The two passengers gave their breakfast orders and handed back the menus. They were seated at a corner table with Dante facing the dining car.

"I can't see the assassin," he admitted after carefully studying the other travellers.

"Maybe he didn't get back on at Nottingham. The train is much emptier today."

"Because all the Cadre Infernale members stayed behind at your boss's estate." Dante bit his fingernails nervously. "No, I'm sure he's still on board. His timetable had the stops at Peebles and Orkney circled. Why would he get off before then?"

Penelope shrugged. "Let's hope you're right, otherwise both of us are in trouble."

The steward returned with their food, giving Dante a fully laden toast rack and putting two steaming plates of food in front of Penelope.

"How long before we reach Peebles?" she asked.

"An hour," the steward replied. "Can I get either of you anything else?"

Penelope shook her head, while Dante kept his gaze fixed on the vast repast opposite him. "Are you sure you've got enough there?"

She smiled. "Breakfast is the most important meal of the day – didn't your mother ever teach you that?"

"My mother was a pirate queen who kicked me off her ship before I reached puberty. All she taught me was how to fight and how to hate." Dante fell silent, deep in thought while Penelope munched her way through a meal fit for someone twice her size.

Sixty minutes later the *Flying Scotsman* was coming in to land at Peebles, a charming lowland settlement next to the River Tweed. Penelope was still belching from her breakfast as the train settled smoothly on to the tracks at the edge of town. It rolled into the station and halted, the tannoy inviting everyone aboard to enjoy the Highland Games nearby. Dante stood quietly beside Penelope in the compartment, looking out of the window at the stone houses of Peebles in the distance.

"Spatchcock and Flintlock will be executed tomorrow unless I clear my name, but I don't feel any closer to a solution than I did when the king was shot three days ago."

"You believe this man on the train is the assassin?"

Dante shrugged. "I'm not sure anymore. The more I think about it, the more I wonder if this whole trip has been a fool's errand."

Penelope frowned. "You told me the man you've seen on board was one of the shooters."

"I said he must be involved–"

"Involved? You convinced me he pulled the trigger!"

"I might have exaggerated," Dante said. "He was definitely standing on Westminster Bridge close to the spot where I confronted the assassin. After I was thrown into the Thames, rising mist made it hard to see, but I definitely heard him talking with someone else. He had an accent I didn't recognise, but it wasn't a dialect from Britannia. He told the other person he would see them soon and there was something about an old man with a short name – Troy? Malloy?"

Penelope shook her head, plainly unable to believe what she was hearing. "You're telling me all of this could have been a wild goose chase?"

"I guess," Dante admitted. "I did see this guy's face, when a skimmer dropped towards the bridge and caught him in its headlights. I'm certain it's the same man I saw at the train station where I met you, the same man who dropped the timetable in the dining car, the same man who was in the other queue at Nottingham – it must be him. It must be..."

"You sound like you're trying to convince yourself," Penelope said.

"I know. Sorry."

Dante!

"Not now, Crest."

"Look, we'll find this guy and interrogate him," Penelope decided. "We'll soon discover what he does know. Maybe you're right, maybe he doesn't have anything directly to do with the assassins – but if he was on that bridge, he probably saw what the assassins looked like, yes?"

Dante, you need to–

"Later, Crest, okay? We're trying to come up with a plan of action. You're the one who always nags me for acting first and thinking second. Well, let me think first for once, all right?"

But the man you are hunting just walked past the corridor outside this compartment.

"He did?"

Yes!

"Well, why didn't you say something before?"

I did, I– Oh, I give up, the Crest sighed wearily.

Dante hurried to the compartment door, dragging Penelope after him. "Which way did he go, Crest? Left or right?"

Left, towards the rear of the train.

Dante tried to run in the same direction, but Penelope was slowing him down. "Come on! He's getting away from us!"

"I can't run," she said, belching heavily as they got off the train. Dante was craning his neck, trying to spot their quarry among the other passengers on the platform.

"Why not?" he asked.

"That second plate of kippers was definitely a mistake. I can feel them churning round inside me." Penelope belched again, clamping a hand over her mouth. "I need a toilet. Fast."

"Can't it wait?" Dante protested. His eyes lit up as a bald man with a goatee appeared for a moment among the crowds marching towards a sign bearing the words "PEEBLES SHOW GROUND". "There he is! Come on!" Dante hurried after the man, pulling Penelope along behind.

"You're not listening to me! I need a toilet – right now!" Penelope stopped, refusing to take another step. "Trust me, this is in both our interests."

Dante looked at the handcuffs connecting them, then at her pale, perspiring face. "Oh. Right." He glanced about, spotting a set of public toilets nearby. "Over there?"

"Over there," Penelope agreed, already striding towards the conveniences. She barged in through the door marked "LADIES", dragging Dante after her. Within were three cubicles, each with a wooden door. Two were occupied but the last was mercifully empty. Penelope shoved her way in and Dante was forced to follow, locking the door behind himself. By the time he turned round she had already peeled her catsuit down past her thighs and was sat on the toilet.

"Bojemoi! You're not going to do that while I'm watching, are you?"

"Right now, I couldn't care less what you do!"

Dante closed his eyes and willed himself not to listen.

Jean Brown loved the Highland Games. Every year Peebles came alive for this event, playing host to thousands of new faces and welcoming as many old friends. Jean might have been eighty but she never missed the Games, no matter what the weather did. Seeing the old traditions kept alive was important to her. Besides, she always hoped for a strong gust of wind when men in kilts were tossing the caber. Alas, old age had played havoc with her bladder control, so Jean kept close to the nearest public toilets. She was still on her way into the show ground when the call of nature forced her to turn aside in search of relief. Into the conveniences she bustled, relieved to find the middle cubicle was free. Jean arranged herself on the seat and let nature take its course, sighing contentedly. Then she heard a most unexpected sound from the cubicle on her left – a man's voice. What on earth was he doing in here?

"Well, is it out yet?" he asked.

"Not... yet!" a woman replied, strain and pain evident in her tone of voice. Jean forgot her own troubles and leaned closer to the adjoining wall, trying to overhear what was going on.

"If it won't come out voluntarily, maybe we need a way of inducing it," the man said.

"I can do this!" the woman snarled back. "Give me another minute, you impatient sod!"

Jean blanched at such language. What in heaven's name was happening? It sounded like the poor woman was having a baby. Of all the times and places she could have chosen!

"I know you can," the man said soothingly. "Relax and it'll come out naturally."

"Get away from me, you bastard. This is all your fault!"

"You're the one who put the handcuffs on us, not me."

Handcuffs? It was a long time since Jean had experienced childbirth, but she didn't recall handcuffs being an intrinsic part of the process.

"Ahhh – it's moving, I can feel it moving!" the woman cried out. "Here it comes..."

"I can't look!" the man said. "I think... I think I'm going to pass out!"

"Don't you dare!" his companion snarled. "We're in this together, remember?"

"I can't go through with it!"

"You haven't got a choice – we're stuck with each other until this thing comes out of me!" A fist banged against the adjoining wall, surprising Jean so much she almost fell off her seat. "Here it comes..." the woman screamed. "Here... it... comes!"

Jean had heard enough. She pulled up her bloomers, flushed her toilet and scuttled out of the cubicle, not daring to look back. Outside she bumped into two men wearing ambulance crew uniforms. "I think you should get inside there – quickly!" she urged.

"Why is that, madam?"

"Some poor woman is having a baby in one of the cubicles. I don't know if that's her boyfriend or her husband in there too, but he's no use at all – she needs your help!"

Penelope finished rinsing the key, then wiped it dry. She held the small slither of metal up for Dante to see. "Who'd have thought such a little thing could cause so much trouble."

He grimaced. "Let's not dwell on the past. Just undo the handcuffs, okay?"

She removed the metal manacles from her own wrist first, then took the other end off Dante's arm. He threw the handcuff into the rubbish chute. "There, you're a free man again," Penelope said happily. "It'll probably take a few minutes for the disabling effects to wear off, but you should have full use of your bio-blades soon enough."

"Good," he replied, rubbing the raw red mark round his wrist where the cuff had been secured. "Now, let's go and search for this assassin. The sooner we discover the truth, the better." But as they moved towards the exit, Dante and Penelope found their path blocked by two men in fluorescent green overalls, both holding pistols.

"You must be the elusive Nikolai Dante," the man on the left said, smiling cruelly. "I'm Dobie and this is Boyle; we've been looking for you everywhere."

His partner took aim at Penelope's heart. "And you must be Agent Goodnight, Britannia Intelligence's most accomplished seductress." Boyle looked Dante up and down, mentally undressing him. "Have you added this one to your long list of conquests? He's not much to look at, I'll grant you that, but I'm sure you must have enjoyed full use of his facilities by now."

"Who the hell are you?" Dante demanded.

"He told you," Boyle replied. "We're Dobie and Boyle."

"Are those names supposed to mean something to me?"

"They're bounty hunters," Penelope said. "Parasitic scum, taking on the cases the Britannia Royal Constabulary can't – or won't – handle. We've got a file on these two at HQ, filled with reports of their illegal exploits. Dobie was a mercenary who travelled the Empire, fighting in petty border squabbles for whichever side paid better. Boyle was a policeman, until his partner died in mysterious circumstances. They've got a reputation for killing without mercy or compunction."

"We're the best there is at what we do," Dobie said proudly.

"Top of the turds, in other words?" Dante asked.

"Kings of the shit hill," Penelope agreed. "Or should I say queens?"

"Our sexuality is irrelevant to our effectiveness," Boyle replied.

"I'll say. How long has it taken you to find us?"

"Shut up!" Dobie yelled, smacking his pistol across Penelope's face. Dante moved to retaliate but Boyle already had his pistol aimed and ready to fire.

"I don't need an excuse to kill you," he sneered. "Our employer made it perfectly clear he doesn't want you coming back to London. At least, not alive."

"How's it going in here?" an elderly voice asked from behind the bounty hunters. An old lady with snow white hair came into the public bathroom, shoving her way past Dobie and Boyle. They hastily concealed their weapons inside their overalls while glaring at Dante and Penelope. The old lady looked about, confused by what she found. "So, where's this baby then?"

"Baby?" Dante asked.

"I heard some poor lass in here, screaming in agony as she tried to give birth. It sounded like she was having the most terrible time of it, so I sent these ambulance men in to help."

"It was all a misunderstanding," Dobie said loudly at the old woman. "You must have been confused, dear."

She shot a stern look at him. "Don't tell me what I did and didn't hear, young man! I may have snow on the chimney, but there's still fire in my belly, let me tell you!"

"Of course there is..." Dobie replied, trying to placate her.

"Don't patronise me, you two-faced so-and-so! There's a terrible stramash outside, with so many people waiting to see you bring out the young woman and her baby. So, where is it?"

"Yes, where is it?" Penelope asked, still nursing the cheek Dobie had pistol-whipped. "You'll have some explaining to do if there's no baby to be seen." She took Dante by the hand and tried to lead him out of the toilets. "Come along, darling, let's go see what's happening outside. I think we've been in here long enough."

"Er... yes!" Dante said, slowly catching her drift. The pair attempted to push past the bounty hunters but Boyle was too quick for them. He pushed the barrel of his pistol into Penelope's ribs, out of sight of the old woman.

"I'll come with you. I need to fetch the ambulance for this baby. Dobie, why don't you stay here and show this delightful old lady what we found in the cubicle?"

"Good idea," Dobie agreed. "Off you go. I'll be out in a minute."

Boyle gave Dante and Penelope a shove towards the exit, then followed them out. As the old woman had promised, a crowd was gathered, waiting for news. Boyle told them his partner was still inside, looking after the baby. "Please, let us past," he called out, nudging his captives through the ring of expectant people. Once they were clear of the crowd Boyle pulled a silencer from inside his overalls and began screwing it on to the end of his weapon. "Keep walking and smiling," he urged. "The ambulance is parked inside the show ground. When we get there, you'll climb in the back. Try anything stupid and I'll kill you both in a second."

"Crest," Dante whispered under his breath. "Have the effects of the handcuffs worn off?"

Not enough for you to survive a mortal wound, it said. *But your bio-blades should be available again any minute now.*

"What are you whispering about?" Boyle demanded.

"He was talking to himself," Penelope replied. "He does that all the time. It's been driving me crazy. You taking him off my hands will be a relief, to be honest."

"Nobody asked your opinion," the bounty hunter said as they entered the show ground. The smell of sweat and exertion filled the air, along with sweeter scents like lavender and cherry blossom from nearby fields. The show ground was a vast field with dozens of events underway and hundreds of people in traditional Highland dress moving from one activity to the next. Kilts were the norm among all the men, with twenty different tartans on display. Boyle pushed his prisoners towards the ambulance, parked in a corner of the show ground. "Keep moving!"

A group of men was standing in front of the ambulance, arguing amongst themselves. A big, bearded man with flaming red hair loudly berated those around him. "This is a disgrace! For three hundred years our forefathers and their forefathers before them have competed at these Games and won more trophies than they had rooms in which to keep them. Now look at us – a clan with not enough men to enter the competitions, let alone win anything!"

The others shuffled their feet and stared at the grass, too ashamed to reply. Their leader glared at them one by one, his nostrils flaring and his cheeks flushed crimson with indignation. "One more man – that's all we need! One more man who can legitimately wear the tartan of the Douglas clan and then we're in business! Can we not find one more man anywhere?"

The youngest of the Douglas clan noticed the trio approaching the ambulance. He pointed at Dante's legs and laughed. "What about that Jessie in the blouse? Will he do, Tam?"

The clan's leader spun round to see where the lad was pointing. "Aye, he'll do, Alistair, he'll do!" Tam marched across to Dante, followed by all the others. "Welcome, brother! I don't know your face but you're a bonny sight for all of us, right enough!"

"Sorry?" Dante asked.

Tam pointed at Dante's kilt. "You're wearing the Douglas tartan, man!"

Say "Aye!", the Crest prompted.

"Aye!" Dante ventured.

"That makes you one of us, doesn't it lads?"

"Aye!" the Douglas clan members roared in response.

Tam wrapped his arm around Dante's shoulders. "What events are your best, laddie? Throwing the weight? Putting the shot? How about tossing the caber, we could always do with another good tosser, couldn't we lads?"

"Aye!" the others shouted back happily.

"Tossing... That's a public event here?" Dante asked fearfully.

"Of course! Once you've had your hands wrapped round a huge piece of wood, you'll be a changed man," Tam promised.

Dante looked over his shoulder at Boyle. "Perhaps you want my colleague, he's more used to wood handling than me."

Tam snorted derisively. "Don't talk pish! You're the one in the kilt, laddie!" He started dragging Dante away, but Boyle intervened.

"I'm sorry, but this man is unwell. I was taking him and his girlfriend to the ambulance for treatment. I can't let him out of my sight."

"Nonsense! Look at him – he's as right as rain!" Tam nodded towards Penelope. "That lassie's got a nasty cut on her face, that needs seeing to all right, but our man is fighting fit!"

"You go, Nikolai," she said. "I'll be fine."

Boyle searched the crowd in vain for Dobie, then stepped closer to Dante. "I'll send my partner to bring you back. Don't try to escape or else your girlfriend dies – painfully."

"What should I care what happens to her?" Dante replied.

Boyle stared at Dante. "You care. I can see it in your eyes."

The other Douglas men had already marched towards the registration desk and Tam was tugging at Dante's arm. "Come on, man, we have to get you entered or we'll be disqualified!" Dante reluctantly let himself be led away, his eyes still fixed on Boyle and Penelope. The bounty hunter was forced her into the back of the ambulance, a murderous look on his face.

Tam rubbed his fingers against the fabric of Dante's borrowed blouse. "Once you're signed up, we need to find you a better shirt. I hope you don't mind my saying, but this one makes you look soft! Now, what's your name? I missed what your girlfriend called you before."

"Nikolai D–"

"Och, you've no need to tell me your last name, I can see it on your kilt, man!" Tam slapped his meaty hand hard against Dante's back. "Welcome to the clan, Nikolai Douglas!"

TWELVE

"Luck is a stick with two ends."
– Russian proverb

"The Tower of London has been the site for a only a small number of executions, contrary to popular belief. Six prisoners were beheaded on Tower Green, among them three wives of the much married monarch Henry VIII. Another sixteen were shot dead, mostly in the Tower's East Casemates Rifle Range. These included three Black Watch mutineers in 1743, eleven spies during the First World War and a German parachutist during the Second World War. The vast majority of condemned prisoners were taken from their cells to others places in London to be beheaded or hung, drawn and quartered."

– Extract from *The Smirnoff Almanac of Fascinating Facts*, 2673 edition

Dobie opened the back of the ambulance, expecting to see two corpses inside: Dante and Agent Goodnight. Instead he found his scowling partner pointing a gun at the secret service agent. "Don't even ask," Boyle snarled. He jerked a thumb towards the Highland Games going on outside the front window of the ambulance. "Dante's out there somewhere, competing for the Douglas clan. You'll have to find him and bring him back here while I guard this one."

"Why not kill her, then help me look for Dante?" Dobie asked.

"Remember what Rucka said in London? We'll have the entire secret service hunting us to the ends of the earth if we kill her. Dante is our target, not her."

"Inspector Rucka?" Penelope smiled. "Of Scotland Yard? So he hired you two idiots."

Boyle lashed out with his pistol, cracking it against her face. "Shut your mouth, bitch! It may be in our best interests not to kill you, but that doesn't mean you get away unscathed."

She glared at him from the floor of the ambulance. "Keep hitting me like that and you'll be the one getting scathed," she promised.

Dobie stepped in to stop Boyle attacking Penelope. "Leave her, Ray, she's not worth it!"

"I'm worth more than both of you put together," she snapped.

Boyle silenced her with a kick to the stomach, then sent Dobie out in search of Dante. "Beg, steal or borrow a kilt and get yourself entered into the Games. If you can't extract Dante, arrange for him to meet an unfortunate accident. I'll bring the ambulance over and we can get the hell out of this place. Got it? Good, then go!"

Dante marvelled at the Games' bizarre range of sporting contests. An area at one end of the vast field was devoted to conventional track and field events like the sprints, long jump and the hop, step and jump. But the rest of the show ground was devoted to more arcane pursuits. Wrestling was a popular spectator sport, with a crowd of excited women watching men in kilts grapple with each other, their kilts frequently flying above the waist to great cheers of approval. Nearby burly men were attempting to toss a mighty weight over a bar that was being raised progressively higher and higher. Others were throwing a hammer, trying to get it the greatest distance. But the most spectacular of the heavy events was tossing the caber. Each man was given a length of wood that resembled a tree trunk and was expected to throw it through the air.

Now the Douglas men had found sufficient numbers to enter themselves as a group, Tam was quickly showing why he was their leader. His hammer throwing easily won first prize, while he proved a demon at wrestling. But the red-haired hurler overdid it tossing the weight over the bar and came away nursing his back. The other Douglas men winced in sympathy, but none were willing to take his place in the caber tossing. "It's a crying shame," Tam said through gritted teeth. "That's my speciality too!"

Dante turned away from him. "Crest, are all my enhanced abilities back at full strength?"

Yes, but that doesn't mean–

"I'll toss the caber!" Dante shouted.

The others looked at him as if he were mad, but Tam smiled and nodded. "I knew you were something special laddie, the first time I saw you!"

When he says special, do you think he means mentally impaired?

Dante strode into the open space where the caber was being tossed. So far, few competitors had managed to lift the six-metre-long wooden pole, let along throw it any distance. A judge asked for his name. "Nikolai Dan– Douglas! Nikolai Douglas!"

"Next to toss the caber is Nikolai Douglas," a loudspeaker announced to the rest of the show ground. "This year the caber weighs more than sixty kilograms, a record for these Games!"

Fortunately for Dante, the caber was already standing on one end, held in place by several organisers. He crouched beside the tall length of wood, making a great show of preparatory puffing and panting to mask a conversation with the Crest. "How do I actually toss this thing?"

You volunteered for this and you don't even know how to take part?

"I didn't want to let the Douglas clan down," Dante said with a shrug.

Of course not. Very well. First, you lift the pole with a swift movement into a vertical position. Dante dug his fingers underneath the caber. *Try not to open your legs too wide while crouching,* the Crest suggested. *You may be dressed like a true Scotsman beneath the kilt, but you haven't got a sporran to protect your modesty.*

Dante glanced across the field and noticed a cluster of young women pointing at him and laughing. "Bojemoi!" he muttered. "As if I haven't got enough to think about." With a mighty grunt he pushed up from the ground, lifting the caber into the air.

Good. Now you start running forwards.

"You've got to be kidding me."

You volunteered for this, remember? You start running forwards...

Dante did as the Crest urged, slowly putting one foot in front of the other until he gradually picked up speed. "Okay, now what?" he gasped between gulps of air.

Evasive action!

"What do you mean, evasive action?" Dante snapped, still running with one end of the caber balanced in his hands, the other end pointing into the sky. "Is that part of the event?"

One of the bounty hunters is on the other side of the field, aiming a gun at you!

By this point Dante was close to the far side of the area cleared for the caber tossing. "Crest, I'm running out of room! When do I toss this bloody tree trunk?"

Sorry, it said apologetically. *I was distracted by the imminent threat to your life. Pardon me for trying to keep you from being shot.*

"Crest!" Dante bellowed. Ahead of him he could see Dobie standing apart from the rest of the laughing spectators, taking aim with a silenced pistol.

You're meant to stop dead and hurl the caber upwards.

Dante did as he was told, launching the mighty pole into the air. It turned over three times before plummeting back down towards the spot where Dobie was standing. The rest of the crowd had already dived out of the way, but the bounty hunter was slow to realise his danger. He dived out of the way with moments to spare, his weapon falling to the ground. The caber slammed into the earth, crushing the pistol beneath it. The judges ran forward with a measuring tape to see how far Dante had tossed, while Dobie melted away into the crowds. Within a minute the show ground's public address system crackled into life. "Ladies and gentlemen, we have a new Games record! Nikolai Douglas has tossed the caber twelve metres further than anyone ever before! Can we have a big round of applause for Nikolai Douglas of the Clan Douglas!"

Having impressed the crowds with his record-breaking efforts with the caber, Dante found himself in demand for all manner of events afterwards. Every time he tried to make his way back to the ambulance, another group would grab his hand and drag him away to a different area of the show ground. He was a useful addition to the Douglas men in the tug of war, helping them reach the semi-final before they were eliminated, but was worse than useless when dragged into dancing a reel with three sprightly youths. Dante staggered off the raised dais where the dancing events were taking place and walked straight into Dobie. The bounty hunter was dressed in a red tartan kilt and was clutching a long sword in each hand. "Going native, are you?"

"You may have buried my gun but I don't need it to finish you off," Dobie snarled. "These ceremonial sabres will do the job just as well!"

Dante smiled as the purple and silver cyborganics extruded bio-blades from his fists. He crossed them in front of his face, raising an eyebrow at the bounty hunter. "You were saying?" The two men circled round each other, searching for an opening.

But before either of them could strike, an adjudicator on the dancing stage saw what they were doing and commandeered the public address system. "Ladies and gentlemen, it seems we have a treat in store. Two of our male competitors are volunteering to perform a Gillie Chaluim!" The crowd gave a collective gasp, everyone nearby looking round to see who the announcer was talking about. "That's right, a Gillie Chaluim! And unless I'm much mistaken, it looks like one of our volunteers is Nikolai Douglas!" Dante and Dobie stopped circling each other and looked up at the dais. The adjudicator gestured for them to come up on stage. "Come on, now, don't be shy!" she called out. "Everybody, give these brave boys a round of applause!"

People left nearby events to join the crowd around the dais, all of them clapping wildly and shouting their approval. In less than a minute more than a hundred spectators were gathered to watch. Dante could see Tam among those joining the throng. "Good on you, son!" the red-haired man shouted over the cacophony. "But you be careful, you hear?"

The adjudicator waved for Dobie and Dante to join her on stage. "Come on," she urged. Trapped by the surging crowd around them, the pair had little choice but to do as she said.

"Try to escape and I promise you a long, slow, painful death," Dobie said into Dante's ear as they climbed up on to the dais. Meanwhile the crowd was shouting, clapping and stomping their approval of this new development.

"Crest," Dante whispered. "What the hell is a jilly charloom?"

I was wondering when you'd ask. A Gillie Chaluim is the oldest of the Highland dances, said to date back to the time of King Malcolm Canmore in the Eleventh Century. After defeating an enemy in battle, the king would lay his sword over that of his adversary in the sign of the cross and execute a dance of victory. The Gillie Chaluim was an exclusively male dance at first, but later it was kept alive by women and particularly young girls. The object was to dance with the feet as close as possible to the swords without ever touching the blades.

"That doesn't sound too bad," Dante said. "From the way it was announced, you'd think we had to dance each other to death."

Funny you should say that. The Gillie Chaluim was outlawed thirty years ago after the name became associated with an altogether more dangerous form of dancing. Men reclaimed the name and used it for a duelling dance where each combatant wields a pair of swords.

"Let me guess – it was made illegal because so many people get hurt?"

Because so many people died, Dante. The winner is usually declared when one of the dancers draws the blood of his adversary. But at its most savage, the Gillie Chaluim is a dance to the death where neither opponent puts down his sword until the other man falls.

The adjudicator called for silence from the hundreds now gathered around the stage. "Ladies and gentlemen, quiet, please! If there are any children present, they must be taken away now – the Gillie Chaluim is not to be witnessed by anyone under eighteen." There were disappointed cries from children clustered at the front of the crowd as parents dragged them away. Meanwhile the adjudicator approached Dante and Dobie. "Well, how far are you gentlemen wiling to go? Will first blood be enough to satisfy honour?"

"That sounds good to–" Dante began.

"To the death!" Dobie interjected. "We fight to the death!"

"You dance to the death," the adjudicator corrected him.

"I dance," the bounty hunter spat, then pointed at Dante. "He dies!"

The crowd overheard this interchange, shocked whispers passing through the throng. "Did you hear that, hen? They're dancing to the death!"

The adjudicator looked both men in the eye. "Are you both agreed on this? Your decision must be unanimous or else the Gillie Chaluim cannot go ahead."

"Well?" Dobie asked his target. "Have you got the guts for this?"

Dante sighed and nodded. "We dance to the death."

"Very well," the adjudicator agreed, then announced their decision to the crowd. A thrill of excitement passed through the people thronged around the stage. The adjudicator made the sign of the cross, then rested a hand on both men's shoulders. "May God have mercy on your souls." She climbed down from the dais, leaving the two enemies surrounded by a thousand people.

"How do I get myself in these situations?" Dante wondered out loud.

Stupidity and stubbornness usually do the trick, the Crest replied.

Inside the ambulance Boyle was getting restless. "What's taking Dobie so long?"

"Finding Dante will not be easy," Penelope said. "He's a master of disguise, able to blend into any crowd and simply disappear. If he is still here, your partner could walk right past him and never even notice. But Dante's got no reason to stick around. Best guess? He'll be a hundred kilometres away from here by now. You'll never find him." She paused, savouring the pained expression on her captor's face. "I'm sorry, was that a rhetorical question?"

Boyle grabbed the front of her catsuit and wrenched Penelope towards him until their faces were almost touching. "Shut your mouth, or else I'll take great pleasure in smashing your teeth down your throat, one by one," he snarled.

"You have the most amazing eyes," she said softly. "A shade of a blue like I haven't seen outside the Mediterranean, flecked with white like shards of ice. A person could lose themselves in those eyes, Ray." She stroked the side of his face tenderly, softly caressing the bruised cheekbones and taut, angry mouth. "Someone hurt you once, I can see in your eyes, the set of your mouth. Someone hurt you and you swore you'd never be hurt again. I could take the pain away, I could kiss it all better." She moved closer, her lips hovering over his, her eyes staring into his, her breasts pressing against his chest. "Let me make it better, Ray..."

He reached a hand up to Penelope's face and shoved her backwards across the ambulance, so her skull smacked against the wall. "Get away from me, you bitch!"

She shrugged while rubbing the back of her head. "Well, you can't blame a girl for trying."

"I can," Boyle warned, aiming his pistol at Penelope's face. "I don't care what Rucka says. Try one more stunt like that and I'll bury your corpse where they can never find it. You won't be dead, just missing in action – one more secret agent who disappeared in the line of duty."

Dobie attacked first, a crude lunge with the sword in his left hand that Dante easily eluded. But the bounty hunter's attempt was merely a feint, drawing his opponent off balance. While his left sword was still in motion, Dobie pivoted on one heel and whipped his other sword through the air. The blade cut through shirt fabric and sliced to the bone, the metal edge gouging into two ribs. Dante cried out in pain, a crimson stain spreading down his left side.

"First blood to me," Dobie crowed. He took a step back and licked the blade clean with his tongue. "It's said the first cut is the deepest – but I promise my last cut will hurt the most."

"Come and have a go if you think you're hard enough," Dante replied. When Dobie stepped in for another attack Dante's bio-blades cut his opponent's shirt into rags, leaving two livid cuts in opposite directions across Dobie's chest. "X marks the spot," Dante said. "That's where I'll bury my blade when I kill you."

"Promises, promises," Dobie smiled. He bowed to Dante, then struck a pose with his two swords. "Enough of the preliminaries. Let battle commence!" Dobie hurled himself at Dante, who danced aside, spinning through the air in a graceful pirouette. The bounty hunter went high with both his blades, but Dante ducked under them. When Dobie went low, his opponent jumped over the top of both swords. "Stand still, damn you!"

"This is meant to be a sword dance, not a sword fight," Dante smirked. "Can I help it if you're not much of a dancer?" He attempted a few dance steps of his own and tripped over his own feet, landing clumsily on his behind.

The bounty hunter laughed, his blades drawn back for the kill. "You were saying?" But when he attacked, Dante rolled aside. Another attack and Dante rolled the other way, narrowly avoiding being impaled. On the third time his luck ran out and Dobie stabbed a sword clear through Dante's stomach so the tip was buried in the wooden dais. The crowd gasped in horror, their new found favourite pinned to the stage, his blood forming a scarlet pool underneath him.

Dobie took a step back, savouring his triumph. "And now, for my next trick..." he announced, turning in a slow circle to look at the audience round the stage, ten-deep in places.

Suddenly Dante rammed his left bio-blade through Dobie's back so far the front half emerged from the bounty hunter's chest. "How do you like your wounds?" Dante said, his teeth flecked with blood. "Straight up?"

He wrenched the blade round through ninety degrees, bringing a scream of pain from his opponent. "Or with a twist?" Dante ripped his bio-blade back out of Dobie's back and walked round so the bounty hunter could see his sword was still wedged through Dante's body. The bounty hunter collapsed to his knees, disbelief clouding his eyes. He tried to swipe his remaining blade at Dante but it fell uselessly to the floor, along with Dobie's neatly severed right hand. The crowd was chanting, baying for blood.

Dante slowly, painfully pulled the sword out of his stomach then let it drop to stage. The dais was awash with blood spilling from his wounds and those of Dobie. The bounty hunter's face was ashen, the knowledge that death was upon him all too obvious. "Please," he gasped, his breath a series of short, wet wheezing sounds. "Don't let me bleed to death."

Dante drew back one of his bio-blades, ready to finish Dobie off, urged on by the crowd around him. Instead he paused and looked up at the sky, studying the clouds as they floated lazily overhead. "Enough," he murmured to himself and turned away.

The crowd booed and jeered, but Dante paid them no heed as he stumbled down the steps to the grass, his knees almost buckling beneath him. Tam was waiting for him, the burly redhead slipping Dante's right arm over his shoulders. "Come on, laddie! You've done the Douglas tartan proud today. I'll see you to that ambulance, get you cleaned up."

On the dais Dobie fell face first into his own blood, splashing those nearest. He gasped a few more times, then made no further sound, his eyes staring lifelessly at nothing.

Flintlock woke to find a dozen guards standing over him. "Spatch, old boy, I think we've got company." The two prisoners were still being kept in the ground floor room looking out on the Tower of London's courtyard, where Princess Marie-Anne had visited them the previous day. By now the air was ripe with the stench of Spatchcock's all-pervasive body odour.

"I had nothing to do with it," Spatchcock mumbled as his eyes opened.

"You say that every time you wake up," Flintlock sighed.

"It's a defence mechanism." He stretched and yawned, then counted the heavily armed sentries filling the room. "All twelve of you to look after the two of us? Isn't that overkill?"

"I'd prefer if you refrained from using words like that," Flintlock whispered.

Spatchcock shrugged, then shifted his attention back to the guards. "I was beginning to think you had forgotten all about us." The sentries remained silent, their faces impassive, weapons aimed at the two prisoners. "Talkative bunch, aren't they?"

"You'll have to forgive them their silence," a man replied from the doorway. He paused to light a pipe, its pungent smoke quickly spreading through the confined space, then made his way through the armed guards. The new arrival had a thoughtful face with piercing eyes, and receding ginger hair. He sucked on his pipe, smiling contentedly. "They are trained not to speak unless given permission by a superior officer or authority figure."

"I'm guessing we don't qualify," Flintlock ventured.

"You guess correctly," the man said. "My name is Rucka, Rucka of Scotland Yard."

Spatchcock grinned wolfishly. "Rucka? That rhymes with mother–"

"Thank you," the inspector cut in. "I'm quite aware of what my name rhymes with."

"Some people have got no sense of humour," Spatchcock complained.

"And other people struggle to elevate their sense of humour from the gutter," Rucka replied. "I can see why Dante chose you two as his accomplices. Both of you are as vile and base as him, a pair of repellent creatures without moral fibre or character."

"I must object," Flintlock spluttered angrily. "This guttersnipe is in no way my equal!"

"You can say that again," Spatchcock agreed. "I've got much more class than you."

"Both of you are as bad as each other," the inspector sneered. "The Raven Corps was kind enough to send me its files on your criminal careers. Spatchcock, your past is littered with sufficient convictions to have you incarcerated for a thousand years – forgery, poisoning and all manner of other felonies."

"Well, I don't like to brag," Spatchcock said with a smile.

"Then there's Lord Peter Flintlock, a man whose youthful exploits were so disgusting, so repulsive, the government of Britannia had no choice but to deport him." Rucka shuddered. "It makes my flesh crawl merely thinking of what you did."

"Both Spatchcock and I have paid for our past crimes," Flintlock replied primly. "Our trespasses were forgiven, in exchange for agreeing to fight with the Rudinshtein Irregulars."

"Where you formed your current partnership in crime with Dante," Rucka pointed out. "Hardly a ringing endorsement for whomever authorised your amnesty."

"What did his lordship do exactly that got him ejected from his own country?" Spatchcock asked. "I've heard how terrible it was, but nobody will ever tell me the specifics..."

The inspector shook his head. "Nor will you learn them from me. I would not sully my mouth by having to speak aloud a description of what your fellow traveller did to deserve deportation. It is enough for you to know his crimes are as bad as anything you've ever done."

Spatchcock looked at Flintlock with a new admiration. "You dirty dog! I never knew you had it in you!"

Flintlock refused to meet his eye, preferring to glare at Rucka. "When the time comes for our execution, I nominate Spatchcock to go first."

"That will not be an option," Rucka replied.

"We've been given a stay of execution?" Flintlock asked hopefully.

"No, you will be executed simultaneously. I've been sent here to keep an eye on you until midday tomorrow. Then you will be transported to the place of execution to await the arrival of her royal highness, Princess Marie-Anne. She seems certain Dante will launch some sort of rescue attempt between now and the moment of your deaths, so I volunteered to maintain a vigil over you both until then. In days gone by I believe this task was known as the death watch."

"Charming," Spatchcock commented. "How long have we got left?"

"Until you die?"

"No, until the summer sales open," he replied sarcastically.

Rucka consulted a pocket watch. "You will be executed in twenty-seven hours."

Spatchcock broke wind loudly. A noxious gas wafted round the room. "Sorry," he said insincerely. "I do that when I get nervous. Expect a lot of that in the next twenty-seven hours."

"I doubt either of us will last that long," Flintlock said despairingly. "Between the biological weapon that is your arse and the fumes coming from his pipe, we'll undoubtedly suffocate first."

By the time he had reached the ambulance, Dante's wounds were already healing themselves. Tam reacted with amazement when he saw the small scars where several brutal incisions had been. "Laddie, that's impossible! You must have the devil on your side!"

"Not exactly," Dante winced, "but enhanced healing abilities can do wonders."

"I'll say!" Tam marvelled. "What was your argument with the man on that stage?"

"Better if you don't get involved." Dante took his hand off Tam's shoulder and shook the Douglas clan leader's hand. "Thank you for all your help."

"No, laddie, thank you! I don't know what we'd have done without you today – they'll be talking about that caber toss for years to come!" Tam shook his head, already marvelling at the memory of it. Beyond him the Games were breaking up, the final events finished and everyone was slowly filing out of the Peebles show ground. "You did us proud, Nikolai Dante!"

"You're welcome. I..." Dante stopped, realising what Tam had said. "You know who I am?"

"Of course! I ken your face from the news, laddie. Most folk round here don't bother with what happens south of the border, but I like to know what's happening in the rest of the world."

"You weren't afraid of having the man who tried to kill the king on your team?"

"Och, no! You'd have been doing us all a favour if you'd pulled it off. The Windsor McKrays are a disgrace, no two ways about it. The sooner we restore Caledonia's own monarchy the better! The day is coming, young Nikolai, you mark my words." Tam shook Dante's hand vigorously while slapping him on the arm. "If ever you need any help, let me know. Ask anyone in the town, they'll tell you where to find me." Tam marched away, laughing to himself.

"Half the country wants to kill me for something I didn't do, the other half wants to congratulate me – bizarre." A whistle sounded in the distance, prompting a surge of movement from those queuing to get out of the show ground. "What was that?"

The Flying Scotsman, *signalling it is getting ready to leave.*

"Diavolo! How long?"

Five minutes at most.

Boyle glanced at his watch. Dobie should have been back hours ago, what was taking him so long? The bounty hunter's eyes narrowed as he glanced at Penelope on the opposite side of the vehicle. Maybe the bitch was right, maybe I did read Dante wrong and he fled the moment we got inside the ambulance. No, I don't believe that, Boyle told himself. I could see the look in his eyes, the same look I've seen in the mirror every morning since hooking up with Dobie. Dante cares about her the way I care about my partner. He wouldn't abandon her.

Boyle's thoughts were thrown askew by the back doors of the ambulance flying open. He spun round, his pistol raised and ready to fire – but there was nobody there. "Dobie, is that you? If you're playing silly buggers out there I'll give you the thrashing of your life!"

"Promises, promises," Dante's voice replied.

"You!" Boyle said. He leaned from one side to the other, trying to catch a glimpse of his quarry, but all he could see were the citizens of Peebles walking away from the show ground. "Where's Dobie? What have you done with him?"

"Your partner had an unfortunate accident," Dante said in a sing-song voice. "He cut himself shaving and bled to death."

"You're lying!"

"Am I? How can you be sure? Your boyfriend was good, but I'm better, much better."

Boyle screamed a curse at the wind. Somehow, in his gut, he knew Dante was telling the truth: Dobie was dead and that Romanov bastard had killed him. "Damn you – come out and face me like a man!"

"I'm not sure I'm your type," Dante taunted him. "Then again, I'm not sure you were Dobie's type either.

He never mentioned you when he was dying, not once."

Boyle could feel an uncontrollable rage boiling inside. He fought to control the fury, to own it, knowing his emotions had the power to destroy him. Attack is the best form of defence, he thought. Make the bastard show himself, that was the only way. Boyle lurched across the ambulance and grabbed Penelope by the hair, dragging her across to him. "I've got your girlfriend here, Dante. She's very pretty, isn't she? She wouldn't be so pretty if I blew her face off."

"I told you before, Boyle – I don't care what happens to her."

"You're lying, I can hear it in your voice. Show yourself or say goodbye to her face!"

A long, protracted silence followed.

"Well?" Boyle demanded. "I'll give you three seconds to show yourself. One!"

Still no sound or movement came from outside.

"Two!" Boyle could feel Penelope's heart pounding beneath his left hand, while his right hand pressed the pistol hard into the side of her head.

A whistle cried plaintively in the distance, followed by the sound of a train getting rolling, slowly picking up speed.

"Three!" But it wasn't Boyle who finished the countdown – it was Penelope. She flung her head back into Boyle's face, breaking the bones in his nose.

As he screamed in pain, Penelope threw herself from the ambulance, rolling away on the grass outside. At the same moment a flash of purple and silver stabbed through the wall nearest Boyle, slicing off his right hand in a single movement. Blood sprayed from the severed limb, changing the air inside the vehicle to a fine pink aerosol. Boyle sobbed in anguish, his left hand uselessly trying to staunch the bleeding from the stump where his right had been.

The bio-blade was withdrawn as quickly as it had penetrated. Within seconds Dante was inside the ambulance, picking up Boyle's discarded pistol. The bounty hunter slumped to the floor, his face a mask of pain. "You'll pay for this, you bastard," he vowed.

"I doubt it," Dante said, shooting Boyle through both kneecaps. "That should slow you down." He climbed back out of the ambulance and helped Penelope to her feet. "Are you all right?"

She nodded, rubbing the back of her head. "I'll be fine, but we've missed the train."

"I know. We'll have to find another way of getting to Orkney."

"What about me?" Boyle demanded. "Why don't you finish me off, you coward?"

Dante shrugged. "I'm not a murderer. I kill to defend myself, but I don't enjoy it – not like you." He contemplated the ambulance. "We could take this, it's got hover-capacity."

Penelope grimaced at the vehicle's blood-soaked interior. "It'll stink worse than a slaughterhouse by the time we reach the island. Let's find something else."

The two of them walked away, leaving Boyle a broken, bleeding mess in the back of the ambulance.

"Orkney is an island?" Dante asked Penelope

"Of course. Didn't you know that?"

"Local geography is not exactly my strongest area."

"There's a whole group of islands, more than seventy of them. Orkney, Hoy, Rousay–"

"Hoy!" Dante exclaimed, stopping abruptly. "That was the name I heard the bald man with the goatee say on Westminster Bridge! He was meeting someone soon and they would see with the old man at Hoy. At least, that's what it sounded like."

"He meant the Old Man of Hoy," Penelope realised. "It's a tourist attraction, quite a famous one. If that is the rendezvous point for our target, we've got to get there first, but how?"

Dante smiled. "I know someone here who owes me a favour."

THIRTEEN

"Pointless to pray when you sin without measure."
– Russian proverb

"The Old Man of Hoy is a legend among climbers. This sandstone rock stack rises more than a hundred metres from the sea, on the eastern tip of the island Hoy, north of Britannia. To the untrained eye it best resembles a rough hewn finger of rock, pointing at the sky. The top of the stack is almost exactly level with the nearby cliffs. For centuries climbers have travelled to this remote island solely to tackle this tricky ascent. An entire tourist industry has built up around the Old Man. Weather permitting, this iconic stack is ascended almost daily during summer."
– Extract from *The Duffer's Guide to Britannia*, 2670 edition

"I never normally get sea sick," Dante whispered, apologising between retches over the side of the ferry. The old wooden vessel was bouncing about on rough water between Orkney and Hoy, pitching from side to side in the heavy swell. "I mean, I grew up onboard a pirate ship, never threw up once. But this..." He unleashed another mouthful of green bile into the churning, restless sea.

"You should have had one of my anti-nausea pills," Penelope commented.

The ferry lurched as it plunged down one side of a mighty wave, then swayed back again as the next wave rose underneath it. Dante swallowed hard but couldn't stop another surge from his unhappy stomach. He retched the results over the nearest railing, then wiped the flecks of vomit from his mouth. "This has to settle down eventually, doesn't it?"

"Let's hope so," Penelope agreed. "You'll be useless on Hoy if you can't stop throwing up."

Seventeen hours had passed since they had left Boyle bleeding to death in the ambulance at Peebles. They had headed for the nearest tavern where Dante asked for Tam Douglas. Three taverns later they found him. He was more than happy to help the saviour of the Douglas clan's honour, but could only offer them ground-based vehicles. Hover-capability was reserved for royalty, the emergency services and visiting tourists in Caledonia. "It's all part of a plot by those holding power in London to stop us reclaiming our rightful place in the sky!"

Dante and Penelope decided against going back for the ambulance, choosing to drive through the night in a borrowed school bus to the north of Caledonia, taking turns behind the wheel. They reached the docks at a desolate place called Scrabster as the sun rose on Saturday. Penelope bought anti-nausea pills from an apothecary's stall at the docks while they waited to catch the first ferry to Orkney. "I'd rather die than get on a boat without these," she admitted.

Once on Orkney, Dante and Penelope raced to the train station, but the *Flying Scotsman*'s passengers had long since disembarked to explore the surrounding islands. Penelope changed clothes in her compartment while Dante searched for Gordonstoun. The head steward was persuaded by having a bio-blade pressed against his throat. Dante described the man he had been stalking since London. "That sounds like Mr Marius Wilderhaber, a Swiss gentleman," Gordonstoun said. "He asked me for directions to Hoy, I think he is meeting friends there later today. I told him the easiest way of getting there was the hover-bus."

"What time does that leave?"

"It already has," the steward had replied with a grim smile of satisfaction. "The next one doesn't leave until Monday. Of course, you could catch the ferry to Hoy, that sails in half and hour – but the seas are very rough today. They might cancel it altogether."

Dante ran to Penelope's compartment and burst inside. "We've got to hurry. The–"

"Do you mind?" She was standing naked in the centre of the room.

"Not at all," he replied, a sly grin on his face. A torrent of obscene and abusive suggestions drove him back out into the corridor. Bojemoi, they had seen each other in far more compromising positions than that before – what was her problem?

When will you learn? There is a time and a place for what you laughingly consider a romantic overture, Dante. That was neither.

Three minutes later Penelope had emerged from her compartment in a fresh black catsuit, zipping it all the way up to her throat. She had a pistol strapped to each thigh in black leather holsters and offered a similar weapon to Dante. "I'll stick with my bio-blades," he said. "I'm not much use with a gun unless it's my Huntsman 5000 rifle, and it's still at the Palace of London."

The pair had caught the ferry to Hoy with minutes to spare. Now, after an hour of being thrown about on the stormy seas, the rocky island loomed ahead of them. Bitterly cold winds sliced at the two travellers, threatening to freeze them where they stood.

Dante wished he had got changed while they were still on the train. His shirt was stained by blood, sweat and now vomit, while keeping his kilt down in these snapping breezes was proving problematic. More embarrassing was the effect of all this cold air blowing beneath his kilt, shrinking a much-loved part of his anatomy to the size of a cocktail sausage.

The ferry made its way to dock with agonising slowness, greasy black engine fumes fighting the brisk sea air for supremacy. Once the vessel was within two metres of the jetty Dante and Penelope jumped ashore, ignoring warnings from the crew. The pair ran towards dry land, searching for information. The hover-bus was parked on a landing pad nearby, some passengers from the *Flying Scotsman* still milling around. "We're lucky," Penelope said. "The pilot must have given them a sightseeing flight round the island before landing." It was Dante who spotted the elusive Wilderhaber. "There!" The bald man was ascending a vertiginous staircase up a nearby cliff. At the bottom a sign bore the words "OLD MAN OF HOY 10 KM".

As the pair watched, Wilderhaber reached the top of the cliff and disappeared inland. Dante sprinted towards the steps, Penelope close behind. "We can still catch him!"

Marius Wilderhaber was running scared. For days he had been unsettled and uneasy, as if something terrible was waiting to happen. His leisurely sightseeing trip up Britannia had passed without incident, yet Marius could not shake a feeling of impending doom, as if everything he saw and did was merely the calm before the storm. Perhaps it stemmed from his failure in London. Yes, the target he had been given was ambitious, but not unattainable. The results were disappointing. He hit his secondary target but the main one had escaped. The man from Basel was not looking forward to explaining his failure.

Marius had been haunted by his failure ever since, but that wasn't the only thing haunting him. Time and again he had felt as though someone was watching him. The first occasion had been on Westminster Bridge. Marius had been on the phone, arranging the rendezvous with his employer. For a moment the Swiss visitor thought he had seen a figure floating in the Thames. His unease had grown after boarding the *Flying Scotsman* in London the next day. Nobody knew how Marius was travelling north to the rendezvous, not even his employer, yet he felt certain someone was staring at him in the dining car that first evening on the train. The same thing happened on Thursday, when everyone got off at Nottingham for day-trips. When Marius dutifully lined up to see the castle, he could not shake the sensation of being observed, as if unseen eyes were watching him. The feeling grew in Peebles yesterday, when they disembarked to watch the Highland Games. Marius's fears had eased after the *Flying Scotsman* departed the border town for a night of feasting and festivities at Stirling Castle. He searched the other passengers' eyes but none of them paid him any attention. With the rendezvous getting ever closer, Marius had let himself relax. The train arrived at Orkney without incident and he caught the hover-bus unmolested, his confidence returning at last. He was nearly home, he was nearly safe.

Marius decided to hike across the island to see the Old Man of Hoy. There were no shortage of local hover-cabs offering to transport passengers there in a fraction of the time the journey would take on foot. But Marius wanted to savour one last trip in his own company, away from the crowds that had hampered his enjoyment of the train journey. Now he was regretting that decision, more than any other choice he had made in Britannia. Two people were stalking him along the windswept path across the island, slowly gaining on him. Every time he looked back, they were closer than before

He risked another glance over his shoulder and froze. I know those two, he realised. The woman had been one of the passengers, blending in with the others, not drawing attention to herself. But the man, that was another matter. He was dressed like one of the stewards in a kilt and white shirt, but his face was all too familiar... Marius gasped as recognition shook him to the core. It was the man he had seen floating in the Thames! The same man who had glared at him in the dining car, who had lingered at the corner of Marius's thoughts and nightmares since London. *He's found me again and now he's hunting me!*

Marius Wilderhaber started running.

"Bojemoi, he's running! The bastard must have realised we were following him!" Dante sprinted after Wilderhaber, Penelope close behind.

"It was inevitable," she shouted after Dante. "This path is so exposed, there's no way he could fail to see us tracking him."

The pair ran through a shallow pool of stagnant water. A cloud of tiny black insects rose from the surface, engulfing them. Dante felt a burning sensation beneath his kilt. He lifted the fabric and saw his groin was covered with minute creatures. "What are these things, Crest?"

Midges – a mosquito-like dipterous insect occurring in dancing swarms, especially near water. They are fond of feasting on human blood by piercing the skin with their mouths and sucking out the desired liquid. Each bite encourages the victim to scratch at the wound, creating irritation and swelling far greater in magnitude than size of the midge.

Dante slapped at his crotch, trying to shift the swarm. "Fuoco, it feels as though I'm being eaten alive!"

"Leave them!" Penelope yelled, dragging him after Wilderhaber. "The more you scratch, the more they itch!"

"Easy for you to say, you're not having your life blood sucked out of your testicles!"

Wilderhaber was breathless and exhausted when he reached the eastern tip of the island. He collapsed by the edge of the cliff, his breath rasping and a metallic taste in his mouth. Close by, the Old Man of Hoy rose from the incoming tide, perhaps ten metres between it and the main part of the island. Wilderhaber peered gingerly over the edge of the cliff, but couldn't see any climbers on the sandstone stack. No witnesses who might intervene, no sign of his employer arriving to extract him. He was on his own, not even a rock nearby with which to defend himself.

The two people that had chased him across the island appeared over the brow of the nearest hill, slowing as they realised there was nowhere left to run. This was it, the end of the line. "What do you want of me?" Wilderhaber asked between gasps for breath. "Money? Do you want money?" He reached in his pocket and pulled out an Imperial Express card. "Here, take it! I'll give you my account code – just, please, don't kill me!"

The woman drew one of her pistols and took aim at Wilderhaber. "Why did you do it?"

"Do what?" he protested. "I don't know what you're asking me!"

"Tell us about the target," the other hunter demanded, one hand rubbing urgently at his groin. "Who chose the target?"

"My employer," Wilderhaber said, shrugging helplessly. "They call me, send me to a different country each time. I only find out my target after I arrive."

The woman stepped closer until she was metres away. "Who's your employer? Who paid for this job?"

"The vice president."

"Of which country?" she snarled.

Wilderhaber frowned. "H-He's vice president of a company, not a country. He works for EuroCorp, the food conglomerate."

Now it was the woman who looked confused. "Why would EuroCorp want the king dead?"

"Sorry?"

The kilted man stopped scratching his crotch and pointed a fist at Wilderhaber. A silver sword extruded from his hand, its tip nearly touching the Swiss man's face. "Why would a food company try to assassinate King Henry? What would it gain from his death?"

"I don't know what you're talking about," Wilderhaber protested. "I was sent here to buy the Britannia Food Corporation, along with its distribution network – that was my target. I secured the network but could only secure one third ownership of BFC."

The woman lowered her pistol, swearing quietly. "Nikolai, he's not the assassin."

"He must be!" her partner insisted. "I didn't chase him all this way for nothing!" The man jabbed his sword closer, the tip digging into Wilderhaber's neck, blood trickling from the wound. "Tell me the truth – otherwise I'll cut out your larynx and you'll never lie again!"

"I *am* telling you the truth!" the tourist insisted, close to tears. "I could never kill another living soul. I'm a businessman, nothing more – please, you must believe me!"

"Crest, can you analyse his heartbeat, detect whether or not he's lying?

Wilderhaber listened but heard no reply. To his amazement, the man in the kilt withdrew his sword and stepped away, cursing repeatedly.

"We came all this way for nothing," the woman sighed. "Now what, Dante? Your friends will be executed in a few hours and both of us are still wanted for a murder we didn't commit."

"Dante? Nikolai Dante?" Wilderhaber asked.

"You've heard of me?"

"Of course, you're the most wanted man in the Empire. Besides, your name has been all over the news for days. They said you tried to kill the king."

"No, I didn't!" Dante insisted angrily. "When will I find somebody who believes me?"

"I believe you," the woman replied, "for all the good it's doing us."

"I also believe you," Wilderhaber said, slowly rising from the ground.

"Why?" Dante asked.

"I heard about the assassination after my final meeting with BFC broke up on Tuesday. I was depressed, I went for a walk. I found myself on Westminster Bridge not long after dusk."

"I *knew* I'd seen you there," Dante said triumphantly.

"Let him talk," the woman replied. "What did you see, Marius?"

"Not much, to be honest. There was a mist rising from the river. As I got near the bridge I heard what sounded like a man crying out in pain, then a splash."

"The sniper's accomplice knocking me out, then probably both of them throwing me into the river," Dante said with a nod. "What next?"

"Two men were talking on the bridge. They had London accents, gruff voices. I couldn't see their faces, they were on the other side of the bridge."

"Could you hear what they said?" the woman asked. "Did either of them mention a name?"

Wilderhaber shook his head. "My employer called, wanting to know the outcome of my final meeting with BFC. When I told him what happened, he suggested I take a few days off, see the country if I wanted. I arranged to be collected from here later today. By the time I finished my call, the two men had gone."

"Another dead end," Dante said hopelessly. But his partner had other ideas.

"Nikolai, you told me a hover-car caught Marius in its headlights – that's how you were able to recognise him as the man on the bridge." She turned to Wilderhaber. "Did you notice the car, see its identity plate?"

He nodded uncertainly. "I did see a hover-vehicle, but nothing I could identify easily."

"What about a colour? Even that would be a start," Dante urged.

"A kind of brown," Wilderhaber ventured. "It looked old but well loved."

Dante stopped talking, his head tilting to one side. "The Crest says there's something coming, a hover-capable vehicle of some sort."

The Swiss man frowned. "It could be my employer's driver come to collect me, but they are not due for another hour at least." The sound of hover-engines rose from beneath the cliff. Wilderhaber moved closer to the edge for a better look. "No, it isn't them. It looks like–"

"Marius – get down!" Dante suddenly shouted, flinging himself towards the tourist.

"An ambulance," Wilderhaber said. He felt two dull thuds in the centre of his chest, then his legs crumpled, pitching him over the edge of the cliff. He would have been terrified, but the Swiss businessman was dead before he hit the jagged rocks below.

"Diavolo!" Dante cursed, his fingers grasping at thin air where Marius had been standing. A hover-ambulance appeared from below the cliff, the same vehicle Dante and Penelope had decided against using at Peebles. Boyle was seated in the pilot's chair, a maniacal grin stretched across his bruised and battered face. The ambulance was side-on to the cliff so the bounty hunter could fire his pistol out of the window at them. He loosed off a fusillade of shots, each bullet smacking the ground ever closer to Dante's precarious position, driving the fugitive nearer the precipice. Boyle's voice boomed at them from the vehicle's public address system. "A piece of advice for the future: if you're going to leave someone to die, don't do it in the back of an ambulance."

"Who says you have a future?" Penelope shouted, opening fire with both her pistols. The rounds smacked into the side of the ambulance, but none penetrated the pilot's door.

Boyle flew his vehicle over the fugitives and came down behind them, cutting off their only escape route. "You should have killed me when you had the chance, like I should have killed you on that bridge. Now I'll make you pay for murdering Dobie."

Dante and Penelope dived to the ground, trying to take cover amidst the rocks and moss. Dante felt naked without a gun in his hands. Bio-blades were fine for close quarters combat, but no use against other threats. What he wouldn't give to have the Huntsman 5000 in his grasp now. "Penelope! Throw me your spare pistol!"

She was trying to shoot Boyle through his windscreen, but her rounds were bouncing off. "What genius put bulletproof glass in an ambulance?" she protested, tossing her other weapon towards Dante. He reached up to grab it from the air but another hail of bullets from Boyle forced him back. The gun floated past, hit the edge of the cliff and bounced over.

Butterfingers, the Crest observed.

Boyle fired again, one of his shots hitting Penelope in her right shoulder. She gave an agonised cry, dropping her pistol. Seeing an opportunity, the bounty hunter sent the ambulance scudding towards his two targets, only centimetres above the ground. Penelope waited until the vehicle was almost on top of her, then rolled out of the way. Dante had nowhere left to go, the ambulance bearing down on him with ever increasing speed. Rather than trying to get out of its way, he began walking towards the oncoming vehicle.

Dante, are you quite insane? Evasive action! Take evasive action!

"I am," he snarled, then spun on his heels and sprinted towards the edge of the cliff. The ambulance was racing towards him, only moments from a fatal collision. Dante launched himself towards the Old Man of Hoy.

"Nikolai, no!" Penelope screamed as the ambulance swept past her.

Dante flew through the air in a gentle arc, arms and legs still pumping, trying to keep his forward momentum going. It felt as if time was slowing around him, each second stretching into an hour. Ahead, the top of the sandstone stack was almost within reach. Dante stretched out for it, his fingers clawing the cold air. He felt a hot blast of exhaust as the ambulance flew low over his head. There was a tearing sound, metal screaming in protest as it fought an unequal battle with nature, but Dante did not have time to look up for the cause. His leap of faith was fast becoming a plunge of death.

His body hit with the side of the stack with a sickening thud, jagged outcrops of rock cutting through cloth and skin, slicing apart flesh and bone. His forward momentum gone, Dante could feel himself tipping over backwards, about to fall to the rocks below. Somehow he clung on to the side of the stack, despite the pain stabbing through every part of his body, despite having the breath punched from his lungs, despite the sounds of mechanical torment above.

Penelope picked herself up from the ground and walked to the edge of the cliff, grimly expecting to find Dante's body smeared across the rocks below next to Marius. What faced her instead defied both logic and belief. "Now that's something you don't see every day," she whispered.

Boyle's ambulance had collided with the Old Man of Hoy, knocking the top section of the stack off and into the sea. The space where the chunk of sandstone had stood for thousands of years was now occupied by the battered vehicle, as if the top of the stack were a natural landing pad. The ambulance had twisted sideways in the collision, Boyle's limp body impaled on the shattered remains of the windscreen. Most remarkable of all was the figure climbing the side of the stack. "You're still alive?" Penelope shouted. "You must be the luckiest bastard in the Empire!"

"Well, you're half right," Dante called over his shoulder. He tried to look at her and almost lost his grip. "Tell you what, let's save the rest of this conversation until I get to the top." Dante resumed climbing, ascending the stack with agonising slowness, hand over hand, a few centimetres at a time. Finally, he reached the top and collapsed, stretching out alongside the ambulance. "Penelope, what was it Boyle said before trying to kill us?"

"He was going to make you pay for murdering Dobie."

"Before that. He said something else before that."

"You should have killed him when you had the chance, like he should have killed you..." Her voice trailed off as she realised the significance of Boyle's words. "Like he should have killed you on that bridge! The men who attacked you on Westminster Bridge – it was Dobie and Boyle. One of them must have been the trigger man for the assassination attempt!"

Dante struggled into a sitting position, leaning back against the ambulance. "That means we've killed the real assassins and still have no proof of our innocence."

A low moan of pain drifted across from the stack. "Dante, you don't sound too good."

"That wasn't me," he replied. "It was Boyle, he's still alive!"

Ray Boyle opened his eyes to find Dante staring at him. The bounty hunter wanted to spit in the Russian bastard's face, but trying to breathe was taking all his energy. He concentrated on his hatred – that would keep him alive.

"You're dying," Dante said softly.

"Go... to hell," Boyle grimaced, the words making jagged, broken things inside him grind together. He screamed involuntarily and that made the pain worse. It was all he could do to keep from passing out. If I close my eyes and I'll never open them again, he thought.

"Probably," Dante agreed, "but you'll be there before me. Besides, I doubt that either of us is much of a praying man." He moved closer, close enough for Boyle to smell the desperation on Dante's breath. "Did you shoot the king, or was it Dobie?"

"Why... why should I tell you?"

"Why not?"

Boyle tried to spit a curse at him but couldn't find the strength.

"You're right, it doesn't matter now," Dante said. "But I need to know who hired you. Was it the princess? Did Marie-Anne pay you to kill her father so she could take the throne?"

The bounty hunter laughed, despite the torture it caused. "You... you couldn't be... further from the truth..."

"Then who?" Dante demanded.

Boyle thought about it. Yes, telling Dante would be fitting revenge against the client who hired them, who set him and Dobie on this doomed path. He swallowed back a mouthful of blood and gasped a last sentence. "Follow... follow the money..."

Dante laid a hand over Boyle's face, closing the dead man's eyes. Professional bounty hunters like Dobie and Boyle would have demanded a huge fee for assassinating the king of Britannia. Such a job would make them pariahs among the criminal underworld, unable to get work again. As insurance the twosome would have asked for half the fee upfront, in case anything went wrong. Follow the money. Yes, of course, Dante realised. Find the bounty hunters' bank accounts, then trace any large payments received in the past month back to the person who commissioned the hit.

Dante got to his feet, grateful for the difference his enhanced healing abilities were already making. He staggered past Boyle's body to where Penelope could see him. "How long have we got until Spatchcock and Flintlock are due to be executed?"

"About an hour, I guess. Last I heard they were scheduled for the chop at six."

He looked at the battered, broken ambulance, resting a hand against its side. "Crest, will this thing fly again?" Wires of purple and silver extended from his fingernails, becoming one with the vehicle's metalwork and circuitry. The engines spluttered, then roared back into life.

You can take that as a yes. Can you fly one of these?

"No, but I'm sure you can teach me," Dante said, before shouting across to Penelope. "Get ready to leave! We're going back to London – now!"

FOURTEEN

"Thoughts may be over the hills, but death is just over the shoulder."
– Russian proverb

"Fought in the Year of the Tsar 2669, the Battle of Britannia devastated much of the nation's capital. The country was of limited strategic importance, but the Romanovs felt obliged to defend their most vocal supporter in the fight against the Tsar. The fact that Captain Nikolai Dante and his Rudinshtein Irregulars were sent in first proved how little firepower the noble house was willing to commit to such a fight. Dante and his troops prevailed over the Tsar's Raven Corps, leaving almost as quickly as they had arrived. Britannia spent the next four years rebuilding London, particularly the area around Trafalgar Square. That same area was to suffer again when Dante returned in 2673. Nelson's Column was toppled for a second time shortly after the attempted assassination of King Henry McKray. Four days later Dante returned to the square once more in even more dramatic circumstances."
– Extract from *Britannia's Lost Landmarks*,
Carolyn Steele

Flintlock ducked to avoid being pelted by a tomato, but straightened up again in time to be hit by an airborne pineapple instead. The impact nearly knocked him out of the hover-cart in which he and Spatchcock were being paraded through the streets of London. "You'd think people would have the decency to throw rotten fruit," Flintlock complained. "That pineapple almost took off my head!" Princess Marie-Anne had purchased all the capital's fruit and vegetables, then given them away free to anyone who attended the public execution in Trafalgar Square. Since Londoners hadn't witnessed such an event for more than a century, the resultant throng had brought the city to a standstill. The Britannia Royal Constabulary was stretched to breaking point trying to control the crowds, policemen lining the route from the Tower of London.

"Stop whining," Spatchcock said between mouthfuls of tomato. "This is the first proper food I've had in days. Ripe will do me fine. Besides, I doubt they'll let you be decapitated ahead of schedule, it'd spoil everybody's fun."

By the time their hover-cart reached Trafalgar Square at a quarter to six, both men were soaked in fruit juice and covered with vegetable pulp. Two warders from the Tower had accompanied them on the journey, walking ahead of the cart. They threw buckets of cold water over the condemned pair until both men were clean. Then Spatchcock and Flintlock were marched to the empty plinth in the square's north-west corner, the shackles binding their hands and feet making each step precarious. The former aristocrat kept his eyes on the ground, but Spatchcock scanned their surroundings, taking everything in.

The square was thronged with people, all of them baying for blood. More crowds spilled out of the buildings overlooking the place of execution, chanting and howling abuse. A giant holographic screen was draped over the front of one building so everyone could witness the execution in close-up. Marksmen were stationed at every vantage point, watching the skies intently. Spatchcock

3ritannia Intelligence and Scotland .

larm sounded from the ambulance's con-
looked out a window and cursed.
ws we're coming," she said. "There's six
meet us."

ys our transmission is being jammed. It's
us are innocent, but somebody doesn't
nation getting through," Dante snarled.

Penelope asked. "Who's behind all of

old her, she still didn't believe him.

Trafalgar Square was getting restless.
me to see an execution, but instead were
a long, self-aggrandising speech from
nne. "This woman could bore for Bri-
muttered. "It'll almost be a relief when
r heads." A sloppy sound emitted from
his fellow prisoner. "Heavens above,
ontrol yourself?"

ok his head. "I fart when I get nervous.
executed isn't doing a lot for my

nasal membranes," Flintlock replied.
e! Having my head chopped off in front
he stench spilling from your arse the
nell!" A single tear spilled from Flint-
d his chin wobbled.

comrade shuffled a little closer. "Are

ely not!"

e at the end, why don't you put me
h? Tell me what you did that was so
d out of the country."

Spatchcock. "Do you promise never
soul?"

nudged his friend. "See? They're still expecting Dante to rescue us. He could be here any minute."

"And dead a minute later," Flintlock said mournfully. "Face it, Spatch. We're doomed."

"Have a little faith! When has the captain ever let us down?"

"Frequently!"

Spatchcock frowned. "Come to think of it, you're right." One of the warders gave them a shove and they stumbled up a flight of stone stairs to stand on the plinth. Waiting for them was the princess in a radiant pink ensemble, and an executioner, clad from head to toe in black, a hood concealing his face.

Spatchcock sidled closer to the executioner. "How's it going, Nikolai? All set to spring your surprise rescue?"

"I don't think so," Marie-Anne snarled, lifting up the hood to show Spatchcock the dull-witted killer underneath. Last time she had been in this position was during the Battle of Britannia, when Dante disguised himself as the executioner to save King Henry from being beheaded. The princess was not making the same mistake twice. "Even if your cowardly comrade is foolish enough to try and save your worthless lives, my sharpshooters will gun him down. Nikolai Dante is as good as dead."

"Is there such a thing?" Spatchcock wondered.

Marie-Anne stroked the blade of the mighty axe held in the executioner's meaty fists. "You'll soon find out, won't you?" The princess's nose wrinkled in distaste. "What is that smell?"

Spatchcock grinned wolfishly. "A hint of things to come."

Penelope was piloting the ambulance south at maximum speed while Dante concentrated on finding out who had hired Boyle and Dobie to assassinate the king. The Crest took a sample of Boyle's DNA from the blood staining the front seat of the hover-vehicle, then created a genetic fingerprint enabling it to pose as the dead bount hunter. The battle computer hacked its way into th Imperial Net via the ambulance's internal computer sys tems and ran a search for Boyle's bank accounts. *N matter where he hid his money in the Empire, I should b able to find it. Proving the money was paid by someon wanting the king dead is another matter.*

"Leave it to me," Dante replied. "A little bluffing goes long way in my experience."

"That explains your alleged success with women, Penelope commented wryly.

He ignored the comment. "How long until we reac London?"

"Fortunately for us, this ambulance is among the faste hover-vehicles in Britannia. Unfortunately, the damage i sustained crashing into the Old Man of Hoy impaired it aerodynamics and this temporary windscreen won't hol forever."

"How long?" Dante demanded.

"Twenty minutes, tops."

"Flintlock and Spatchcock will be dead in less than fif-teen."

Penelope grimaced. "I'll do what I can but miracles ar beyond even me."

Found it, the Crest announced. *Boyle, Raymond. Bank with the First Imperial Bank of Vanuatu – a somewha obscure tax haven in the South Pacific. A joint account shared with Dobie, first name Lewis. A wire transfer fo twenty million roubles was paid into the account las week.*

"Where did the money come from?" Dante asked.

Checking... Alas, whoever commissioned the hit has cov-ered their tracks rather well. The funds were originall held in an account controlled by the Britannia civil service. Beyond that, it's impossible to say.

"King Henry's own government paid to have him mur-dered?"

You misunderstar
government funds.
and how they did
said to Penelope.

"So Princess Mar
all?" she asked.

"Or anyone else w
"For all we know, i
she would have ha
money."

"If F wanted som
Rippers and then la
veniently covered u
vehicle's navigation
ham."

Dante, I've found son
details at the bank. I'
tained a virtual safe

"A what, Crest?"

The principle's th
a bank vault, but
computer files, i
ments.

"Can you get a
Already done.
ing: dates, prices
McKray. Yes, thi
hired to make th
assassination to
could be a scap

"Who hired
head when the
take. Check it

"Passing W
Dante. "Well,

"The Crest
nodded. "Ok

information to
Well, why not?"

A proximity a
trols. Penelope
"Somebody kno
Rippers here to

"The Crest sa
got proof all of
want that inform

"Who is it?"
this?"

When Dante

The crowd in
Everyone had c
being treated t
Princess Marie-
annia," Flintloc
they chop off o
the posterior o
man! Can't you

Spatchcock sh
Waiting to be
intestines."

"Nor for my
"What a way to d
of millions with
last thing I ever s
lock's right eye ar

His malodorous
you crying?"

"N-No. A-absolu
"Look, since we
out of my misery,
bad it got you kick

Flintlock glared
to tell another livin

"I'll be dead any minute, if her royal bitchiness ever shuts up – who could I tell?"

"All right." The former aristocrat leaned closer to Spatchcock and whispered in his ear. The flatulent runt's eyebrows shot upwards and his mouth dropped open in amazement. When Flintlock finished, his partner in crime looked at him with new-found respect.

"I... I..." Spatchcock spluttered, shaking his head. "I've never heard anything so disgusting, so degrading, so completely and utterly revolting in my life! I'm shocked, honestly, I am shocked! I didn't know you had it in you."

"Remember what you promised!"

"Well, I lied," Spatchcock said. "Now, all we need is Dante to save our ugly asses and then I tell the world what you just told me – you dirty dog!"

The princess finally brought her speech to a close. "Now, I shall hand proceedings over to our royal executioner..." A cacophony of cheering came from the crowd as Spatchcock and Flintlock were shoved towards the twin chopping blocks at the front edge of the plinth.

Spatchcock searched the sky hopefully. "Come on, Dante, don't let me down – not now!"

The ambulance was flying less than a metre above the Thames, its hover-engines screaming in protest as Dante piloted the vehicle with reckless abandon. He had swapped places with Penelope, freeing her to shoot at the swarm of Rippers pursuing them. She leaned out of the passenger window, firing her pistols at the murderous hunters on their hover-bikes. Trying to target them was not easy with Dante flinging the ambulance about in the air. "Hold it steady!" she howled. "I can't shoot these bastards if you don't hold it steady!"

"Easier said than done!" Dante shouted back. He pulled back on the controls, sending the vehicle's nose up into the air so it skimmed above one of the bridges crossing the Thames, then flung it back down towards the water.

No sooner had he straightened out again than a sailing ship floated directly into their path, forcing an abrupt swerve.

Penelope got lucky with her next shot, exploding the nearest Ripper's engine. The fireball of debris claimed two more Rippers behind it, leaving only three in pursuit, She tried to fire at them with one weapon, then the other, but both clicked repeatedly. "I'm out of ammunition!"

Dante glanced at his mirrors. "Let's see if I can't shake off the last of these bastards." He grinned at Penelope. "You might want to strap yourself in." Once she was secure, Dante wrenched the controls backwards. The ambulance shot underneath Westminster Bridge and then up into the air in a tight arc. But instead of levelling out again, Dante maintained the trajectory.

"These things aren't designed to loop the loop you maniac!" Penelope said, g-force pulling her lips back from teeth into an involuntary grin. Around them the vehicle was threatening to shake itself apart, glass fragments flying through the air inside.

"Now she tells me!" Dante replied through gritted teeth. The ambulance was upside down but it kept going, starting to plunge towards the Thames. "Hold on, this is going to be close!" Dante snarled, keeping the controls tight to his chest. The ambulance seemed certain to smash into the river's surface but somehow righted itself, once more racing along above the water. Ahead of them the remaining Rippers were looking back, astonished by Dante's death-defying manoeuvre. They didn't notice the barge crossing the Thames in front of them until it was too late. All three flew straight into the ship, exploding in a trinity of fireballs. Dante grinned at his wide-eyed passenger. "You know, I wasn't sure that would work."

Penelope shook her head in disbelief. "I can't decide if you're the bravest man I've ever met or the biggest fool in the Empire."

Probably both, the Crest observed.

Dante slowed the ambulance to a halt, then told Penelope to swap places with him. "Are hover-vehicles required to carry parachutes in case of emergency?"

"Of course, there's one under each seat – why?"

Dante removed the parachute from beneath his position and began strapping it on his back. "You'll have to drop me off over Trafalgar Square, we'll never land this thing close enough."

"Then what?" Penelope asked.

"Knowing the person who hired Boyle and Dobie, they won't be satisfied with leaving the king alive. I'm guessing they'll use the diversion of the public execution to take matters in their own hands. You're Britannia's best secret agent – you have to stop them!"

"What about a last request?" Spatchcock asked, stalling for time. "As condemned men, don't we get a last request? We haven't eaten in days!"

"If you're worrying about losing too much weight, I believe the imminent removal of your heads is, perhaps, a more pressing issue," the princess replied. Those in the crowd who could hear what she was saying laughed a little, but the rest were growing ever more impatient. Marie-Anne nodded to the executioner, who shoved Spatchcock's head on the chopping block next to Flintlock. The prisoners' manacles were attached to a taut chain on the plinth, preventing them from squirming around or escaping the axe when it came.

"That axe isn't sharp enough," Spatchcock complained. "I don't think it's been cleaned since the last time an executioner used it. If the blade isn't sharp enough, we'll be here all night with him hacking away. I don't want him finishing me off with a pocket knife."

"The axe is sharp enough to split hairs," the princess said, "as you will soon discover!" She turned to the crowd and smiled magnanimously. "Do the condemned men have any last words they wish to say before the sentence is carried out?"

"Yes," Flintlock replied. "I'm too young and too pretty to die!"

"You wish," Spatchcock cackled.

"Anything else?" Marie-Anne demanded.

"There was one thing," Spatchcock said. "Did you know there's a madman falling out of the sky towards you?"

The princess sighed. "I didn't think there were still people alive foolish enough to believe that 'look behind you!' misdirection still worked."

"I'll take that as a no. Oh, hi, Dante!"

Marie-Anne spun round but there was nobody behind her. She turned back to face the two prisoners, her expression sour enough to curdle milk.

"Made you look," Spatchcock smirked, winking at her.

"Kill them!" the princess shouted at the executioner. "Kill them now!"

Then the sharpshooters around Trafalgar Square opened fire.

"Your majesty, you should not be exerting yourself like this," Doctor Bhamra insisted, gesturing at the chaos surrounding her. The king had demanded a holographic display for his hospital room, along with a camera crew on standby in case he wished to broadcast a proclamation.

"Nonsense, my dear! How can I be expected to rule if I don't know what's happening in my kingdom?" Henry summoned the pretty young physician closer, so he could whisper in her ear. "This is still my kingdom, isn't it?"

"Yes, your majesty, of course it is."

"Jolly good show!" The king pinched the doctor's buttocks and gave her a friendly wink. "Now, what's on today? Not one of those dreary films about the royal family – can't stand them!"

"It's the public execution," one of the camera crew chipped in, "from Trafalgar Square, Your Highness. Two of the men who tried to kill you are being beheaded."

"Really? I don't remember signing any such decree."

"Your daughter did it, while you were incapacitated," Doctor Bhamra explained.

"Did she now? The cunning little vixen! We'll see about that. Start those cameras!"

The odds that none of these sharpshooters will hit you or disable your parachute are slightly greater than seventeen thousand to one – against.

"Never tell me the odds, Crest!" Dante shouted, struggling to hear his own words above the volleys of gunfire coming at him from every possible angle. He was dropping towards the place of execution in Trafalgar Square, having jumped out of the ambulance as it passed overhead. "One more minute and I'll be safely on the ground. These marksmen couldn't hit water if they fell out of a boat."

They may not be able to hit you, but eventually they'll realise your parachute is a considerably larger and easier target, the Crest predicted. Not sooner had it spoken than the sharpshooters shifted aim upwards. *So much for beating the odds.*

Dante's descent began accelerating with each fresh hole put through his parachute. "What I need is something soft to cushion the impact of my landing…"

Like everyone else in the square, the executioner was watching the spectacle of Dante's daredevil descent. He found it all but impossible to tear his gaze from the Russian renegade's groin, fully displayed thanks to the wind tugging Dante's kilt upwards. It took a slap across the face from Princess Marie-Anne to get his attention. "Chop off the prisoners' heads now or your head will be next on the block!" Eager to please her, the executioner drew back his axe in the air, preparing to swing it down on Flintlock's scrawny neck. But the sudden arrival of Dante's feet in his face proved something of a distraction. The executioner tipped over backwards, falling on to the blade of his own axe. It sliced neatly through his spinal column, proving just as sharp as the princess had promised.

Dante dropped into a crouch, his bio-blades already extending from each fist. He sliced one sword through the air, severing the ropes and straps linking him to the parachute. The other blade cut apart the manacles holding Spatchcock and Flintlock in place. The two men scrambled to their feet, all too aware of the numerous sharpshooters nearby.

"What took you so long?" Spatchcock asked wryly.

"Traffic was a bitch," Dante replied before turning his attention to the princess. "Well, your royal highness? What have you got to say for yourself?"

Marie-Anne pointed at Dante accusingly. "This is the man who tried to murder my father!" She shouted at the crowd of thousands upon thousands gathered around them. "This is the man who butchered your beloved Queen Mother, Babs!"

"You know I had nothing to do with those attacks, princess. You know who pulled the trigger and you know who paid the assassins. You've known it all from the start, but made sure it happened far enough away from you so you could maintain deniable culpability!"

"Will nobody rid me of these lies, these falsehoods?" the princess screamed. "Marksmen! At my signal, kill this accursed Russian dog and his accomplices where they stand! Ready!"

"Wouldn't this be a good moment to take cover?" Flintlock suggested.

"Aim!"

"I think she fancies me," Dante replied.

Marie-Anne stepped aside, giving all the sharpshooters a clean target. "Fi–"

"Hold that order!" a regal voice boomed around Trafalgar Square from the vast holographic display suspended on the northern side. The crowd dropped to one knee in homage. The familiar face of King Henry smiled down upon his subjects, a mischievous twinkle in his eye. "Hello, everybody!"

"Your Majesty," Dante said, breathing a sigh of relief before joining the others on bended knee. Only the princess remained standing, a pout on her face and both hands on her hips.

"Now, what's all this nonsense about you trying to kill me, Nicola?"

"I don't know, sire," Dante replied.

The king turned away from the camera. "I can't hear what he's saying. Can't you get a microphone pointed at him out there?" Satisfied with whatever reply he got, Henry looked at the camera again. "What were you saying, Nicola?"

"I did not try to kill you, sire – I saved you from the assassin's bullets. I only wish I had been fast enough to save your mother as well."

"Old Babs had a good innings. For what it's worth, I can confirm young Nicola had nothing to do with the attack on me, nor did her chums. I invited Nicola to Britannia to protect me from assassins and that's exactly what she did."

"But, father–" the princess tried to protest.

"Tish and pish, my girl, I'll hear nothing more from you. You've caused enough trouble while I've been laid up. Once this is all over you're going straight back to the Tower. Consider yourself well and truly grounded, my dear!"

"Your Majesty," Dante called out. "Another has been falsely accused of conspiring to assassinate you, a blameless operative from your secret service known as Agent Goodnight. But she possesses evidence that will show the identities of the true killers and the name of the person who hired them to attack you."

Marie-Anne flung herself at Dante, her fingernails flailing the air like a bird of prey's talons. "I'll kill you! I'll kill you," she vowed. But Spatchcock and Flintlock stepped in front of Dante to protect him, keeping the princess a safe distance away.

"The assassins were two bounty hunters named Boyle and Dobie," Dante continued. "Both have since died in violent circumstances, and nobody need weep for them."

"Dashed glad to hear that, Nicola," Henry said. "But who hired these bounders?"

"That was me," another voice cut in from the king's bedside. A gun appeared on the edge of the holographic display's picture aimed at Henry's head. The crowd gasped in horror. Few of them recognised the voice that was threatening the king, but Dante did.

"Why did you do it?" he demanded of the unseen voice. "Why did you hire two bounty hunters to murder the king... Inspector Rucka?"

The inspector stepped closer to the king, putting himself into the picture. He wanted to be certain everyone could see his face at the moment of triumph. "For years I worked my way up through the Britannia Royal Constabulary, proving myself over and over again. But what recognition did I receive for all my hard work? Next to nothing. And why? Because I refused to become one of the silly handshake brigade who still control so much of our life in this once great nation! Finally, I decided enough was enough. I would strike a blow for the decent people of Britannia. I would have the king murdered, so her royal highness would take her rightful place on the throne."

"So why not pull the trigger yourself?" Dante demanded from Trafalgar Square.

"Because I was ambitious and a fool," Rucka replied. "I knew this would be seen as the crime of the century. What better way to ensure my advancement by solving it, proving once and for all my genius as a detective. When the king invited you to Britannia, I knew it was the perfect opportunity. I was foolish because I entrusted the task to two bounty hunters and they let this old man escape them."

"And my daughter knew about all of this?" Henry asked.

"I gave her hints, enough to know her time was coming, but not enough to incriminate her. She is innocent, for once in her life," the inspector replied.

"Why come out of hiding now?" Dante demanded. "Why tell us all this?"

Rucka smiled. "Because after I murder the king, I will turn the gun on myself. You already have the proof of my guilt, there was no hiding place from that – but I can still rid Britannia of this old fool! He has been an embarrassment to us all for far too long. When he dies, a new era will begin." The inspector pressed the gun against the side of Henry's head. "Goodbye, your majesty – and good riddance."

A single shot rung out, a shot that was heard all across Britannia.

EPILOGUE

"Touch what hurts, admire what's pretty."
– Russian proverb

"Midge bites are painful and irritating, no more so than when they occur on sensitive parts of the anatomy. For example, a single bite to the male genitalia can cause itching, redness and unsightly swelling. In such cases, all sexual activity should be avoided until the swelling has gone and the bites have healed. Certain creams can be helpful in speeding this process, but take care during application not to cause unnecessary arousal as this only leads to further frustration."
– Extract from *The Duffer's Guide to Britannia*, 2670 edition

"I was beginning to think you wouldn't make it in time," Dante said. "I mean, could you have cut it any closer before you put a bullet through Rucka's head?"

"Probably not," Penelope conceded. "There, how does that feel?"

"Better, but now the front is starting to itch again."

"Already? I only just finished putting ointment on there."

Dante shrugged. "Can I help it if I'm extra sensitive below the waist at the moment?"

Two days had passed since the death of Inspector Rucka ended Dante's latest adventure in Britannia. The king had granted royal pardons to all those previously accused of trying to assassinate him. Princess Marie-Anne was back in the Tower of London, still vowing to have her vengeance against Dante, and the money Rucka had embezzled to pay Boyle and Dobie was back in the proper civil service accounts.

To celebrate not being a fugitive anymore, Dante had checked into the bridal suite of London's most expensive hotel. Spatchcock and Flintlock were given the room next door, but had been warned not to disturb their friend. "I've spent the past week being chased, hunted, shot at, bitten by bloodthirsty insects and generally put through the wringer," he told them. "Right now, all I want is a bath, a good meal and a bed to sleep in. Do what you like but don't disturb me! Got it?"

He waited until both men were out of the hotel before calling Penelope on her private line and inviting her over. He had hoped her acceptance signalled a thawing in relations between them at last. His hope had risen further when she arrived with a large tube of cream and a determined look on her face. "Show me your crotch," she said once they were in the bedroom.

"I thought you'd never ask," he replied, stripping off all his clothes in the time it took Penelope to remove her jacket. For once she was out of her ubiquitous catsuit, preferring a short black silk dress over matching stockings, a neat seam running down the back of each leg. She gasped upon seeing the state of his groin. "Impressive, isn't it?" he asked rhetorically.

"Have you been scratching?" she asked sternly.

"Why? Will you promise to give me a spanking if I say yes?"

"Nikolai, you've almost rubbed yourself raw! The swelling is... considerable."

"Well, I don't like to brag."

"That's not what I'm talking about," Penelope snapped. "Lie down on the bed. I'll apply some ointment to the worst areas and you should start to feel some relief almost immediately."

"Sounds promising," he agreed.

"That's not what I meant and you know it!"

"A boy can always hope, can't he?"

Penelope settled down on the bed beside him, then quickly stood up again. "And keep your wandering fingers to yourself!"

"Spoilsport," Dante said, sulkily removing his hands from beneath her.

"That's better," she said, sitting down once more. Penelope turned the tube upside down above his groin and began squeezing the thick white cream all over him. After emptying half the ointment out, she cast aside the tube and began gently massaging the cream into his swollen areas.

"Oh, yes," Dante sighed. "I'm feeling relieved already." He winked at her playfully. "You never told me whether you got any midge bites while we were on Hoy."

"A few," Penelope admitted, her hands stroking the cream back and forth on the most swollen area of his groin. "Those bloody things always bite you in the most inconvenient places."

"I hope you haven't been scratching."

"Maybe a little."

Dante smiled. "Let's see if I can guess where..."

Spatchcock and Flintlock were returning from a hard day's drinking in the taverns of London when they heard a terrible moaning sound from Dante's suite. "Bojemoi, it sounds as if he's in agony!" the shorter man said, leaning closer to the door.

"Dante told us not to disturb him under any circumstances, Spatch!"

"But what if he's dying in there?"

Flintlock shrugged. "I guess we could have a peek, see if he's okay."

"Me first!" Spatchcock was peering through the keyhole before Flintlock could object.

"What is it? What's happening?"

"I think Dante is attempting the entrance exam for the Britannia secret service." Spatchcock muttered under his breath. "But I'm not sure he'll ever get in that way..."

ABOUT THE AUTHOR

David Bishop was born and raised in New Zealand, becoming a daily newspaper journalist at eighteen years old. He emigrated to Britain in 1990 and was editor of the *Judge Dredd Megazine* and then *2000 AD*, before becoming a freelance writer. His previous novels include three starring Judge Dredd (for Virgin Books) and four featuring Doctor Who (for Virgin and the BBC). He also writes non-fiction books and articles, audio dramas, comics and has been a creative consultant on three forthcoming video games. If you see Bishop in public, do not approach him – alert the nearest editor and stand well back.